Devil by the Tail

Caroline Lavoie

Winnipeg, Canada

Developmental editor: Craig Gibb
Proofreader: Margaret Larson

Published October 2024 by Deep Hearts YA.

Deep Hearts YA
PO Box 51053 Tyndall Park
Winnipeg, Manitoba R2X 3B0
Canada

Visit deepheartsya.com for more great reads.

For my daughters, Marie-Eve and Rafaële.
You are the two most amazing girls I know.

Devil by the Tail

When the French settlers came across the ocean, they brought not only the smallpox and the Devil. The *chat-cornu*, a shapeshifting deceiver, followed too. Those who see the beast are cursed, for it will steal from them someone dearest to their heart.

— *The Legend of Fort Castor.*
Paper placemat, Beaver Lodge Pub & Grill

Part I

Devil by the Tail

Chapter 1

All of Fort Castor, northern British Columbia—population 968—is assembled in the snowy field behind the community centre for the Lumber Games, in which junior and adult competitors show off their lumberjack skills. Chatty, the horned lynx mascot, prances around giving little kids candies and high-fives. Not to mention fodder for nightmares with his threadbare fake fur and stained velvet fangs.

So far, I took first in the axe throw and second in the bow sawing contest. I'm going for the gold, so I *must* win the underhand chop.

I grip the axe handle with both hands, fingers winter-cold, palms clammy. The peeled log beneath my feet is a smooth, pale neck awaiting its fate. The crowd buzzes in the bleachers, and my blood sizzles in my veins. I will turn this piece of wood into kindling.

Like I should have done with the letter stuffed in my back pocket. The words scrawled in purple ink still swim behind my eyes.

Dear Alexia,

My name is Alex.

You must think I'm the worst person ever.

No, no. We're good. Just leave me alone.

The megaphone crackles. "Contestants, get ready for the tiebreaker."

"You go, girl," Dad shouts.

Breathe. You've got this.

I raise the axe over my head. In my peripheral vision, Caden swings his own axe between his legs a couple of times then imitates my pose. He's Fort Castor's golden boy, right down to his golden-brown hair and green-gold eyes. Even though he's one of my favourite people, too, I hope he's ready to eat wood chips because I'm totally winning the underhand chop.

The grand prize sits on a snowbank, a Moto-Ski snowmobile, orange with a black seat and a 440cc engine. It's about three times older than me, but I want that sled more than I've ever wanted anything. A junker of my own to get my hands dirty on and my happiness will be complete.

I thump the tips of my boots against the log to dislodge snow from the soles. I can't afford a single slip-up.

The folded paper shifts in my pocket.

Sometimes, bad things happen and force us to make the most painful decisions.

Yeah, I agree. Today was the worst day to find this letter. I should have thrown it in the wood stove unread.

The air horn rips the air. The first impact of blade on wood shoots up my arms and raps the back of my skull. My world shrinks to a snow globe. It's just me, my axe, and the log I'm about to annihilate.

I chop left, chop right. My braid escapes the collar of my sweater, an ash-blonde rope that flays the air.

The chat-cornu got under my skin. None of it is your fault…

Damn right it's not my fault.

Left. Right. Left. Right. Splinters fly everywhere. I'm halfway through. My muscles are on fire, and each strike feels like my wrist is shattering. Caden and I are neck and neck. I can't stop—*won't* stop hacking even if my body falls apart. I said I'd beat him, and I will.

Dammit, Alex. Focus.

Three more blows and victory is mine. The axe hits sideways and flies out of my hands and into the snow. Cheers erupt. Between my feet, a finger-thick strip of wood still connects the two halves of my log.

Damn. I can't believe it. Caden won. He's strong, but so am I. I trained so hard for this—fell asleep every night picturing the gold medal hanging on my neck. So much for the power of visualization.

I hope you can forgive me someday.

Hell, no. I'm not forgiving anyone.

Panting and drenched with sweat, I hop down from my log and kick some snow with the edge of my foot, which does nothing to cool the lava rolling beneath my skin. Caden holds his axe high and waves at the crowd, so pleased with himself. But then he cuts a glance at me and his brow furrows.

Hey, no need to worry. I *am* a sore loser, but I'm not going to throw a tantrum. He won fair and square.

He finally strides over, hair burnished with sweat. "Good job, Alex. You didn't make it easy."

"Congrats on beating me." I offer him a fist bump and hiss in pain as our hands connect. My wrist feels like it's made of broken glass.

"You okay?"

On a good day, his attentiveness would wrap me like a warm hug, but right now it rubs me the wrong way. Before I spew a reply I'll regret later, Chatty—who never speaks a word, by the way—saunters over with his grinning lynx face and googly eyes, and sweeps Caden away to the winner's circle.

Some people are scared of clowns or dolls. This ridiculous mascot fueled my childhood nightmares. It doesn't matter who's wearing the costume. Even if it were Caden, I'd have to resist the urge to shove him away from me. Mr. Tanuyak volunteered for the job this year, but someone must have had to replace him, for whatever reason. I doubt he'd be freezing off his toes in those scuffed combat boots.

"Nice work, Alex," Dad says.

I swivel around. He's stomping my way, boyish and ruddy-cheeked. We have the same blue-grey eyes, my favourite thing about myself. He was only nineteen when I was born, and people regularly mistake him for my big brother. To me, he just looks like Dad.

"I'm proud of you." He wraps an arm around my shoulder and pulls me close.

"Thanks, Dad."

Beyond him, the sled I just lost sits on its dirty

snowbank with the sunset-tinted Rocky Mountains in the background. The Devil's Tail reigns among them, not the tallest peak but definitely the sharpest. The one Chatty's evil twin supposedly haunts.

You've been cursed, Alexia. The chat-cornu was going to steal from you a person you loved. Your daddy deserved you more than I did, so I had to leave.

I shudder, imagining Chatty's black mouth stretching to swallow me whole. It's silly, but the visceral fear from my nightmares when I was little is still etched on my brain.

"You all right, sweetie?"

"Yeah." I step back. "Why does everyone keep asking me if I'm okay?"

He ruffles my toque. "You'll get over it."

I'm sure he means losing the contest, not my mascot-phobia. I bat off his hand. "I have to go find my parka. See you later."

Whatever you do, stay away from that mountain. Love, Mommy

Got it, Karine (sorry—not calling you Mommy). The Devil's Tail isn't haunted, and it's not cursed either. Sure, random people have died up there over the years. Because, like every other mountain on Earth, it can freeze you, bury you, skid you off a cliff. The list goes on. There's a hundred ways to die on the Tail, and only one way not to. Stay off it.

She's right about one thing, though. I have Dad. I don't need anyone else.

"Your axe." Caden is back, holding it out. A gold medal hangs on his neck.

I have him, too—my oldest friend. I'm glad he cares enough to pretend he's not put off by my mood swings.

I take the axe and inspect the cutting edge, the handle. No chip in the metal, no crack along the hickory wood. My loss is a hundred percent on me. Well, ninety-nine-point-nine percent. I could have done without Karine's distracting letter.

"Let's go check out your prize," I say.

In the declining afternoon, the Moto-Ski isn't as shiny as it appeared in the sunlight. Fort Cass (as most of us call Fort Castor) doesn't hand out brand-new sleds to kids, of course. This one has been pulled out of some barn or junkyard and restored to reasonable condition. Like concealer on a pimple, the fresh coat of orange paint does only so much to hide the years of abuse by the elements. Still, it would've been nice to have my own sled.

"I was hoping you'd beat me," Caden says. "You know I don't really need that thing."

Right. He has a sweet-looking Polaris that's just a few years old. But now I'm suspicious. "You'd better not have been trying to let me win."

"I'd never do that to you." He widens his eyes, like he's offering me his soul to read. It's not necessary. I believe him.

"Well, you won. By the way, I heard that Moto-Skis are all-around crappy."

Caden bumps my calf with the edge of his foot and smiles. "Sore loser."

Coming from his mouth, it sounds like the best of compliments.

"Contestants," a woman's voice screeches from a

speaker. "Don't forget to come in and grab a bowl of chilli and your winnings."

My stomach growls. I get too jittery to eat during a competition and my breakfast is long forgotten. "Let's go in. I'm starving."

We're the last ones outside. We stride across the field toward the community center. I lost the big prize, but I should still take home a few bucks for placing in all my events.

A flash of genius hits me. "Hey. If you're interested in selling, I could take that Moto-Ski off your hands."

"That all-around crappy sled?" He lifts a mocking eyebrow. "Make an offer."

"Whatever's in my money envelope?"

"Deal."

Sweet. Caden is gold.

After the meal, I find Dad at the crowded table he's sharing with old high school buddies.

"I'm heading home," I shout over the din.

"On your shiny new ride?" he teases.

"It's a fine sled. Bye."

I step out into the frigid, navy-blue dusk. The quiet feels good after a day hectic with the cheers of the crowd, the thwacks of axes, and the whines of chainsaws.

The Moto-Ski is dull in the remnants of daylight. I slide a gloved hand over the peeled-off logo stickers, the rubber grips worn smooth from decades of use.

My snowmobile.

It's perfect.

I pump the gas primer and yank the starter cord. The engine purrs but doesn't catch. That's nothing abnormal. This thing has been sitting out in the cold all day. I prime some more, crank a few times, prime, crank.

"Did you flood the engine?" Caden is coming my way, a fleece-lined aviator hat on his head but no jacket over his grey wool sweater.

How many times did I pump that primer? Eight? Twelve? Way too many, obviously. Dammit. I'm incompetent through and through today. "Yeah."

"Happens to the best of us. Can I help?"

"Sure. If you want."

"You hold the throttle, and I'll crank?"

He waits for me to say, *no, I'll crank*, because cranking is the most intensive part and I'm not a slacker, but my right wrist is screaming, and my left arm is just about dead.

"Okay." I hold down the gas lever with my thumb.

The excess gas burns off in a dozen pulls, and the engine coughs to life. We stand back, enveloped in a cloud of exhaust.

"Thanks, you're the best." It's true, and I'm not the only one to think that. Caden is just about everyone's favourite guy, one of those rare people who are almost perfect in every respect.

"No worries," he says.

His eyes evade mine, showing me he's pleased I told him that. I'm not sure when his feelings for me began to change, but I know he likes me.

I poke my finger into his chest. "Don't let it go to your head. Next year, I'm beating you at every single event."

He leans into the pressure of my finger. "We'll see about that."

"Ooh. I'm so scared."

We're standing so close. I can think of a way I could wipe that little smile from his lips. The flush of winter on my cheeks turns to a burn. What if I like him more than I think, and I really am cursed to lose someone I love? It's not like we hang out all the time, but Caden has always been there. I don't want that to change.

I climb onto the snowmobile and gun the engine. "See you tomorrow."

He steps back from the pungent cloud of exhaust. "See you."

The sled crawls into motion. It doesn't have power steering, so I clench my teeth against the pain shooting up my arm and head for the trails. I ride along the town's backyards where junk cars, kid swings, and trampolines sleep under a thick blanket of snow. The Moto-Ski's headlight sucks, but I could drive home with my eyes closed. This is just something people say, but I'm sure I could do it. The road is perfectly straight right up to the bottom of my dead-end road.

As I leave the town behind, thick forest funnels me in. A few stars peek out of the sky as I glide downhill into a patch of icy fog. My warm, cozy house awaits up the other side. A chill creeps down my spine, though the frigid night air couldn't possibly get past my goose-down parka. I've never liked this section of the road at night. If I were playing in a movie, this is where the swamp monster would slither out of the ditch.

Or the chat-cornu would disembowel me.

The fog swallows the last glimmer of dusk and the engine sputters as I approach the bottom of the hill. My heart squeezes in my chest.

Come on, you piece of junk. Now's not the time to quit.

I max out the throttle and advance lurch by lurch. One of the fuel lines must be sucking air. I'll check it out when I get home. Which won't be anytime soon, as the engine dies at the lowest point on the road and, along with it, the headlight.

Crap.

My ears are still buzzing from the engine's rumble while utter silence descends on me like a polar vortex, and exhaust fumes fill my nose. On the left side of the road, the forest is mostly aspen and subalpine fir. On the right, the old-growth forest that covers the Devil's Tail has never seen a chainsaw or a feller buncher, and probably never will. For one, there's a moratorium on old-growth logging. Also, this mountain has a bad aura.

Across the ditch, two massive tangles of willows cling to life like mouldy skeletons, marking the head of an abandoned trail that used to lead to a trapper's cabin. According to legend, this is where the chat-cornu lurks, waiting for the opportunity to curse people with losing someone they love. People like me, supposedly, even though I never set a foot on that mountain except in my nightmares.

Anyway. I'm not spending one more minute down here. I step off the sled and wrench the crank. In the short-lived blink of the headlight, a shadow slinks across the fog. I crank again. Another blink of light. The shadow's still there, but there's nothing to cast it. It's only a denser patch of fog. In my mind, it takes the shape of a patchy-furred lynx with ear tufts and a bobbed tail like the real animal, and, impossibly, two black horns sprouting out of its head.

It's the beast from my nightmares, and it's coming for me.

I throw my whole weight into the next pull and the next. The starter cord snaps, launching me backward into a snowbank. Snow tumbles into my collar and trickles down my back, grounding me.

There's no monster here. The only curse is that I'll have to walk home, which I could also do with my eyes closed, walking backward.

Even if I had a cell phone, there's no reception here. I'll have to trust Dad's power of deduction. I set the starter's rubber handle on the seat so he sees what happened when he drives by. Tomorrow, we'll tow the sled together and have a good laugh about it.

The fog is so thick down here that I barely see my feet. A breath from the Devil's Tail kisses my cheek. The willows' brittle boughs scratch against each other, sounding like wails. Or like the cries of a lost little girl calling for her mommy. The chill the melted snow left along my spine spreads to the rest of my body and clings like a clammy second skin.

This is all giving me a freaking *déjà vu,* but everybody knows that's a trick of the brain. I've never been alone here in the dark, never stood listening to cries come out of the forest.

They're gone now. Everything is silent except for my hammering heart. The wails must have been a hare getting caught by a regular lynx—no horns. Gruesome, but part of life.

I breathe evenly and rein in my pace to a brisk walk, but the more I tell myself I'm not being watched, the more my muscles tingle. My metabolism must be starved for sugar after hours of activity, and there's leftover chocolate cake in the fridge at home.

I break into a run, but it's not the call of chocolate that lends me speed. The breathing that rasps in my ears, is it mine?

The amber glow of the porch light blinks through the trees like a beacon. I fly across the yard, trip on the porch steps, and rush into my house, nearly knocking the big aloe vera plant off its stand. Shit, I should quit the Lumber Games and take up sprint events. Wins guaranteed.

My rational brain takes over, and my pulse returns to normal. The sled's fumes must have messed with my senses. I dump my winter layers and go up to my room. As I take off my jeans, the letter sticks out of the back pocket. It's damp with the snow that melted down my back, and the ink has bled through the paper.

You've been cursed.

Yeah, right. She left, but how big's the loss? I mean, she abandoned me.

Dad's the best—I don't need anyone else. Maybe I should show him the letter. He'd agree it's rubbish.

Wouldn't he? But it might hurt him, too, like the ghost of Karine coming back to haunt him. He doesn't deserve the grief. I slip it in between the pages of my Cabela's outdoor gear catalogue and grab some fresh clothes. I need a shower.

Afterward, I settle on the couch with an ice pack for my tender wrist and a giant slice of cake. I turn on the TV and pick a non-scary documentary about an Old West outlaw named Zwing Hunt. Sounds like something you'd call a lousy snowmobile that quits on the first ride. So, Zwing it is. Caden should consider himself lucky I took it off his hands for seventy-five bucks.

I almost fall asleep, exhausted after the long day of axe throwing, log chopping, and pole climbing. The letter keeps drifting back into my mind like a cloud of vile smoke. *The chat-cornu was going to steal from you a person you loved.*

What was Karine thinking all those years ago when she tucked the envelope into that box of hand-knitted stuff? Did she know I'd run out of warm socks one of these Lumber Games, and Dad would be on the porch yelling at me to freaking hurry up, please, we're going to be late for registration? And then what?

Karine is long gone, back to Quebec where she came from. Probably hiding in a large, stinky city, safe from the fictitious chat-cornu getting under her skin.

I'm not letting anything—or anyone, for that matter— get under *my* skin.

Chapter 2

I shuffle into the kitchen, eyelids glued nearly shut with sleepiness.

Dad is a blur at the table. "Good morning, sweetie."

"I'm not sweet." I ruffle his ginger crew cut as I squeeze between the back of his chair and the counter. The French press is half-full and steaming. I drop a handful of sugar cubes into a cup, drown them with coffee, and top up with lots of cream.

"Since when do you drink coffee?" Dad asks.

"I'm starting right now." Well. I've had Frappuccinos and Iced Capps before. The formula is simple enough: coffee-flavoured sugar and fat. I sit across from him. My sled's recoil assembly rests between us on the pockmarked pine table, a new rope wound on the reel. "You kept me up late. I'll need a boost to stay awake in class."

"Serves you right for buying junk without your daddy's professional advice."

Dad takes a gulp from his own brew. Mine is so sugary my teeth hurt as I sip.

"Give me a couple years, and I'll have my own shop right here in Fort Cass," I say.

"Is that so?" Dad's forehead wrinkles as he raises his eyebrows.

"I'll hire you, and then you won't need to work shifts at the mine anymore." Not that he has to walk into the bowels of the Earth, never knowing whether he'll see the daylight again. The mine he works at is open-pit. But still.

His lips set into a line, and the coffee's sweetness turns bitter in my mouth.

"It's all right," I hurry to add. "I know you have to work there. I get it."

"It's not so much that I *have to*, Alex."

He raised me by doing odd jobs around Fort Cass, but he's a Red Seal heavy-duty mechanic, and the real money is out there in the mining industry—destroying the planet one chunk at a time. But hey. Everybody wants cars and cell phones and stuff.

We've never had much cash until he took this job last fall, but some of my best memories are of tearing into gifted boxes of non-perishable food and garbage bags of hand-me-downs like it was Christmas in July.

He raps the table top with his knuckles like he does when something's bugging him. He's been doing that a lot lately.

"What is it?" I ask.

"I got a job offer at one of the big shops down in Prince George."

"Please, no. I don't want to start at a new school in the middle of grade eleven."

We've had this moving-away conversation before. Dad's remote job means he's not home a lot, but I'm seventeen—old enough to babysit myself a couple weeks at a time. Also, leaving Fort Cass would feel like I've turned into Karine and let a spooky legend scare me away.

"Besides losing the Games and my sled starter rope quitting at the worst moment last night, nothing bad has ever happened to me here.

"You'd miss working on those giant dump trucks and shovels." I smile down at my coffee. "And maybe that Melody-person you've been talking about a lot?"

"She's a co-worker." Dad's skin flushes easily, but I'm sure I'm onto something,

"For now."

"You come first, Alex. I want you to be happy."

"I am. You have a right to be happy, too." I down the last of my syrupy coffee and slam my cup on the table for emphasis. "This is our place. We belong here."

"All right, boss." Dad glances at his watch. "But you'd better get a move on or you'll be late for school."

I grab a protein bar from the pantry, then hug his shoulders from behind. "Sorry, Dad. I wasn't trying to guilt you."

"Then you'd better stay out of trouble." He takes my hand and examines the bandage he made for me last night. "How's the old wrist?"

"I'm sure I'll live." I try to pull away, but he catches my thumb with his vise-grip mechanic's fingers.

"Don't downplay your pain, Alex."

He looks at me—I mean, really looks—like he's poking around inside my head and sees a corner of Karine's letter sticking out from the folds.

"I'm not."

"You can't heal properly if you ignore the hurt, right?"

It's a sprain—nothing to cry about.

"I'll be careful. Now you're the one making me late." I kiss his stubbly cheek. "Wait for me before reinstalling the starter for Zwing."

"For who?"

"Zwing, my sled."

He laughs. "Will do."

I shrug into my parka, a snow-camo with a twigs and dead leaves design, and head out into the cold, white morning.

Dad has nothing to worry about—the shooting ache in my wrist is impossible to ignore as I shift the truck into gear.

In the early light, the dip in the road is the same as usual with the fog, the forest, and the tangled willows. An animal's tracks dot the roadside, round with no claw marks. It's *Lynx canadensis*, with its unique snowshoe-paws. If my European settler ancestors had really brought the chat-cornu along with them, the beast would look like the Eurasian *Lynx lynx*—but with horns. Anyway, I'll believe it when I see it. Which doesn't happen on my drive to school.

I park in the lot beside the wood-and-glass modular building and pick my way over a snowbank into the icy school yard. People hang around in small groups, but we all know each other. Fort Castor is small and remote. In a crowded year like this one, the entire high school population is no more than seventy-five students, with a single class for each grade.

At the back door, pink-haired Chloe is chatting with

Caden, never missing an occasion to flaunt the sexy mole above her lip with a cute pout. She was my first crush ever. I liked her brown curls when we were twelve or thirteen, but I don't like much about her these days. We're not enemies or anything, we just don't talk much anymore. I have no idea what she's yammering about, but Caden nods and smiles because he's such a nice guy.

I wave, and his smile lights up. He says something to Chloe and strolls my way. I hide my bandaged wrist deeper into my sleeve as he approaches.

"Hey." His breath puffs out in a cloud of condensation. "How was your ride home last night?"

I give him a friendly push. "On that piece of shit you sold me?"

"What's wrong with it?"

"It stalled on me then the starter broke. My dad towed it on his way home last night."

"I can give you your money back if you want." He shoves his hands into his coat's pockets as if he's looking for the bills.

"No way. That baby is mine. I'll finish fixing it tonight."

The first bell rings. We go inside to our lockers together, and then to class where there's a traffic jam in the doorway. We hang back while it clears.

"Can you give me a ride after school?" Caden asks. "My mom dropped me off, but she has to work late."

"Sure."

Caden's mom, Tina, is Fort Castor's nurse in residence. Out here, people have to be extra mindful of angry moose and grizzly bears, out-of-control chainsaws, and excess speed on the snowmobile trails. The nearest hospital is a three-hour drive away, so Tina picks up the slack. It's her job, but she's nurturing by nature. Babysat me a lot when I was little.

The traffic jam clears. A tawny-skinned girl in a yellow dress and black leather jacket is sitting at the first desk.

Who the heck is that?

Caden steps aside to let me go first, but I push him ahead. Like everybody else, I want more time to check her out.

She tugs at a strand of her smooth, black hair and gives Caden a slow once-over. From her dimpled smile, I guess she likes what she sees. No surprise—this is Caden. I stare until she switches to me. She blinks, and her smirk flickers away. What, she doesn't like me?

Sue me, I don't have to like *her*. I stride to my desk in the middle row and take out my pencil and notebook.

"Good morning, everyone." Ms. Lewis leans her ample hips against her desk and smiles. "I hope you had fun at the Lumber Games. And I see you've noticed a new student has arrived."

Well, duh. Half the class is practically drooling.

"Meet Miss Amka Tanuyak," Ms. Lewis says.

What? Who knew Mr. Tanuyak had a daughter? Not me. But he only moved in last fall, and I don't know him all that much.

Amka turns in her seat and gives a half-hearted wave. A silver bracelet with an oval mood stone gleams on her wrist. I saw similar ones online when I was looking up ideas for our class Christmas gift exchange. But I drew Chloe, so she got a matching hat and scarf from the box in the basement. Hand-knitted with love, never worn. In defence of re-gifting, I gave her the soft wool set in a brand-new store-bought tote bag, complete with a gift receipt in case she hated it.

If I'd dug deeper into the box, I might have found the letter then, but maybe I hadn't racked up enough bad karma yet.

The stone on Amka's bracelet is greenish-grey. I don't know what mood that is, but judging by her vacant expression, she's unimpressed by the lot of us.

Ms. Lewis passes some papers around. I pretend to read along, but my eyes keep straying to Amka's purple-painted nails tapping the phone hidden on her lap with urgency, like she's telegraphing for someone—anyone—to whisk her out of here.

She sits with Mickey at lunch, maybe because he's the only other Indigenous kid in our otherwise white class. Not that I could tell just by looking at her, but I know her dad is Inuk. Mickey's showing her his black sketchbook, which no one else ever gets to see—even me who's been a friend for years. He's probably the best artist in school, but he's always been private about it.

At the end of the day, Amka takes off the microsecond the bell rings. Most guys dash after her like a pack of stray dogs after a steak. Caden sticks around and leaves with me.

"So?" I ask as we cross the parking lot. He'll get what I mean. We could always read each other's minds pretty well.

He pulls a blank face. "She seems…nice."

I snort. More like sizzling hot.

Feet stomp the snow-packed ground behind us.

"Hey, guys."

We turn as one unit. Amka—wherever she came from—struts our way, sizing us up.

I'm Fort Cass's undisputed champion of the staring contest. I may have outgrown the game sometime between primary and high school, but right now, I can't help but stare. Her eyes are so deep and dark. A flush burns across my face. I extract my keys from my pocket and unlock the driver's door. Which I never bothered locking earlier.

"Got room for one more?"

I'm not the only one driving to school. A whole crowd of licenced teens—well, at least four—idle around their parked vehicles, looking our way. Why single out Caden and me? Because we were the only ones pretending to not pay attention to her?

She builds a little mound of snow with her boots while I take my time to decide. And, oh my god, she's in scuffed combat boots.

"It was you in the mascot costume yesterday?"

"Yeah." She pretends to gag. "My dad got food poisoning on our way back from the airport, so I had to fill in for him."

Poor girl. I'd chose throwing up my guts over wearing that foul thing any day. I gesture to the truck with my chin. "I'll give you a lift."

She points down the street. "My house is that way."

"I know. I mean—I know where your dad lives, so."

She follows Caden to the passenger side. He steps in

first and scoots to the middle of the bench seat. I'm grateful he chose to sit next to me. Then Amka climbs in and, of course, he's sitting next to her, too.

I exit the parking lot and cruise along the town's main and only street. Caden's hands are in his lap. Nobody talks, and the radio drones too low to relieve the awkward atmosphere in the cab. I turn it up. Amka crosses one leg over the other. Her yellow dress rides up her thigh, revealing a sliver of skin where her black knee sock ends.

"You should watch where you're going." Caden reaches up and adjusts the steering wheel for me. I was crossing the centre line—not that anyone could see much of it through the patchy ice.

"I *am*." I focus on the road after that, all the short way to Amka's house at the edge of town. It's yellow, like her dress.

I pull over on the side of the road. She pops the door but doesn't get out yet, taking a moment to survey the dilapidated picket fence, the snow-covered swamp speckled with stunted black spruce beyond her backyard. "This place is such a hole."

"Then why'd you come here?" I ask.

"My mom couldn't stand me anymore, so she shipped me off to my dad's." Her voice is hard, her smile fake.

Me and my big mouth. "Sorry."

She shakes her head. A trace of hurt lurks in her eyes. "Don't be."

I have to make it up to her somehow. "Do you need a ride tomorrow?"

"Thanks, but I'll walk." She smiles at Caden. "See you around."

Don't count on me to offer her any more rides.

She saunters across the street to her house, the ruffled dress dancing along with her steps.

"She might want to review the dress code."

Caden appraises her hem. "And the weather forecast."

"Let's go," I say, even though I'm the one lingering. I jam the shifter into gear and gasp as an electroshock shoots up my arm.

"How's your wrist?"

"Not bad, Doctor." At least it wasn't too achy a moment ago.

Caden wants to become a paramedic, actually. We played with this toy medical kit when we were kids, which had a working stethoscope. He probably knows the sound of my heartbeat better than I do.

"You should ice it when you get home," he says.

When we arrive at Caden's place, Misfit, the blue heeler he's fostering, crawls from under the porch, her three puppies in tow. Their fluffy coats come in a mottled array of grey, tan, and black. The former owner suspects they're coydogs. If the daddy's really a coyote, it did pass on its slanted eyes.

"These little guys are sure growing fast," I say.

"I hope we find them homes soon. The mom is getting spayed and adopted next week."

"Aren't you going to keep one?"

He shakes his head, looking at the floormat. "Nah."

"Oh." His childhood Newfoundland dog, Floof, died

two years ago. The whole family took it pretty hard. He was a gentle giant, but for some reason, I could never relax around him.

"Well, thanks for the ride." Caden climbs out and whistles his dog pack onto the porch. The pups trail clumsily after their mother. When they're safe from my truck's wheels, I wave at Caden and shift into reverse. As soon as he's out of sight, my thoughts wing back to—what's her name again?

"Amka."

It sounds sweet and hard, like a jawbreaker candy. She's acting tough, but I've gotten a peek at the hurt hiding beneath the surface. If she has mommy issues, we have more in common than she might think. Even if for me, it's more like non-issues.

Chapter 3

Does unravelling a bandage from one's wrist count as distracted driving? I'm driving perfectly straight, so I think not. Dad says I should wear the itchy thing for a few more days, but it's been over a week and I'm fed up with it. I toss it on the passenger seat as I roll into Fort Cass.

March has only begun, but the morning is mild and spring-like. I cruise past Amka's house. She's jogging out of her yard and onto the road. The muddy slush will stain those tight little jeans of hers. Now that's distracting, but I don't slow down. I'm almost late for school, so she will be late for sure, but she said she didn't want lifts. Who am I to throw a wrench into her gears?

As I push the school entrance door, the glass reflects Caden's red Tacoma rolling into the parking lot. I pause long enough to see that he has Amka on board. A burn spreads from my elbows to my fingertips. The traitor. I stalk inside, bang stuff in my locker, then hurry to class.

I snub them when they come in, and all through English. They're sitting to my right, so I gaze left past two rows of desks and out the window. The mountains are skirted in fog. The Devil's Tail lurks among them, all pointy and smug. I curse in my mind and go back to stabbing notes about literary devices into my notebook. No problem if I end up losing the page. The words are etched three sheets deep.

What's up with me, anyway? I'm not jealous but pissed. I blame it on hormones—I'm on the gross day of my period. Caden can pick up girls off the roadside all he wants. And he can play the knight in shining armour all he wants, too. I've never let him rescue me, even when we played paramedics as kids. Got a leg squashed under the track of an excavator, AKA the couch? He'd have given me limb-saving treatments, but I was more the field surgeon-type. Bring on that saw from the toy carpenter kit.

He catches up with me at my locker after class, an apology at the ready. "She flagged me down."

"She lives like five steps away."

"She was late. The road was slushy."

Who cares? My feet are still wet from stepping into a puddle and I haven't melted or died. "You're too nice. Someone's going to take advantage of you someday."

I yank my science textbook from the shelf. An avalanche of stuff tumbles out along with the book. Caden catches a pencil case and picks things off the floor. I'm about to tell him I've got this, but I change my mind and let him help. He's done nothing wrong and doesn't deserve my crappiness.

"You're too nice with me." I shove everything back in. "But thanks anyway."

We fall in step with each other as we head down the hallway to second period. Amka is at her locker, checking her phone. No one has sent her a rescue helicopter yet.

Caden bumps into me to avoid her. I don't budge, and we walk to the science lab with our arms touching. My annoyance vanishes.

"Are we partnering up for the rat dissection?" he asks.

"You bet."

I hunt with Dad every fall. The insides of a rat are not so different from those of a snowshoe hare, but the poison-pickle smell of formaldehyde is something else. It's still in my nose at noon, so I grab my lunch pack and go outside.

The ice has melted off most of the picnic tables. I sit on top of one and close my eyes for a minute, tuning out the slight chill in the air to enjoy the caress of the sun's rays on my face. I hope there's more cold weather ahead. Zwing's back up and running, but I've barely had time to ride it because of my sprain.

Caden and Mickey come out with basketballs and shoot hoops on the wet blacktop. Mickey is as thin as a fishing rod, with deep-copper skin and the best eyes in Fort Cass—so dark they're almost black. I'm a sucker for dark eyes.

"Mind if I sit?" Amka asks.

I don't own the table, I think of saying, but she doesn't wait for my answer and hauls herself up beside me. Her knee peeks through a frayed rip in her jeans. A nasty, white scar cuts across her whole kneecap. I have various marks on my body from tool-mishandling and barefoot running, but none as impressive as hers.

"What happened?" I ask, hovering a finger above it.

"Climbed a cemetery fence at night with a couple of

friends." She brushes a finger over the scar. Her nails have a fresh coat of black polish.

"What were you doing in there?"

"Summoning spirits," she says, matter-of-factly.

I lean my upper body away from her to get a better look at her face. Her cat's eyes narrow, and her dimples flash.

"Kidding." She bumps my leg with hers. "We wanted to see if the White Lady was real, but she didn't show. We almost got caught by the security guard, though."

"You believe in ghosts?" It seems to me like every town except Fort Cass has its version of a ghostly lady in white.

"Maybe."

I lift my peanut butter-and-cheese sandwich to my mouth and take a bite. After today's lab, I'm glad we were out of pickles.

"Ugh," she sighs.

"What? It's an acquired taste."

"It's not that, but yeah, gross." She moves her palms in the air, painting a scene. "I mean, I feel like I've landed in some low-budget movie. City girl stuck in small-town, middle of nowhere. Will she survive the boredom?"

"Everywhere is the middle of somewhere."

A moment passes before she replies. "True."

I hear the smile in her voice, and I'm pleased she agrees with me. Then I'm annoyed at being pleased. What does she want with me? I meet her eyes—almost black and surrounded by about two million mascaraed eyelashes. I take it back. Mickey isn't the one with killer eyes.

She's close enough that she can probably smell the

peanut butter on my breath. I stash away what's left of the sandwich and bite into an apple.

"So…where are you from?" I ask.

"Mississauga, Ontario."

"Oh, yeah?"

"What? Did you think I used to live in an igloo on the Arctic Circle?"

"I didn't say that… Maybe it's that I'd hate living in a city myself."

"Fort Cass is home for now, I guess," she says without enthusiasm.

"Using the town's nickname already? You were calling it a hole the other day."

"Sorry if I insulted you, but this isn't my place. Being forced to live here sucks."

"I live with just my dad, too. We're doing fine."

She shrugs, and I take another bite of my apple.

"You remind me a lot of someone." She twists her bracelet around her wrist. A dreamy sheen glides across her eyes. "It's really weird, actually."

"Um, thanks?" At least, I think it's a compliment.

A gust of wind whips down from the mountains. A lock of Amka's black hair mingles with a lighter strand of mine. I can be nice when I try. Maybe we could be friends?

"Caden says he has puppies at home," Amka says. "Is that his pickup line?"

Or maybe we can't. "Nope. There really are puppies."

"A puppy sounds like fun. I'm getting one."

On the blacktop, Caden glances our way and misses the hoop. Maybe he does like her.

"I'll give you a ride there if you want." There. Alex Watts, role model of kindness and generosity.

"Sure. I'd like that."

The day seems to slow to a crawl after that, but after hours of poring over the most unexciting moment ever in Canadian history, and then the lousiest game of volleyball, the last bell finally rings. Amka's not at the lockers when I get there. Has Caden whisked her away again?

My disappointment is short-lived. I find her waiting by my truck as I step outside. We head to Caden's house. The Rockies loom as if they're following us as we move. I see them every day, but their frosty majesty never ceases to amaze me.

"The Devil's Tail, eh?" Amka says. "That tree up there looks creepy."

I don't need to look to figure out which tree she's talking about. I know exactly where the giant, twisted western hemlock stands, towering above the rest of the forest.

"Mickey's little sis says if you go there at midnight, it will come alive and eat you," she continues.

Mickey's kid-sister just turned eleven, but she can't possibly believe that crap. "That story has been going around since my dad was a teen. Whoever made it up watched *Poltergeist* one too many times."

That tree's always been there, and it's always been dead. But still, it's giving me an idea.

"Have you seen the movie?" I ask.

"*Poltergeist*? I've seen the remake."

"You should come to watch the original one at my place sometime."

A few seconds pass. She doesn't accept my invitation but doesn't say no either. There's hope.

I signal and turn onto Caden's slushy, bumpy road. We pass a farm and some fields before reaching his log home. As I'm pulling into the driveway, the fuzzy, tri-coloured pups trundle around the corner of the house.

"*Oh my god!*" Amka sings. She opens the door and jumps out before I've come to a full stop. "They're so cute!"

She crouches on a brown patch of frozen grass to meet them. Her light jeans are patterned with muddy paw prints within minutes. Caden steps out the door and cocks an eyebrow as I join him on the porch.

"What? *I'm* not allowed to give her a ride?"

He picks up Misfit's chew rope and taps my thigh with the frayed end.

"Just make sure you don't end up being taken advantage of." He grins, but he looks half-serious.

I rip the toy from his hand and toss it to the dog. "You forget people only take advantage of *nice* people."

Amka shrieks as one pup attempts to climb onto her chest to lick her face. I like that she's not obsessed with her clothes and makeup, like I imagine most city girls would be.

The puppies grunt and squeal as she lifts them one by one and covers them with kisses. She takes forever to choose. I wouldn't mind watching a while longer. She eventually picks the male with a speckled nose and mismatched eyes: one blue, one yellow.

"I'm calling you Blue," she says.

Not the most original, but it fits.

Caden packs a couple of days' worth of kibble into a plastic bag and hands it to her. "You can buy more at the Trading Post."

She turns toward me, hugging Blue in one arm and the bag of kibble in the other. "We can stop there on our way back, right?"

She talks like we're best friends already.

I shrug. "Sure."

We stop at the barn-shaped Post, which sells everything from fuel to animal feed, hardware, local arts and crafts, and snacks. You name it, they have it. She gets some puppy food, a dog bed, a matching collar and leash with a skull-and-crossbones pattern, and a chew toy.

Blue pees in her lap as I park in front of her house. She laughs it off.

I think I like her a lot.

Chapter 4

The blacktop gleams with frost and the sky is overcast, but a narrow band of blue sky far to the north announces an upcoming cold snap. Our P.E. teacher, Ms. Tanguay, removes her fogged-up cat-eye glasses to inspect our class of sixteen.

"Miss Tanuyak, is that your definition of warm clothing?"

Everybody turns to Amka except me, because my eyes were already on her. Jeans aren't the best for an afternoon stroll in the snow, but she looks real fine in a red hoodie—even if it's baggy and fraying at the cuffs.

"I've got an extra sweater underneath." Amka does a little twirl, but she'll learn soon enough that cute doesn't work on Tanguay. Works on me, though.

Tanguay shoves her glasses back on. "Well, I hope you got your long johns on because there's no going back inside until this thing is done."

"Yeah, sure." Amka bends to pick up Blue, who's chewing at her boot laces. She's only had him for a little over a week, but he's grown almost too big to be carried like a baby. He squirms in her arms, grunting his objections.

The why-the-heck-did-you-bring-your-dog-to-school

argument has already happened, and Blue's staying. Amka claimed it's never too early to train a future rescue dog, though the real reason is that he pees all over her house when he's left alone. There's no time for her to take him home if we want to be done by the last bell, anyway.

"Team up with a partner and put your snowshoes on." Tanguay grabs the milk crate she had set on the ground and sorts through its contents. "Then come grab an instruction sheet, a whistle, and a compass."

I take one step toward Amka, but I don't know how good she is on snowshoes, and Blue will be a liability. I have a streak to keep going.

"Alex?" Caden wriggles an eyebrow—meaning, let's win this thing together again.

Hell, yeah.

The *thing* is a treasure hunt, and I bet the prize will be something lousy and low-budget—this is Fort Cass, after all. We've won the hunt together every single year since we started high school. Last year's prize was a small stack of stale chocolate bars left over from our September fundraiser for a field trip that ended up being cancelled for lack of sufficient funds. But victory is sweet in itself, and Caden and I are a perfect team.

"Let's do this." I lift my hand for a fist bump, but he knocks me lightly on the shoulder instead. "Stop worrying about my wrist. It's healed."

I glance at Amka as I bend down to strap on my snowshoes. She's teaming up with Chloe? The two of them are already bickering.

"Good luck to them," I mutter.

"What's that?" Caden asks.

"Nothing."

It is nothing. Doesn't bother me. At. All. Amka eats lunch with me every day now, and I drop her off at her house most afternoons, too.

As it turns out, we're both horror-movie fans, though she's into paranormal while I'm more into slasher. Why? I'm always rooting for the one savvy girl to survive, of course, but you've got to admire a guy like Michael Myers, who gets stabbed and blown off and run over by trucks yet comes back a dozen more times for revenge. Amka says I make her ghost-chasing school friends look like nerds.

I don't point out that her school is Fort Castor Secondary now, not Mississauga-whatever. I've got nothing against city people, but there's more to life than hanging out at the mall.

"Let's go, let's go," our teacher calls. "We don't have all day."

Caden stuffs the whistle in his pocket and hands me the compass. The class heads across the school playing field. I'm pleased that the footing is ideal for minimal effort and maximal output: a fluffy layer over a weight-bearing base.

Blue struts behind Amka, stepping onto the tails of her snowshoes. She falls on all fours, her arms sinking to the elbows.

"Let me help." I hook my arm around hers and lift her up to her feet.

"God, I hate snowshoeing," she says, brushing snow off her knees. Wet patches stain her jeans.

"Do you really have long johns on?"

"Nah. I just wanted Tanguay off my back."

"There's an abandoned school bus over there." I point to a graffitied, yellow patch in the trees ahead. "You should hide inside while Tanguay isn't looking. Caden and I are winning, anyway."

I startle as Chloe parks herself beside us and says, "That bus is nasty."

"Nasty stuff happens all the time in the tractor tires on the playground and you didn't mind crawling in there when we were younger," I tell her.

Amka looks at us in turns. Yeah, Chloe and I have a *history*, but she doesn't need to know anything about it.

Chloe's not going to talk either. She huffs and stalks away.

"Come on, Blue." Amka stumbles after her.

I pass the two of them in about three steps and catch up to Caden.

"I thought I'd lost you in my dust." He unzips his army surplus parka to reveal the grey wool sweater he looks so good in.

"Not a chance."

We reach the barbed wire fence at the end of the school grounds and file out through the open gate. Every post is marked with different colours of tape.

"Find your colour-coded post and get ready," Tanguay says.

I check our sheet, then hand it to Caden. "We got *pink*."

"Your favourite."

"You know me too well." I don't own a single piece of

pink clothing. My palette is in blues, greys, blacks, and camos.

We step to our starting point and wait for the cue.

"First team to find the treasure, blow one long blast of your whistle. As soon as this happens, everybody heads back here," Tanguay says. "If anyone gets lost, blow three short blasts. Don't get lost. Ready, set, go!"

"Forty-two degrees, eighty-nine steps," Caden reads from the sheet.

I set the compass dial to forty-two, swivel on my feet until the needle lines up with the red arrow, then close an eye to aim the sight. "We're going toward that dead spruce over there."

There are lots of dead spruce in the boggy forest ahead, but Caden just knows which one I mean. It's nice never needing to explain things to him. I don't have that with anyone else, not even Dad. Certainly not with Amka. But I'm not against a little mystery.

We start at a relaxed pace, counting steps in our heads by unspoken agreement. At least, I hope Caden is counting because I'm distracted by Chloe and Amka, arguing by their fence post.

We enter the woods of spruce and aspen. Navigation is effortless, with the cows having tramped down the undergrowth all summer and fall.

"That's eighty-nine," Caden says.

He reads the next step in the directions. We walk to our next point, then the next and the next, without speaking much so we don't lose count of our steps. Now that Amka is out of sight, I'm on top of my game.

The going is easy, but the course is convoluted. After a while, we cross other teams' tracks. Mickey passes a dozen strides away with his teammate Kyle. He waves at us and counts out loud. "Twenty-nine, sixty-two, twelve, nineteen…"

"Nice try," I shout.

We pause to trade gear when we reach the next point. A little flock of chickadees flits in the tree tops checking out what the action in the woods is all about. They are the cheeriest birds I know, as happy as I am with the long, cold season.

"We're halfway there already," Caden says.

"How do we share the prize? Sixty-forty?"

"I bet it's some old candy bars from last fall's fundraiser. I can eat all of it for you."

"You're so nice."

He gives me the sheet, and I hand him the compass. I'd hold on to it if I'd teamed up with anyone else, but I trust his accuracy with the compass as much as my own.

"Okay. Our next destination is two-hundred-twenty—"

A flash of pink between the trees—Chloe's hair. No*t* my favourite colour, and definitely not my favourite person. She rushes toward us. "I lost Amka."

I plant myself in front of her. "What do you mean you lost Amka?"

She sidesteps and spills out her explanations to Caden. "Her dog took off after a rabbit. She went after him, and then I couldn't find her anymore."

Their shared orange whistle dangles from Chloe's neck.

"You took the whistle so now Amka has no way to

signal if she's in trouble," I say. I should have teamed up with her. I'd never have let something like this happen.

"This lot is fenced," Caden replies. "There's no way to get lost."

We look at each other and come to an agreement. I let him do the talking since Chloe isn't done ignoring me.

"Go warn Ms. Tanguay," he says. "Alex and I will look for her."

Chloe purses her lips like she's looking for words to argue, but she knows as well as anybody else that Caden and I are the best at trekking through the forest. "Fine."

"Let's follow the tree line," Caden says.

I nod. "She won't be hard to spot in her red hoodie."

We walk fast, now that we no longer have to count our steps. It's not about winning anymore. I just want to find Amka.

We reach the fence line that runs south to north. The snow is pristine here, except for a single line of hare tracks. We head north for a few minutes and are about to turn west for another pass.

"Wait. Is that..." I point to a tree that has fallen onto the fence. Snowshoe tracks lead to it and across the broken barbed wire.

"Yeah, those must be hers," Caden says.

We follow her tracks downhill to the swamp, which doesn't always freeze solid in the winter. The trees thin, and Caden jogs ahead. "There she is."

Amka stands thigh-deep in a patch of swampy slush. Blue lies whining at the edge, ears perked and mismatched eyes trained on her.

Visceral dread comes out of nowhere, like a knife in my guts. It makes no sense. I don't know why this sight should freak me out. It's not the first time in my life I've seen a filthy puddle. Amka has got to be cold, but she looks fine otherwise.

"What are you doing in there?" My voice trembles.

"Just sh-shooting the breeze with Blue, you know," she quips. A big shiver shakes her shoulders. "I'm stuck!"

"Hang on, we'll pull you right out." Caden nudges me. I should have sprung into action already.

I snap out of whatever has gotten hold of me and cautiously step toward the half-frozen bog, testing the ground as I approach. I hold out my free hand. "Whatever you do, don't lose your boots in there."

"This is f-freaking cold, by the way," she says.

We each pull one of her arms, and she works her legs. After much bog-sucking protest, the swamp releases her to us. We half-drag her to a fallen tree and sit her on the trunk.

"What the hell were you thinking, going into the swamp?" I glare at her. "Are you trying to lose your toes?"

She only pouts.

Caden removes his parka and lays it on the ground. I kneel before Amka and remove her boots, snowshoes still attached. Then, I pull off her thin ankle socks. The nails of her pretty toes are painted sparkly purple. It would be a shame if she lost some of them.

I won't let that happen.

I wrap her feet in the parka and rub them to get the blood flowing, while Caden empties the water-filled boots.

Blue gives one of the drenched socks the death-shake, oblivious to the trouble he caused. Some rescue dog.

In the distance, a whistle blows.

"Sorry I made you lose the hunt," Amka says.

"Never mind that," Caden and I say at the same time.

We shrug at each other. I'm sure we'll be winning some other race together, some other time.

"Can you pass me my socks?" Amka asks.

"You can't put these back on." I sit on the log and unlace my boots. I've been good and did a ton of laundry yesterday, so I have my best Smartwools on over a pair of liner socks. I give her the woollen ones.

"Thanks." She pulls them on. "Warm. Feels so good."

"I'm sorry to say that you can't have my boots. You'd just be floating around in them."

She wrinkles her nose as she sticks her feet into her wet leather boots. "*That* doesn't feel good at all."

Voices start calling Amka's name. Caden blows three short blasts of the whistle.

"Let's get out of here," I say.

Caden grabs a squirmy Blue, and we head out to the squishy sound of Amka's boots. To shake off the strange dread that overtook me earlier, I make myself think about Amka's cute little toes.

Chapter 5

It's Friday, Dad's gone to work, and I've got plans.

"Are you sure you don't want a ride home?" I ask Amka by the lockers.

"Yep, but you'll have to pick me up tonight."

"What time?" I've never taken anyone on a date, and somehow, this feels like one. Because I do like Amka *a lot*, and it's not just that she likes horror movies and has the prettiest feet. She acts aloof, but I can still glimpse the hurt inside of her. I yearn to be the one to show her it doesn't have to be this way. She could be like me—happy in Fort Cass with just her dad and a few friends.

"Text me later?" she says.

Great. "I don't have a cell phone at the moment."

"What?" She looks at me as if I just announced I was raised by a wolf pack.

"Long story," I say, though there isn't much to it. I could use the landline, of course, but I say, "How about eight?"

"Sounds good. Am I sleeping over?"

Ooh. "You bet!"

She waves and then strolls down the school hallway in a black lace dress that would look goth on anyone else. On her, it simply looks gorgeous. When she's out of sight, I open my locker and switch my sneakers with my boots. Caden shows up as I shrug on my parka.

"What's up?" I fuss with the zipper caught in the lining while he scrutinizes me. I've been having qualms lately about him reading my mind.

"We're playing hockey on the lake tonight." He steps closer. "Wanna come?"

Something flickers in my belly, and I'm not sure what it is. If our friendship is like paddling on a quiet stretch of river, hanging out with Amka is like jumping into a hole in the ice. I'm thrilled and exhausted, like I've been shivering nonstop for days.

Suddenly freed, my zipper lurches up and pinches my chin. "Um, sorry. Amka's coming over tonight."

"She can come along to the lake." It sounds like a statement, but it's actually a question in disguise: what am I wanting from Amka?

The answer is *everything*. Yup, Alex is thoroughly infatuated. But I say instead, "You've seen how she dresses. She'll be freezing in five minutes."

His slow nod shows me he's totally reading between the lines. "If you change your mind, you know the way."

"Hey, Caden." Chloe barges between us, her pink ponytail sweeping across my face. "Can I ride to the lake with you?"

"Sure," he says, because he's such a nice guy.

"Did you get my text?" Chloe smirks at me as if she just noticed she's almost standing on my toes, then her cool eyes slide right back to Caden. "Everybody's coming to my place afterward."

I'm sure I'd have gotten her text, too, if I still had my phone. Like, snubbing me is below her and our falling out is purely my fault. I shut my locker door, ready to take off, but she beats me to it.

"See you tonight." She spins around and saunters away to bother someone else.

Caden looks at me like he's expecting me to say something nasty. He knows me too well.

I bite the inside of my lips, take a breath. "See you on Monday."

"Have fun with Amka." He gives me a knowing smile. Not judging, but…disappointed?

I shoulder my backpack and head toward the exit, feeling like a two-faced bitch. A couple weeks ago, I was wondering what it would feel like to kiss him, and I'm pretty sure he'd have let me try. It would have been good, too. No doubt about that.

Then, Amka happened.

The extreme cold slaps me in the face as I open the school door. Blowing out clouds of vapour and guilt, I trudge across the parking lot and climb into my truck. The frozen seat is hard as concrete. While I wait for the windshield to defrost, I think of the other time I saw that knowing smile from Caden.

During our last summer before high school, our favourite game was Tracker, a kind of hide-and-seek that didn't involve counting to a hundred or staying hidden in one spot.

That July evening, when full dark wouldn't come until eleven, Caden and Mickey were the trackers and the rest of us, the fugitives. I'd bumped into Chloe around the back of the elementary school building. My fingers somehow twined with hers, and I pulled her across the dewy grass to one of the pastel-painted tractor tires standing on the playground.

The inside was dim and full of spiderwebs. Chloe's hand was still wrapped in mine, and she didn't pull away. My heart beat so fast, and not only from running. On a wild impulse, I leaned toward her and kissed her on the lips, real quick.

"You're dead," Caden said, throwing himself onto his knees in the tire opening.

Chloe giggled and wiped her mouth as if I'd been gross and embarrassing. I blushed so hard my cheeks should have blistered.

Caden held my gaze briefly, then just shrugged. Chloe and I stopped talking after that, but Caden didn't judge, or mock, or tell.

I should be more like him—I mean, being nice, and not just to others but also to myself. Besides, I haven't promised my heart to anyone. Why should I feel guilty for liking Amka?

The full moon throws the shadows of bare trees across the road. Blue stretches on the truck seat between Amka and me. He was a fluff ball when she got him, but he's in an awkward phase now. His puppy fuzz looks like a teddy bear that has gone into the wash too many times.

I hadn't specifically invited him, but aside from school, Blue goes everywhere Amka goes. It's fine. He's a good boy when he's not using your big toe as a chew toy.

We approach the down-and-up hills with the fog and the willows at the bottom. I can't believe my guts still quiver when I drive here after dark. The silly incident when Zwing broke feels like one of those nightmares that linger long after waking up because it felt so real. I press the gas pedal to give my insides something worthwhile to quiver about.

"Woohoo!" Amka lifts her arms to the ceiling as we hit the bottom.

We swoop safely to the other side. I laugh, half because this was fun and half because I'm ridiculously relieved the truck didn't sputter and die. I ease off the gas and coast all the way to my house. As soon as I've come to a stop, Amka steps outside.

"Hurry up, Blue!" She runs to the front door, her leather jacket creaking in the cold.

"It's not locked. You can go right in." I jog after them, hands stuffed in my pockets. We stomp on the mat, and I shut the door behind us. The crisp aroma of winter lingers, tainted with chimney smoke.

"It's colder than Nunavut on New Year's Eve," Amka says.

"You've been there?" I'd love to see seals and polar bears.

"Was born in Iqaluit, but my mom hated the cold. My grandparents still live there." She shrugs out of her jacket.

All she's wearing underneath is a sleeveless, lacy top that shows the lovely slope of her tan shoulders, and black skinny jeans.

Feeling overdressed, I remove my hoodie, accidentally knocking her into the overgrown aloe vera on the console table.

"Ow!" She rubs her arm. The plant's serrated leaves have left a scratch on her skin.

"Sorry about that. This is Vera."

"You name your snowmobiles *and* your plants?"

"She's the only plant in the house. My dad and I don't have a green thumb, but *Vera* just won't die."

Amka clucks. "That's not nice. Aloes get rid of negative energies."

If that's true, Vera is failing at her life mission. Amka hasn't been here for five minutes and I'm already losing points.

I grab her jacket and stuff it in the closet. "Let's go see if I have any treats for Blue."

He's already investigating the kitchen, but Amka hangs back.

"Aw." She parts the dusty leaves of the aloe and stoops toward the dustier picture frame behind it. "Baby Alex. You were a cutie."

I lean against the wall as she gawks at little-me, wondering what she thinks of me now.

In the photo, I'm three years old and sitting on a log with Karine's arm wrapped around my shoulders. She's wearing a purple-and-green scarf that matches my unlucky socks (no idea where it's at—it wasn't in the box with the socks), and her white-blond hair shines like spider silk in the sun. I can almost feel the soft tickle of it on my cheek.

Enough about this. I push myself off the wall. "You coming or what?"

"Your mom was really young," Amka says. "You look exactly like her."

"No, I don't." My eyes are lighter than hers, and my hair is several shades darker.

Amka turns away from the artifact that neither Dad nor I are willing to get rid of. Her smile is gone, and her manicured eyebrows arch with something like pity. "Did she die?"

"No, she's just gone." I trip over our discarded boots and stumble into the kitchen. "Do you want popcorn for the movie?"

Finally, Amka gets the hint and follows me in. "Maybe later?"

A movie without popcorn is just wrong, but the idea of a movie with Amka on my cramped loveseat cheers me up. I root for two cans of iced tea in the fridge while Amka wanders into the living room, Blue on her heels.

"Wow, is this for real?" she calls out. "Nobody watches DVDs anymore."

"Welcome to the Stone Age. We're stuck with 'rural high-speed internet,' so streaming is problematic."

I set the cans on the coffee table and join her in front of the bookshelf that holds Dad's massive collection.

"What are we watching?" she asks.

"Your pick. Horror is on the bottom shelf."

Amka kneels on the floor, and I sink down beside her.

"Decisions, decisions." She pulls out a few titles, pushes them back in. Her arm, softer than I thought skin could ever be, brushes mine with each move.

"Take your time."

"*Last House on the Left*," she reads on one of the plastic cases. "Don't you ever get scared when you're alone here at night?"

"I must've watched these movies a dozen times each. I'm immune to fear." I swallow the sour taste on my tongue. This wasn't a lie. Sure, mascots creep me out, and maybe I freaked a little when Zwing quit on the roadside, but I'm sure my "middle of nowhere," as Amka called it, is safer than any city.

She slides out *Psycho* and chuckles, but it seems forced. "That's my mom when we get into a fight."

I catch that glimpse of hurt behind the dark gloss of her irises. "If she's that bad, I'm glad you're here."

"She's white, like Norma Bates, in case you're wondering."

"You're half-white?" Now, I'm the one sounding like I just learned she was raised by wolves. Or just plain ignorant.

"Not when I go to Dollarama with my white friends." She passes a palm over her tawny arm. White people pay money to get spray-painted in such a lovely shade. "Guess who the staff keeps an eye on?"

"That sucks."

"I never shoplifted a thing in my life, but who cares." She shoves the DVD back into its slot and resumes her perusing. "How come you don't have a stepmom? Your dad's good-looking."

I stay silent for a few seconds, to adjust to the sharp turn our conversation just took. "Don't you get a crush on my dad. That'd be creepy."

"Sheesh, just saying. Besides, I don't get crushes on guys."

My belly does that roller-coaster thing it did on the road earlier.

"He has a girlfriend, sort of," I say belatedly. "Melody. She drives a rock truck at the mine."

I chew the inside of my bottom lip, wondering how to go back to her not-getting-crushes-on-guys revelation. Maybe—just *maybe*—she was trying to tell me something? Or else, why would she want me to know that?

"Ooh, *Poltergeist*. Like your tree."

"It's not *my* tree."

"But that's the 'original one,'" she says, mimicking the snobby tone I used to say that the other day. She thrusts the DVD in my hands. "Let's watch it."

The room spins as I walk to the player. Maybe I stood too fast, or it's all the shifts in our conversation that are dizzying me.

Amka plunks down on the loveseat. Blue tries to climb beside her, grunting with effort.

"Sorry, but my dad said no pets on the furniture." He's made no such rule—we've never even had pets—but there's no way I'm sitting alone in the recliner in the corner.

"Stay down, Blue." Amka lowers his front paws to the floor then pets him with her foot. He rolls onto his back and falls asleep, mouth half-open like a crocodile.

I sink into my rightful spot beside Amka and skip the

previews. She quickly becomes absorbed. When things get a bit spooky, she folds her legs onto the couch, seemingly unaware of the effect she has on me when she tucks her feet beneath my thigh.

The scene where the tree comes alive to eat the little boy traumatized me when I was too young to watch horror, but now it's underwhelming. Generally, trees tend to not eat people. But why am I even wasting time thinking about this when Amka's feet are so nice and warm beneath me?

I pretend to watch, but my attention is not on the skeletons (real, human ones, by the way) bouncing out of their coffins. If I let my fingers slide off my thigh, my knuckles would come to rest on that strip of bare skin between Amka's ankle sock and the hem of her jeans. Would she find me creepy? Brush me away like a fly? I have no problem coming at a log with an axe, but I have no idea how to come on to someone I like when I don't know whether they like me back.

The movie family packs their stuff, and Amka retrieves her feet from under me before I can act. While I put the DVD away, she wanders into the kitchen.

"How about that popcorn now?" she asks.

I nuke a bag of kernels while she's in the bathroom, getting into her pyjamas. Blue guards the door as if I might break inside. Silly pup.

The microwave beeps. She comes out in heart-print lavender boxers and a matching long-sleeved shirt. The soft colours give her an air of innocence, but the badass scar on her knee suggests otherwise. I like both aspects of her. And then there's everything I don't know about her. I've opened up a little about Karine—which I usually avoid at all costs because it's just not worth it. Maybe she'll tell me more about what she misses so much in Mississauga, if not her mother.

I dump the popcorn into a bowl. "Let's go up."

Blue leads the way up the stairs like he owns the place and enters my fern-green room.

I grab my moose-print pyjama pants. "I'm just gonna change quickly, if you don't mind."

"Sure."

I'm not shy about my body, and we've changed in front of each other after P.E. at school, but this feels a bit different. Maybe Amka senses it, too, because she turns her back to me, checking out my Lumber Games medals from past years, the titles on my bookshelf, the pocket knife serving as a bookmark in my Cabela's catalogue.

By the time I pull on a hoodie and slip my bra out of one sleeve, she's done with her inspection and hops onto my bed. Blue tries to climb on, but his legs are too short. I grab his middle and haul him up.

"He's allowed?" she asks.

"My room, my rules."

I turn off the overhead light. The room feels warm and cozy in the glow of the bedside lamp. I sit cross-legged facing Amka and set the bowl of popcorn between us. Blue stretches out and lays his head on her lap.

She pulls out her phone from her pocket. "What's your Wi-Fi password?"

"Five-four-three-two-one."

"Are you kidding?"

"It's not like anyone's going to freeze their butt off outside my window to steal data."

Weirdly, Caden pops into my mind, standing alone in the cold dark. I get up to lower the blinds. The back porch light is turned off, but he wouldn't be huddling there. No one would have lasted over two hours at the lake in this cold, either. He must be at Chloe's, and I bet she's making a pass at him right now. Not that it's any of my business.

I return to the bed. Blue twitches in his sleep. I cup his hind paw in my palm, rubbing my thumb over his soft footpads. I wonder where his mind is running off to. Or Amka's. I wish her attention was here with me instead of on her phone.

"Jeez." Amka pouts. "Your internet is so slow."

I should go downstairs and turn off the router. Pretend it's an outage.

"What happened to your phone?" she asks. "You dropped it in the toilet?"

"In a tub of used motor oil. My dad bought it for me with his first decent paycheck, and I'm not allowed a new one until I go to college."

"That's awful. How do you keep in touch with everyone?"

What is she doing on that phone, anyway? Playing a game? Texting with someone?

"There's the landline," I say. "And I have a laptop."

"I would die stuck here without my phone."

"Stuck in Fort Cass, or stuck at my house?"

She looks at me from beneath her multimillion lashes, a cheeky smile pulling at her lips. I'm about to spontaneously combust when Blue startles awake and kicks the bowl. Popcorn flies everywhere.

"Blue!" Amka cries.

I scoot off the bed. "It's okay, I'll go get the broom."

While downstairs, I quickly brush my teeth and go to the basement to stoke the wood stove for the night. When I walk back into my room, broom in hand, Amka is sitting at the edge of my bed reading a crumpled piece of paper in the lamplight.

What the hell?

I fling the broom against the wall. It clatters to the floor as I stomp through a minefield of spilled popcorn. "What are you doing with that?"

"Oh, Alex." She lifts her arms toward me. "I just saw it sticking out of the magazine and—"

"It's bullshit." I snatch Karine's letter from her fingers before noticing how soft her gaze has gone. She was about to wrap me in her arms.

She drops on the bed and hugs Blue instead. "I'm sorry."

"Never mind." I shove the paper to the bottom of my underwear drawer.

Amka gets up to grab the broom. I wave her off.

"I'll do it," I say, gentler this time.

"Blue needs to go outside for a few minutes," she says, eyeing the popcorn-littered floor.

"You can borrow my parka. It's in the closet."

"Thanks." She and Blue crunch out of the room.

I clean the mess while they're gone, then unroll my sleeping bag on the floor. When she returns, flushed and shivering, we tiptoe around each other without speaking. She settles on the bed with Blue. I punch my pillow into shape and slip inside my bag. The mattress creaks as Amka reaches for the lamp. The light goes out. I lie on my back, watching silver pinpoints dance on the ceiling. Icy snowflakes clink against the window. I should say something—apologize for being rude. It's not her fault I didn't hide the letter better.

"I'm sorry I read your mom's letter," Amka says in a small voice.

"Don't be. It's no big deal."

"Do you miss her a lot?"

"There's nothing to miss. I remember next to nothing about her."

I was her curse, I guess. As an exchange student from Quebec, all she wanted was to learn English for a few months, but then she got pregnant with me and was stuck here. Then I was born, and her homesickness turned into depression.

That's what Dad told me—the part about the depression. He said nothing about curses.

"Do you wish she'd taken you along with her?" she asks.

"No way." Can we talk about something else now? "What about your mom?"

"She used to be cool," Amka says, "but then she started going through my things and taking away my phone privileges because she thought I was hanging out with the wrong friends."

I twist the drawstring of my sweatpants around my finger. "I wonder what she'd think of me."

"She wouldn't care." She huffs. "She doesn't care about anyone I love."

Wouldn't, doesn't. Is she saying loving me is within her realm of possibilities?

"You're free to love anyone who cares about you." I practically strangle my waist with the drawstring. "I care."

"You're sweet, but she's wrong if she thinks I'll rot out here forever."

My heart pinches. She's thinking about leaving already? She just arrived. Wouldn't that make the chat-cornu happy. I picture it lurking on the back porch licking its chops. As far as I'm concerned, it could move right on to his nether regions.

But there is no chat-cornu, so there can't be a curse.

I'll prove it. Fort Castor is the best. Amka just hasn't seen it the right way yet. I'll show her there's a lot to love about this place.

And maybe a couple of things to love about me.

Chapter 6

I wake up to Amka standing above me in the muted morning light.

"What are you up to?" I ask, my voice rusty.

"Had to let Blue out." She nudges my ribs with her foot and smiles, all traces of awkwardness from last night's bedtime gone. "You sleep like a rock, by the way. If I was a dangerous criminal, you'd be toast."

"You think so?" I grab her ankle as she steps over me.

"Totally!" She collapses with a high-pitched cry and goes for my throat with tickling fingers.

"I'm not ticklish," I lie, laughing and grabbing at her wrists.

Her fingers somehow twine with mine, and she tries to pin me down. She's kneeling close enough to my head that I can see the subtle, almost opalescent stretchmarks on the inside of her thigh and smell her warm, sleepy skin.

My body goes soft. If she tries a move on me, I won't fight back. Then, I realize our little scuffle has turned me on, and it shows through my tank top.

"Fine, you win," I say.

She narrows her eyes, and her smile turns sly. "I heard through the grapevine that you're a sore loser."

No point in asking who told her that. I'm borderline famous for it, so it could be anyone. I might even have told her myself and forgotten about it.

"I give you a free pass out of the goodness of my heart," I say. "There will be no retribution."

Her grip relaxes, and I quickly reach for my hoodie, which I tossed sometime during the night.

Amka stands. "Blue must be ready to come in."

I don't know if she noticed anything, but she seems unperturbed as I follow her out of my room and down the stairs. We haven't made plans for the day, but I'd like her to stick around. "Do you like banana-chocolate chip pancakes?"

"Sounds delicious."

I hop down the last two steps. "I'll make you some, and then we'll do something fun."

Operation Charm Amka starts now.

A wickedly cold breeze blows a translucent sheet of snow across Pecan Lake, stretching white tendrils over the grey square of ice Caden and friends cleared for hockey last night.

"I wish Fort Cass was on Vancouver Island," Amka says through her scarf. I lent her my snow-camo parka and black snow pants. She looks good in them. "Winter wouldn't be so freaking cold."

"But then we couldn't ice fish." I bear my weight down on the manual ice-auger, sweating in one of Dad's insulated work coveralls. I'm tall, but he's taller, and he's lean, but I'm leaner. If anybody spots us from a distance, they'll think I'm a sasquatch.

The blades pierce through the ice, and I set the auger in the toboggan hitched to Zwing. Amka moves in with the oversized slotted ladle to scoop out slush from the hole.

I kneel and open my tackle box. Blue sticks his nose inside, sniffing at the ghosts of fishing past.

"A one-day licence wouldn't have cost much, you know." I remove my mittens to attach a lure to my line.

"I'll be happy to watch." She tosses the slush ladle and slumps down beside Zwing, calling Blue to her side. "And after your undercooked-slash-burned pancakes, I'll be more than happy to cook whatever you catch."

"Yeah, I'm a bad cook. Thanks for rubbing it in." But if Amka's happy, I'm happy.

Is she? While I cast my line into the hole, Amka's mind seems to be drifting elsewhere. In Mississauga, maybe— even though she claims her mother is like Norma Bates. Does she miss those friends her mom hates? That person I weirdly remind her of?

I wiggle my line. After twenty minutes, I haven't gotten a single bite.

Amka twists toward the mountains hugging the eastern edge of the lake. "Mickey said the Devil's Tail used to be round."

"Yeah. There was a landslide in the eighteen hundreds."

"He said it was called *Tsa* before the settlers came around and renamed everything."

"I know. It means 'beaver' in Dakelh. That's how Fort Castor got its name, too."

"Sounds better than Fort Beaver." She chuckles. "What's the story, anyway?"

"You haven't been to the Beaver Lodge Pub and Grill yet? It's printed on their placemats."

"Come on. It's a colonizer story, no?" She gauges my face.

I wipe my leaky nose with the cuff of my mitten. "I guess."

It's not like I crossed the Atlantic Ocean myself to come and settle on this land, but I can't claim I'm not part of a colonizer society and benefiting from it.

"Tell me, and maybe I'll tell you an Inuit story someday."

I do want Amka to tell me things. Anything. I know she keeps lots to herself.

"Fine, I'll tell you the story." I stare at the sky as though the words are written in wisps of clouds. "Once upon a time, a trapper named Gabriel trekked up Tsa Mountain on bewitched snowshoes to steal the chat-cornu's pelt and impress his fiancée Atwanet."

"Bewitched snowshoes? I need a pair of those so I don't fall into any more gross water holes."

"They were pretty useless in the end. Without its skin, the chat-cornu became a shadow, but it didn't lose its powers. It triggered the landslide for revenge. Gabriel couldn't outrun it and was buried in the rubble. Since then, anybody who sees the beast is cursed to lose someone they love."

"Aww." Amka bats her frosted eyelashes. "Handsome Gabriel and his soulmate Atwanet were cursed to be apart for the rest of eternity."

"A guy named Gabriel really died in the freak landslide, but Atwanet's probably made up, like the rest of the legend, because who doesn't like a story about star-crossed lovers, right?"

"Do you believe in soulmates, at least?"

I reel in my line to see if the bait is still on. It's gone. "I don't know about soulmates, but I do believe hot chocolate is food for the soul."

I stick my fishing rod into the snow and grab my backpack from the toboggan. I sit beside Blue, who's leaning into Amka. Zwing's bulk at our backs makes a decent windbreak. Amka fishes the thermos from the pack and fills the two cups I'm holding away from Blue's inquisitive nose.

"How did you end up being cursed?" she asks.

"Uh?" Oh, right. She read the letter. "It's just a cautionary tale to keep people off the mountain. It's not my fault Karine believed every word of it."

Amka gazes into her cup and says, "All stories have some truth to them."

"Well, true story: she left."

My words echo in my mind, harsher than I intended. If I want to charm Amka, I should try harder to be charming. Honestly, I have no idea why I thought I could pull it off. But since we're talking about this curse nonsense, I can tell her something real I've never told anyone, even Dad.

"I used to have this recurring nightmare about her." The cold air makes my voice sound raspy. Maybe Amka thinks I'm being vulnerable because she reaches around Blue to set her mittened palm on my knee. I steel myself and keep going.

"I'm little in the dream, having a tantrum in my car seat. There's a fallen tree across the road at the base of the Devil's Tail. Karine gets out of the car to move it but then she sees something in the forest."

An unexpected lump blocks my throat. I choke it down with a swig of hot chocolate.

"Just before disappearing into the trees, she turns to look at me, but then her skin peels off, and she transforms into Chatty the mascot. Except it looks more like a real lynx, and its fur is dripping with blood." I snicker. "I know. This is silly."

"My god, Alex." Amka pats Blue's rump to get him out of the way. He takes off to sniff around and pees on the mound that holds my fishing rod. Amka scoots over and looks at me, all doe-eyed. "The nightmares must have been some kind of coping mechanism."

I shrug. Why does it still upset me? The chat-cornu didn't steal Karine. She packed her suitcases and drove away. Dad returned from hunting to a silent house, with me fast asleep in my crib. All she left was that box of knitted stuff with the damn letter in it. That's the real curse. Since I found it, it has kept stirring up things I thought I had long put behind me.

"I'm coping fine."

Amka frowns like she doesn't buy it. "You know what? We should go up there sometime."

"On the Devil's Tail?" Nobody believes in the legend, but no one goes there either.

"Mickey says his ancestors had a trapper's cabin up there. We should check it out. It might help you exorcise your ghosts."

My ghosts? I don't have any ghosts.

"That cabin must be a rotten pile now."

She leans into me. "We could bring a tent in case we don't find it and camp overnight."

Amka and me alone in a tent up on the Devil's Tail? Ice-fishing clearly isn't her thing, but if she's into chasing after ghosts, I'm willing. Extra point if it helps her forget about skipping town.

"I don't have any bewitched snowshoes, so we'll have to wait until the snow melts."

Hot chocolate sloshes on her mittens as she knocks her cup against mine. "It's a date."

Blue trots over, tongue lolling and tail wagging like he's excited about our plans. With his yellow eye in view, he looks more coyote than dog. His head tilts to one side as if he's listening to the elusive fish swimming beneath the ice.

Amka digs into the snow with the heel of the spare winter boots I gave her, uncovering a patch of grey ice. "You think the lake might break and swallow us?"

"No way. That ice is two feet thick." The idea of falling in and being stuck under the ice gives me a chill, though. "Are you ready to go?"

"I thought you'd never ask." She pulls her scarf over her face again. "My nose is ready to fall off."

She packs up the thermos while I gather my fishing gear. Blue barks his head off as Zwing's engine sputters to life. Amka pats the seat between us, but he won't hop on like he did when we rode over.

"Fine, then," she says and slides forward to wrap her arms around my waist.

With her holding on to me like this, I'm in no rush to go anywhere fast. Blue escorts us as we head safely to shore. If the lake is hungry, today's not the day it will swallow me.

Chapter 7

Ms. Tanguay blows her whistle. "Alex, we're playing *ringette*, not rugby. Go sit for five."

Chloe gives me the stink eye, her pink ponytail hanging askew.

"It's not my fault she was in my way," I mutter, jogging to the bench along the far wall. And like I care that she's been buzzing around Caden like a fruit fly around a banana ever since they played hockey on the lake.

This isn't even real ringette. Like hockey, it should be played on ice. Personally, I'd rather be practicing real-life skills, like splitting firewood and pushing stuck cars out of snowbanks.

I don't mind sitting and watching, though. Amka is a fierce player. I bet she'd hate playing anything on ice. Our fishing outing two weeks ago was a flop, and she didn't want to give snowshoeing another try even though I promised we'd stay away from the swamp.

The teacher switches up teams. I start getting up, but the searing look she gives me says I'm benched for the rest of P.E. Mickey and Amka jog over and sit on the bench, one on each side of me.

Mickey rakes his fingers through his black hair. Sweat

makes it stick up like the crest on a Steller's jay. "My parents are going away on spring break. I'm having a party. What d'you guys think?"

"Yeah, sure," I say.

"I'm spending the week in Mississauga," Amka says. "Sorry."

That's news to me. She didn't mention this when I suggested we binge-watch the entire *Halloween* franchise on spring break.

"You could have told me," I tell her as we head out of the gym.

"I was going to. No need to be pissed."

"I'm not pissed." I push the changing room door, and it bangs against the wall.

"Then why are you like this?"

"Like what? I'm trying to plan my spring break." I know exactly what I'm being like but can't stop myself. I open my locker door and sort through my change of clothes. "I mean, if you're not around, I could go ice fishing with Caden and stuff."

I don't know why I bring him up. It's not like that'll make her jealous. To top that off, Caden has been too busy fending off Chloe's flirting to pay much attention to me lately.

"Jeez," she says. "I wouldn't want to ruin it for you. I'll go right ahead and buy my plane ticket." She slips on her leather jacket over her tank top and heads out, still in her gym shorts.

"What's up with her?" I mumble. My heart is racing.

"She's homesick," Chloe says. She's fixing her ponytail

and looking at me from the magnetic mirror on her locker. "Wouldn't you be?"

"She has her dad right here, her dog, and…" By now, I thought I mattered to her a little bit, too.

Chloe applies some pink gloss that matches her pink hair and smacks her lips. "With you, it's always all or nothing, isn't it?"

"What's wrong with that? I know what I want."

She shakes her head. "For someone who hates losing, you sure know how to jinx yourself."

"What's that supposed to mean?"

"We used to be friends." She shuts her locker door and turns to face me. "We could still have been friends."

After she laughed at me because I kissed her? "I don't think so."

"What about Caden? You just about ditched him for her."

"Convenient for you, right?" I grab my stuff and stalk out.

Her words are still stabbing me as I get into my truck. But Chloe's wrong. I'd never ditch Caden. He's my friend, and we'll always be friends.

I get into my truck and skid off the schoolyard. Amka is tramping up her walkway as I drive past. I should stop and make up with her right away. She turns to look when I ease off the gas but climbs her porch steps without pausing. Why waste her time if she's not up to listening to me? I speed up again and go straight home.

Dad is in the backyard, enveloped in a cloud of chainsaw smoke, cutting a pine trunk into logs. I go inside to pull on my winter clothes and join him, axe in hand. The frozen wood splits easily. I go at it like this is an event at the Lumber Games. I'd be winning for sure at this rate, but I only feel like a loser.

My arguments with Chloe and Amka are still on my mind as I slip into bed that night, muscle sore. The peachy shampoo smell Amka left on the pillow that one time she slept over is long gone, like a dream you know you had but can barely remember. I can't fall asleep, mulling over what Chloe said. Apparently, it's my fault our friendship went out the window.

That line from Karine's letter about the chat-cornu stealing someone I love bleeds into my mind. How long does it take to know that you love someone?

I turn on my bedside lamp and step to my dresser. The crumpled letter is pushed all the way to the bottom, tucked behind the plastic package of beige, full brief underwear Grandma Watts gave me last Christmas.

This letter is the curse—I've known it for a while. Now's the time to take care of it.

I creep past Dad's bedroom and all the way down to the basement without bothering to turn on a light. The fire in the wood stove casts a dancing orange glow across the unfinished room. I kneel on the warm concrete and unfold the paper.

You've been cursed, Alexia...I had to leave.

When I search my feelings for Karine, I don't find any love. It's hard to have deep sentiments for someone you barely remember. If I really was cursed, would that mean I still stand to lose someone?

I love Dad more than anyone. He could get crushed by a forty-ton rock truck at the mine. A bull moose could go through his windshield when he's on his long drive home. I make up a couple more scenarios, but I'm not feeling it. Dad is strong, healthy, and down to earth. Plus, he used to hunt on the Tail every fall before the area was closed to protect the mountain caribou, and nothing bad happened. Curses can't touch him.

But Amka? She believes in ghostly white ladies and stuff. What if she decides she'd better stay away from cursed-me? The mere thought of her not returning after spring break crushes me. I want more time with her.

I want her to fall in love with me. Is that too much to ask? I'm a good-enough person, most of the time.

I open the stove door a crack. The rush of air stokes the flames, and the fire growls in the chimney. I toss the letter inside and latch the door. Behind the glass pane, the paper catches instantly, curling up at the edges. The words turn to smoke, meaningless particles sucked out into the night.

There. It's done. Curse broken.

I stand and dust off my knees as the flames flare a greenish white. My breath catches, like the instant you drop a glass and know there will be no picking up the pieces and gluing them back.

My letter-burning ritual didn't make Amka and me magically fall into each other's arms in tearful apologies. We didn't speak over the weekend, and she's been throwing me some you-break-it-you-fix-it looks for the first half of the school week.

After what Chloe said, I've been too proud to fall back on my friendship with Caden. She's always around him and I can't stand her, so I've been spending all my free time alone in the school library. Who would have thought I'd become *that* girl.

We have early dismissal on Wednesdays, but today I stayed to scour the shelves one last time. I've been looking for books on Fort Castor's history but haven't found any. I can picture Karine sitting at a table reading such a book and filling her gullible mind with crap about the chat-cornu. It's ridiculous, but I can't let it go.

I shoulder my backpack and head out into the gloomy afternoon. It might rain, or it might snow. I leave my truck in the parking lot and jog across the street to the white-painted Our Lady of Sorrows Church. I don't believe in ladies of any kind—ghostly, saintly, or otherwise, but I believe I might find what I'm looking for in the basement public library.

The stairs are on the side of the building, narrow and shaded. As I start going down the worn wooden steps, someone comes out.

Amka.

She climbs the stairs, a frown aimed at her feet. I hesitate between spooking her now or letting her jump when she notices me.

"Hi, Alex."

I'm the one who's startled. My name sounds almost

sweet in her voice, but her tone is tired, as if she's already been forced to say hi to me a hundred times today.

"Hey." I press my back against the wall to give her a chance to pass. She does, so it's really up to me to fix what I've broken. My worthless pride is just a bad taste in my mouth now. I grasp her fingertips while she's still within reach. "Do you have a minute?"

"What?" Standing one step up, she faces me with the kind of polite smile you give a cashier at the grocery store.

"I'm sorry I was pissed the other day."

She considers me for a long moment. "It was kind of childish."

I don't know if she meant what *I* said was childish or if the whole argument was. It doesn't matter if she's willing to hear me out. "I was surprised you weren't staying for spring break, that's all."

"Okay."

"And I guess I was a bit hurt you didn't tell me."

"Okay."

I don't dare sigh with relief just yet. "So…are we good?"

She sucks in her cheeks, maybe to hold in a smile. Her face is inches from mine, and her breath smells like mint. "I was annoyed with you for, like, fifteen minutes. You sure can hold a grudge for a long time."

"Sucks to be me." I grin back at her. "When are you leaving?"

"Not sure yet. I'm keeping an eye out for last-minute deals on flights."

A deal during spring break seems unlikely, but what do

I know? I've never shopped for plane tickets myself—never even been on an airplane.

"I gotta go." Amka's smile is gone and the frown has returned. "See you tomorrow?"

"Sure. Good luck with finding a deal."

"Thanks." She swivels around and jogs up the stairs.

I continue down because I've got nothing better to do at home. Dad's gone to work, and dinner will be something out of a can. Mickey's mom volunteers here on weekdays. She might know something I don't about Fort Cass and its history. Maybe she'll remember Karine—not as the mother who left me behind but as the carefree teen she must have been before I crashed the party.

A smell of incense and musty books hits my nose as I push open the door. I take in the five rows of bookshelves, the dismal fluorescent lighting, the dehumidifier whirring in a corner. Perfect setting for a horror movie.

Mickey's hunched over his sketchbook at the librarian's desk a few steps away. He doesn't look up but quickly yanks off his thin wire glasses. "Forgot something?"

"Hey, it's me."

"Oh. *Bonjour, mademoiselle*," he says. "I'm filling in for my *maman* today."

You'd think French would have been in my blood, with Karine being from Quebec and all, but he's the one who aced grade eight French while I passed by the skin of my teeth.

"*Hadih*," I say in Dakelh. There are so few fluent speakers of his traditional language left—because of colonization and everything—that I know almost as much of it as he does. It's ironic. Or maybe not. I was never forbidden to speak my mother's French—I just didn't put any effort into it.

He squints at me. "Did you see Amka on your way in?"

"Yeah."

"Did you two finally make up?"

I shrug. "I hope so."

"You like her that much, eh?"

Heat blooms on my cheeks although Mickey and I already share a few secrets. Like, how he wears glasses instead of contacts when no one's looking. Or that we fooled around after the school year-end party last year. He's the first (and only) guy I've kissed. It was fine, but things didn't go any further. No tears, no hurt feelings.

From the sketchbook on the desk, a character in black ink winks at me, looking a lot like Mickey—wild hair, dark eyes, and a skinny frame.

"A graphic novel? That's your top-secret project?"

Mickey taps the page with his pencil. "Meet Mickey Man, demon slayer,"

I take in the finely detailed sketches. "That is really cool."

"Thanks." He covers the page with his palm, and I feel intrusive. I leave him to his work and wander between the aisles. There's nothing about Fort Castor at first glance. I open random volumes and read the names on the obsolete checkout cards. Some ring a bell, but Karine's name isn't there. Perhaps she wasn't into history. Maybe all there is to the legend is written on those Beaver Lodge placemats.

A shadow crawls along the floor and up the far wall, Nosferatu-like. I turn as Mickey leans over my shoulder.

"Are you looking for something in particular?" he asks.

"What do you know about the chat-cornu?"

"It's a—"

"I know. It's a colonizer story."

Mickey snorts. "It's not what I was going to say, but good for them for making up their own trickster instead of appropriating one."

"Yeah. My dad has about twelve different wendigo movies in his collection."

Mickey pulls a few books from the shelves, but I don't think he's looking. He confirmed the chat-cornu is made up—of course it is.

"Thanks," I say, though I'm not sure what I'm thankful for. For listening to me, I guess, and for not being bothered that I like Amka so much.

"Anything for you, Alex."

"Are you sure? Could I be Mickey Man's sidekick in your book?"

"Hm…maybe in the sequel." He scratches his hair, his gaze lost in space as if he's really considering it. "Awesome Alex and her magical axe, Axcalibur."

"Ah, sweet." I swing an imaginary axe but stop short when my belly growls. "I'd better go fill up before going off to slay demons."

I leave empty-handed but grateful. Mickey's a true friend.

Outside, darkness has fallen. I run back to my truck and drive home. As per my new habit, I speed up across the hills near the Devil's Tail, giving myself no time to dwell on uncanny shadows. My stomach lurches as usual, but it's just the combination of hunger and lingering incense-and-old-books aftertaste.

Chapter 8

"Come on, Alex. You're no fun." Amka leans back into her closet. The clothes are so packed on the rod that she doesn't fall through. She wants us to go to Mickey's party dressed up as each other.

"It's April Fool's, not Halloween."

"This shitty town is boring me to *death*." She pouts, then swivels on her feet and resumes riffling through her clothes, yanking out dresses and tops that she examines before stuffing them back inside.

Amka never found a good deal on flights, and her parents couldn't agree on who should pay for her plane ticket. She ended up stuck here for spring break, and she's been in this crappy mood *all* week. I'm relieved the letter is gone, but I also feel guilty, as if by burning it I cast a spell to make her stay in Fort Cass against her will.

"Still waiting," she says, tapping the tip of her foot on the carpeted floor. "Are we doing this or not?"

I want Amka to stay, but I also want her to be glad to be here. And, who knows, maybe she can coax an inkling of charm out of me. "Fine, let's dress up as each other."

"Fantastic." She pounces on me and clutches my shoulders. "Let's do you first. You'll take the longest."

"Gee, thanks."

"I didn't mean it that way. If you want to achieve my signature look, you must suffer a little."

She plugs in the flat iron and finger combs through my hair. My scalp tingles at her touch—not suffering much so far. Then, she smooths strand after strand with the iron until they flow like honey.

Blue snores on the bed, catching a few moments of beauty sleep. I grab Amka's phone from the bedspread to check the time.

"It's getting late." I wouldn't mind her playing with my hair all night, but it's almost nine.

"What time's the curfew around here?" She steals the phone from my hand. "Ten o'clock? Are Mickey's mommy and daddy going to hang out with us?"

"They're out of town. His older sister will be there. She's nice."

"Is she as good-looking as Mickey?"

I know Amka's teasing, but this bugs me all the same. "I haven't seen her in a couple years. Come on, hurry up."

She paints my fingernails black and takes forever to apply creams and makeup on my face. When she's done, my eyelashes are so heavy with mascara I can barely keep my eyes open.

"Ta-da!" Amka guides me to the mirror on her closet door. "You're a masterpiece."

"Whoa." I don't look like Amka at all, and I barely look like myself. I could probably walk into a bar without being carded. "Maybe we'll fool everyone into thinking I'm one of your girlfriends from Mississauga."

Amka's smile vanishes. "Don't say stuff like that."

"Stuff like what?" I glance at her bracelet. Clearly, that thing doesn't tell moods—the stone is a cool turquoise while Amka's irises gleam like gunpowder.

She shakes her head. "Never mind. It's nothing."

It doesn't feel like "nothing" when she jabs the hoop earrings into my earlobes. Note to self: do not mention girlfriends from Mississauga ever again. I have a theory, though. Maybe her mom isn't as bad as Amka says and never kicked her out. She ran away from heartbreak. Maybe she was hoping to go to Mississauga to patch things up? It's not a good idea. She should let go and move on. I'll help her as best as I can.

"Put this on." She flings me a black skirt that's way too short for the school dress code.

I don't dare argue. Anything to restore Amka's good mood. I'd shamelessly go fetch or roll over for that treat.

The skirt feels silky on my skin as I pull it on. I'm narrower than Amka, so it sits low on my waist. The hem flares mid-thigh, but I still feel half-naked. "If I drop anything on the floor, you're picking it up for me."

"Sure. Whatever." She then hands me a soft, dove-grey sweater.

I toss my T-shirt aside and put on the sweater, which leaves a stripe of belly exposed. I try to pull it down over my midriff, but she brushes off my hands.

"That's how it fits."

"I'm going to freeze dressed like this."

"It's not a backyard party, is it?"

"I don't think so." I slip on the long, black socks that

complete the outfit and glare at the strange girl in the mirror. I do dress up sometimes, for family gatherings and school photos, but never like this. And usually not for hanging out in someone's basement.

"Why are you doing this to me?" I whine.

"You want to be Amka? You have to rock it."

Okay then. Now that I'm supposedly Amka, I'll be flirty with the real Amka as soon as she turns into Alex, and see how she reacts. Maybe she'll be subliminally compelled to imitate me after we return to our usual selves.

She upends my backpack on the bed, shaking it to see if any more clothes will fall from it. Her bracelet glints. I've never seen her without it, and I'm apparently not getting to wear it tonight.

"Are you kidding me?" She lays out my black jeans, tank top, and hoodie. "That's what you were planning to wear?"

My turn to be smug. "That's how you rock being Alex."

I fuss with my hair while Amka changes, catching glimpses of her in the mirror. She jumps up and down, but my jeans won't go up her curvy hips.

"How do you fit into these?" she says.

"Why don't you just wear your own black jeans? No one will know the difference."

"No cheating." She trades the jeans for the leggings I was planning to sleep in, and then gathers her hair into a ponytail without even brushing it.

"That was easy." She twirls. "How do I look?"

"Exactly like me." Of course, she doesn't, but she's as stunning as usual.

She rubs her palms together. "Ready to fool everyone?"

My stomach clenches. I've tobogganed down rooftops and kissed toads on a dare, but I've never pulled a stunt like this. "Sure. Let's go."

Amka gets to wear my warm parka while she forces me into her leather jacket and combat boots two sizes too small for me.

"Bye, Blue." She kisses him between the ears. "Be a good boy."

Mickey lives only a few houses over, so we walk. A handful of stars shine between drifting patches of darkness. The lawns in front of the houses are still under snow, but the road is bare and glitters with frost. We stroll along the yellow line. There's hardly any traffic in Fort Cass after nine.

When we pass under the streetlight in front of the barn-shaped Trading Post, our shadows slink ahead. In their dark version of us, I could really be Amka. I wish it would give me some insight into her mind.

Shadow-Alex grabs my hand with her icy fingers. I give them a squeeze, and she squeezes back. I don't know what it means, but I like it.

We walk up the concrete walkway to Mickey's front door. Caden's Tacoma is parked in the driveway among a few other vehicles. A bass beat pulses through the walls of the house. There's no point in knocking, so we go right in. Hip-hop music drifts up the basement stairs. I hang back, and Amka goes down first. When she enters the room, the chatter stops—not that we could actually hear it over the music, but lips are set in smiles or pouts or gasps.

"Nothing to see," Amka shouts over the music, hands cupped around her mouth. "It's just me, Alex."

"Where's Amka, then?" Mickey shouts back.

Pretend-Alex steps aside and pulls me down the last two steps. The basement is packed. All faces turn to me. Someone whistles.

Mickey navigates his way over to us, his head sticking out of the crowd like a periscope.

"Hey, Al—I mean Amka." He gives me a once-over.

"Hi." I'm not usually shy, but my face feels hot. I'm glad the room is dim.

"Can I help you with your coat?" he asks.

"I got it." I toss the leather jacket onto a pile with my parka, then Amka parades me around, which means bumping into people and getting my toes stepped on a lot. Most of our classmates are here, plus some older siblings, home from college, and a bunch of friends and cousins from out of town. Some guy with dreadlocks and thick-framed glasses gawks at me as if he's never seen a girl before.

I stare him down and slip my arm around Amka's waist. And she slips hers around mine. Well. This might turn into a fantastic evening.

Caden's at the pool table in the far corner, leaning forward to play his turn. His gaze finds me as he knocks the ball. He looks from me to Amka and back and smiles when our eyes meet. We haven't been talking much lately, and I guess I've been missing him a little. I should go say hello, but Amka drags me through a dancing crowd. Some of the girls are flashing twice as much skin as I am, and Jonas, a guy in our class, is twirling his sweaty T-shirt above his head. I flinch away from him. He needs a shower, or at least a drench in Axe body spray.

"Is that Mickey's sister over there?" Amka asks at the top of her lungs.

"Yeah. Charlie."

She's in faded black jeans and a dark-black crop top. Charlie and Mickey look a lot like each other, but Charlie has multiple piercings on her face, and her hair reaches down to her waist.

"Amka wants to be introduced," Amka says.

This is getting confusing. Who wants to meet Charlie, Amka-me or Amka-her?

"Just so you know, she has a girlfriend," I say in her ear.

Amka throws me an impish smile. "Doesn't matter. Amka and Alex are leaving together when the party is over."

My pulse skips—or maybe it's the beat of the music that bounces around in my ribcage. Whatever that feeling might be, this might just be the night I finally work up the nerve to kiss her.

Charlie gets up from her stool as we approach and sets her phone on a counter loaded with a rainbow of cans and bottles.

"Hey, Charlie. Remember me, Alex?" Amka says. "This is my gorgeous friend, Amka."

Charlie knits her brow.

I smirk. "April Fool's."

She laughs, eyes still on me. "Neither of you looks like the Alex I remember."

I introduce them. Amka asks Charlie what she does, and Charlie inquires about Amka's family. Amka's hand is still around my waist, and she bumps me with her hip from time to time to punctuate what she's saying.

"Are you thirsty?" Amka asks. "I'll be right back."

I yell-chat with Charlie until Amka returns and pushes a can of Twisted Tea into my hand.

"Amka's favourite." She kisses my cheek and drifts away again.

I take a few sips, savouring the lingering feel of that kiss. Charlie excuses herself, so I plow my way toward the pool table, only to realize Caden is done playing. I locate him on a couch across the room. Chloe sits on the armrest, leaning down to speak to him. I can see her cleavage from here, framed by her low-cut shirt and cascading pink hair. She looks good, and it's obvious who she primped herself for.

Mickey nudges my arm with his pool stick. "Want to play a round of eight-ball?"

Does Amka play pool? I'm not even sure where she's at. She's not being a very good Alex right now, because the real Alex would be hanging out with Amka.

"Sure." I grab a stick. "One game."

The hem of my skirt keeps riding up my thighs each time I lean over the green velvet, and I keep playing fouls. I catch Caden watching me when he thinks I'm not paying attention, but he looks away each time I notice.

The party unfolds, and like all parties, there's some horsing around, some dancing, an almost-fight, and plenty of making out. The windowless room is getting stuffier by the minute. Amka comes by the pool table to give me another drink and hang out for a bit, but she spends most of her time hovering around Caden and getting in Chloe's way, throwing me a mischievous wink from time to time. Odd way to have fun, but at least she's not moping anymore.

I finish my second losing round of pool and my third Twisted Tea. If the music wasn't so damn loud, I'm sure my ears would be buzzing because I'm dizzy as I head toward the couches. Caden looks like he needs saving. Chloe and Amka are having some kind of sexy dance-off practically on his lap.

Dreadlocks-guy moves into my path as I worm my way between dancing bodies. I give him a death stare, but he's undeterred. In no mood to deal with this rando, I prepare to shove past him, but then Mickey appears out of nowhere and blocks him.

"Mickey Man to the rescue." He does a little dance move. "Wanna dance?"

I'm flattered by the way his eyes move over me. It softens my two losses at eight-ball, so even though I don't have a dancing bone in my body, I give it a try. This is another hip-hop song I don't know, and I have no idea how to dance to it. I probably look like a short-circuiting robot.

He leans down to speak in my ear. "Is this your Awesome Alex outfit?"

I show him my empty palms. "Minus Axcalibur."

"You're still looking pretty awesome."

"Don't get used to it," I say. "I'm turning back into plain Alex at midnight."

"It's two a.m."

I laugh. Is it even funny? Who cares.

"How are things with Amka?" He loosely drapes one

arm around my waist. Our dancing slows though the beat of the music picks up.

"I dunno."

"If I were her, I'd be all over you."

I throw him a mock flirty glance from beneath my mascara-heavy lashes. Maybe that'll motivate Amka to come and steal me away.

"Just so you know, I'm drunk," I say. "I won't remember any of this tomorrow."

He smiles and shrugs. As we move around, I notice new people occupying the couch. Amka and Chloe are disappearing up the stairs, laughing. Huh. Are they besties now? I scan the room. Who else is missing? Caden. Charlie. Dreadlocks. A few others.

I need a minute to myself. I push away from Mickey. "I'm going to the bathroom."

"Sure. See you later."

Unsteadily, I climb upstairs and lock myself in the cramped room. I lean into the sink, the ceramic coolness soothing beneath my palms. With all the makeup I'm wearing, my reflection in the mirror is a stranger's. I glower at her until she blurs at the edges. She blinks, the blue of her eyes oddly familiar though a lighter shade than my own. For a fraction of a second, Karine stares back at me.

"Shit." I blink hard and return to being me. I'd love to splash cold water on my face to clear my head, but if the mascara runs, I'll look like a hot mess.

As I step out of the bathroom, a patio door slides shut in the dining room beyond the archway to my left. It's too dark to see anyone, but a whiff of weed floats by and voices fade away into the backyard. It's Chloe, I think, with some guys and a girl whose laugh sounds a lot like Amka's.

Is that what they're all up to? I'm too goody-goody for drugs, but they could at least have invited me.

Does Amka still think we're leaving together? I did what she wanted—let her dress me up like a damn Barbie doll. She left me alone most of the night and now this? I'm ready to take off right now, with or without her. We didn't lock the door on our way out. I'll let myself into her house and go to bed. She can come home whenever she's good and ready.

I stalk away from the dining room and bump into Caden at the top of the stairs.

"Whoa, there." He catches my arm to steady me. "You all right?"

"I'm just so tired." And also relieved he's not in the backyard doing whatever. My legs feel weak, like they're made of pipe cleaners. I close my eyes and lay my forehead on his shoulder. He does nothing at first but holds my hips when I tilt to one side. His fingertips graze my skin, and he doesn't move them off. I don't mind them there. I'm so lonely all of a sudden.

"You need a ride home?" he asks. "I'll give you one if you want."

"I don't know." I want to stay like this until morning. I wrap my arms around him and wonder how he manages to smell so good after hours in a boozy, crowded basement. Being this close to him feels like floating on a lake, with water so clear you can see right to the bottom. Caden is like that. No games.

"Don't ever change," I mumble into his shirt.

"What was that?" he asks.

A new set of fingers flit across my waist. I flinch.

"Sorry for interrupting your little moment," Amka says, "but I must steal Alex from you, Caden."

She pulls, and I have to step back to keep my balance. Caden's hands still hold me. He questions me with his eyes—do I want him to let Amka win this tug of war?

I resist, undecided. I love winning, but I don't know how I feel about being the prize.

How long has she been spying, anyway? I didn't even hear the patio door open and close. Maybe she wasn't outside after all.

"I thought we were leaving together," Amka whines.

My skin feels hot beneath the pressure of her fingertips. She presses herself against me, and just like that, my body lets me know she has won.

I let her drag me away. Caden's arms slide off me and fall to his sides.

"My stuff is at her place," I say, avoiding his eyes.

He clenches his jaw and says nothing. I send him a pitiful wave as Amka pulls me down the stairs by the hand. He turns and walks out the door.

As I dig through the coats piled on a chair, anger crowds out the twinge of guilt. I put on my parka, tight-lipped. Why did she make me choose between Caden and her, especially when she chose to hang out with everybody but me all evening?

"How was your night?" I snap. "Haven't seen you in a while."

She pulls at the fabric of her leggings. "Some asshole spilled a beer on me. Sorry."

"It's okay. I wasn't going to sleep in them, anyway."

Amka finds her leather jacket and follows me out. I start down the street, keeping ahead of her. My toes are killing me in the too-small boots, and the chill in the air is cruelly sobering.

"Are you angry with me or something?" she asks.

"I thought we were going to this party together." A fresh wave of annoyance surges. "I barely saw you after we got there."

She jogs to catch up with me. "Aw, you think me-Alex should have followed you-Amka everywhere like Blue begging for a treat?"

"You're such a tease." We've reached her house, but I keep walking.

"Where are you going?" she asks.

"Home." I should have taken Caden's offer for a lift.

"You can't do that. It's too far."

"You don't know me."

"What about the chat-cornu? What if it's waiting for you?"

I snort, but when I look at the woods down the street, a shiver runs beneath my skin.

"Alex, please." She runs to overtake me, forcing me to stop. We face off, the steam of our breath hanging thick between us.

"Let's go inside, c'mon." She grabs my hand, like earlier when I let myself believe this would be a great night.

The cold seeps under my skirt. My feet hurt. It would

be a cold, lonely trek home. And I would have to walk by the old trail at the base of the Tail. Wasted as I am, I'd probably mistake a coyote wail for a little girl's cries or my own shadow for a monster.

Amka's fingers warm up in mine. I don't want another fight with her because then she might decide she's done with me once and for all. Besides, the night isn't over yet. I pull my hand away but turn around and head back toward her house.

"Thank you," she says.

"For what?"

"For coming back with me."

"No problem," I say, though I wish I'd have come up with a better platitude.

We get back to her house. Blue greets us in the mudroom, prancing around and whining. After he returns from his bathroom break, we tiptoe upstairs. My legs ache. I'm relieved not to be alone on the dark road. Blue jumps onto the bed, and Amka throws herself beside him.

"How do I get this gunk off my face?" I ask.

"There's makeup remover on the shelf above the sink."

I clean up, trying to be quiet because her dad sleeps downstairs, but I keep dropping stuff and knocking things over.

Amka knocks softly. "Can I come in?"

I open the door for her. She has peeled off the beer-soaked leggings and wrapped herself in a fuzzy blanket.

"Found everything all right?"

"Yeah."

She sits on the edge of the bathtub. "Are you still pissed?"

I interrogate my face in the mirror. I'm back to being Alex, though with red splotches on my skin from all the scrubbing. I don't seem angry anymore—can't feel the angry burn on the inside, either. Amka said we'd leave the party together, and we're both here now, so I guess I'm sort of forgiving her for ghosting me.

"You were right. Fifteen minutes of being pissed are plenty."

She smiles and hugs me, quick and impersonal. "I need a shower. See you in a bit."

I shuffle back to the bedroom. Since my leggings are ruined, all I have to sleep in is a T-shirt and my underwear. Amka has a queen mattress, and she said no need to bring my sleeping bag. I slip between the sheets, turning my back to Blue sprawled in the middle. I close my eyes. The room spins. I'm almost asleep when Amka returns.

"Off the bed, Blue," she hisses. "Go lie down on your blanket."

The light clicks off, and the mattress creaks. Amka lies quiet beside me. My body and mind sink deeper into sleep.

Until she inches across.

I lie still, but I'm wide awake now. I hold my breath as she pushes my hair up on the pillow then spoons me, one arm around my waist. Her fingertips slowly travel down my ribs, my belly button, and then the other place they've explored in my before-going-to-sleep daydreams, making me glow like an ember stoked by a wind.

I want more. I want to do this for her, too.

"Amka," I whisper, trying to turn into her arms.

"Shhh." She clutches me tight, keeping my back pressed to her.

I hold still, willing her to return to her exploration of my body, but her grip soon relaxes, as if she's falling asleep. Her lips touch my neck. She says something. A name. It starts with an A, but doesn't quite sound like Alex.

Then her breathing becomes long and deep.

The night is over now, and whoever she's dreaming about, it's not me.

A knock at the door wakes me. I blink in the soft morning light, my heart pummelling my ribcage. Amka snores on her side of the bed, and Blue is wedged between us.

"Amka, wake up," a gruff voice says in the hallway. The door opens, and the harsh ceiling light switches on.

Shit. Her dad stands in the doorway, bright-eyed and dishevelled, and I'm in my freaking underwear. I yank the comforter over my bare legs.

"What?" Amka mumbles. She sits up, pushing her hair away from her face.

I don't move, now hidden from her dad's view by a mound of blankets.

"Your grandmother is in the hospital," he says. "Pack a suitcase. We're going to Iqaluit."

"Oh, my god." Amka jumps out of bed. "What happened? Is she going to be all right?"

"I don't know. We'll see." He leaves the door ajar as he

heads down the hall, shouting, "Hurry up, we're leaving in twenty minutes."

Amka shoots out of bed and flies to her dresser. Drawers screech open and bang shut. By the time I've sat up and pulled on my pants, she's fully dressed in her ripped jeans and my hoodie.

"Can you pull my suitcase from under the bed?" She yanks a brush through her tangled locks.

"Yeah, sure." My head pounds, and the light hurts my eyes. I kneel and wrestle the black luggage from among cardboard boxes and dust bunnies.

I open it on the bed, and Amka drops in a handful of socks and underwear. Blue gets in the way, riled up by the anxiety stuffing the room. I don't know what to say or how to help. The best I can do is squish the clothes to make room for more as she tosses random items into the suitcase.

While she goes to the bathroom, I pack my backpack with the few things I brought that I can find. I think I'm in shock.

Amka's leaving.

But she momentarily comes back to the room, zips up her suitcase, and sits on the mattress.

Blue hops beside her, and she hugs him. "What am I gonna do with you?"

"I'll babysit him," I say, jumping on the opportunity to remind her I'm still in the room with her.

"Thank you." She gets up and throws her arms around me.

"If you need anything, all you have to do is ask," I say

into her hair, taking in the peachy smell as if it were my last breath.

"Keep him on a leash when he's outside, okay?"

"He wouldn't run away."

"Please? I couldn't stand it if anything happened to him."

"Okay. Don't worry."

"Amka, let's go," her dad bellows.

I carry the suitcase downstairs and out on the porch. Amka hands me Blue's leash. She kisses him on the head, then kisses me on the cheek, so fast I barely feel it.

"Bye." She hugs herself, looking lost in my oversized hoodie—that piece of me she chose to take along.

"Good luck," I say, realizing they're probably the wrong words, but she's already climbing into the car.

"Thanks for keeping the dog, Alex," her dad says, waving at me over the Honda's roof.

I nod and wave.

They take off the moment Amka shuts the door.

I stand in the frozen dawn with Blue whining at my feet.

"Don't you worry." I scratch the top of his head. "If she doesn't come back for me, she'll at least come back for you."

Chapter 9

I pick my way alone across the muddy parking lot after school. Amka has been gone forever—a full two weeks. Caden and I still hang around each other because his friends are also my friends, but he's been pretty much ignoring me since Amka wrenched me from him at the party.

I climb into my truck and search my pockets for the keys. Not there. Root inside my backpack. Nada. I'd have heard them clink if I'd dropped them somewhere. As I mentally retrace my steps, my hand goes to the ignition switch. There they are. Silly me. I twist the key, but it only turns one notch.

Crap. I thump my forehead on the steering wheel. In addition to forgetting the keys in the switch, I left them on the accessory position, with the heater blasting and the radio playing. Dad warned me the battery wasn't holding its charge too well anymore. Great. Now, I've killed it.

What was I thinking?

Oh, right, I was thinking about Amka's hands trailing all over my body.

I pop the hood, hop out of the cab, and fish out the jumper cables tucked behind the seat. Caden's truck is parked beside mine, but he hasn't come out yet. Of course, he'd never leave his keys behind. Will I drain his battery if I use it without the engine running?

I don't get the chance to find out. Here he comes, with Chloe hanging onto his arm. They both glance my way. She laughs—if it's at me, I don't care—and tells him, "I'll text you tonight."

She knows what happened to my phone—no need to rub it in. I haven't even heard from Amka since she left. I wish I could ask how she's doing. Text her that I care. Phoning would be too weird. I've been hoping she'd contact me, but I understand this is probably not a good time. I'm not family or anything. I'm not even sure what I am to her.

Caden strides to his truck, arching an eyebrow at the cables in my hands. He gets in and starts the engine. Please don't just drive away. Maybe I'd deserve it after blatantly choosing Amka over him, but between the two of us, he's not the sore loser. Lucky me, he unlocks the Tacoma's hood, comes over, and grabs his end of the cables.

"Thanks," I say.

"Least I can do."

He'd do the same for anyone else, too, and probably with a smile. I'm not getting one today.

We hook the clamps to the battery poles in our respective vehicles, then I sit behind the steering wheel, turn the key, and *voilà*. The engine rumbles to life.

Caden is already coiling the booster cables when I step out. He hands them to me and asks, "Have you heard from Amka?"

"Nothing yet." Not having news to share feels like a defeat.

"I hope her grandmother's okay."

"Yeah, me too."

We linger near each other for a few awkward moments, me absorbed in polishing the Ford crest on the grill of my truck. I keep myself from saying I hope she comes back soon, because I don't want him to hope she doesn't come back. Because this is what I think his curtness is saying. I could be wrong, though.

"I should go home before Blue has another *accident*." Dad's on his time off, but the locals still call him for odd jobs, and he won't pack Blue around on a leash. "Apparently, he's only house-trained for Amka."

Caden chuckles. "Good luck."

This sounds like a bit of forgiveness. I'll be happy to clean up any dog messes if it means our friendship is intact.

"Thanks for the boost," I say.

"No sweat."

He leaves while I'm still tucking the cables back behind the seat. I drive off a minute later, slowly making my way along Main Street. As I drive by Amka's house, I spot her dad's silver Honda in the yard. My heart jolts in my chest. She's back. Maybe I should go get Blue first, but I wouldn't mind having her all to myself for a few minutes.

I park beside the car, leaving the engine running. I'll just go in and say hello. No doubt she'll want to come home with me to reunite with Blue. I knock at the door and wait, chewing a fingernail.

A shadow moves through the frosted glass. The door opens, and Mr. Tanuyak stands in the doorframe, dressed in a rumpled plaid shirt. His stiff, black hair sticks out every which way.

"Hi, Alex."

"Hi." I flush, remembering him barging into Amka's room with me lying half-naked in her bed. "I, um, saw you were back and…"

I glance at the stairs behind him, hoping Amka will show up and rescue me from this embarrassing situation.

Mr. Tanuyak must notice because he says, "Amka's in Mississauga."

"Oh."

"She should be back next weekend."

Should? Like there's a chance she won't? But I have Blue, so…

"Okay," I say.

He grabs his car keys from their hook on the wall. "I'll come pick up her dog."

"No, no. It's all right. I don't mind keeping him a while longer. I mean…if it's okay with you."

"Sure, if you'd like. I'll tell Amka to call you when she gets back."

I say goodbye and head back to my truck, realizing I didn't even ask how his mother was doing. How rude of me.

The road to my house is an even muddier mess than the school parking lot. Down here the snow is gone, but the mountaintops still shine a brilliant white. The Devil's Tail stabs the sky. I imagine Chatty the mascot sitting on a log somewhere up there, picking a flea from its matted fur and asking me, "Lonely much?"

When I walk inside my house, the carpet is spotless—phew, no accident.

Dad sits at the kitchen table, transcribing notes from his dog-eared black notebook to his mechanic's log. "Hi, sweetie. How was your day?"

"Great. I left the key turned on and drained the battery. Caden gave me a boost."

He tuts. "You live, you learn."

There's a yellow puddle beside one leg of the table.

"Where's Blue?" I ask.

"Probably eating the couch or something."

"He peed on the floor."

"The little bugger." Dad half-stands to witness the latest mess. "I took him outside twenty minutes ago."

"He must miss Amka. He never pees in her house." I grab the paper towels from the counter.

"When's she coming back?"

"I don't know," I say, mopping up the puddle. "Her dad's back, but she's at her mom's."

"How's she doing?"

"How would I know? If I had a *phone*, maybe she'd text me once in a while."

"Then you shouldn't have dropped yours in a tub of 10W30."

I look at him over the edge of the table. "You'd be antsy too if you couldn't keep in touch with your *girlfriend*."

He blinks. "Is Amka your girlfriend?"

No challenge there, just curiosity. I don't know what gave me away. Maybe it's that I've been moping around a lot.

"No," I say. "At least, not yet."

"Well." He shrugs and goes back to his notes. "I'm sure she'll be back soon."

Blue trots over from the living room. He drops and rolls on the spot I just finished cleaning, then goes for Dad's bare toe with his teeth.

"Ouch, you little coydog!"

I ball up the yellow-stained paper towels and stand.

"Did Karine ever try to contact you?" I blurt.

Dad finishes scribbling a line in his logbook, then looks up at me. Minus the laugh lines at the corner of his eyes, he looks younger than his thirty-six. But he's not laughing now.

"Any reason you're bringing that up?" he asks.

I shrug. I'm disappointed Amka isn't back, and I have an urge to spread the crappiness. "Sorry, I don't know where that came from."

"If you want to find her, I'll help you. I've told you before."

He'd do it for me, but he's already done so much for both of us after she left. She wouldn't even talk to him, and neither would her parents. As if he were the bad guy in the story.

"Forget about it." I toss the paper towels in the garbage can and wash my hands. As far as I know, Karine might be living on another continent or have a new daughter who isn't cursed. Why should I care?

"Are you worried about me being with Melody?" Dad asks. "You know you'll always matter to me the most."

"No, it's fine. I'm sure Melody's nice. Can't wait to meet her."

No longer in the mood for a heart-to-heart, I stomp up the stairs and slump on my bed to stare at dust dancing on a shaft of light from the window. All I want is Amka. What's she doing in Mississauga, anyway, if she can't get along with her mother? Ghost-hunting with that person whose name she whispered in my ear?

Serves me right. Burning Karine's letter while wishing Amka would be stuck here for spring break was as good as black magic. Anyone who's watched witchcraft movies knows that whatever darkness you put out into the universe will come back at you threefold.

Needle teeth prick my ankle.

"Ow!"

Blue's open-mouthed grin seems diabolical, like he's the enforcer of the threefold law. I'll accept my fate, as long as Amka comes back soon.

"Let's go for a walk, you little devil."

Six days later, I get my wish. "I'll be right over," I say into the phone and hang up.

"Blue, guess who's back!" I sing at the top of my lungs. "Let's go for a ride."

Blue looks at me out of the corner of his yellow eye and cracks a dog smile. I clip on his leash, and we race to my truck. Dad put in a new battery, so it starts like a charm.

It's not like my dead-end road has speed-limit signs, but it takes all I have not to floor the gas pedal.

When I get to her house, my heart melts. Amka sits huddled on her front steps, dressed in my black leggings she never gave back and a white tank top. Underdressed, as usual. We're on the last stretch of April, but the leaves aren't out yet.

Blue yips and bounces all over the seat. I reach over to the passenger door to let him out. Amka's face lights up as he jumps on her, licking her face all over. Ew. She hugs him and buries her face into his fur while I stand on the concrete walkway, pathetically waiting my turn.

Blue finally lies down at her side.

"Hi," Amka says quietly. Her eyes tear up.

"How was your visit?" I don't think her tears are happy ones.

She looks down to scratch at the chipped polish on her thumbnail, shakes her head, and swallows.

"I'm so sorry." I sit beside her on the steps and pull her into me.

I wish I could absorb her grief. I'm strong enough to bear it, but that wouldn't be fair. It belongs to her. She goes soft against me. All I can do is hold her for as long as she needs. I'm glad she lets me do it.

She shivers. "Let's go inside. Come on, Blue."

In her room, her open suitcase has spewed out an avalanche of clothes all over the floor. The bed is unmade, just as we left it weeks ago, with the pillow I used bunched into a lump. Does she remember how sweetly she touched me? My skin certainly does.

She fixes the blankets, then falls onto the bedspread and pats the spot beside her. I take one step, but Blue beats me to it. I rock back on my heels. She was calling him, not me.

"Did you behave for Alex?" She scratches his ruff.

I sit on the corner of the mattress. "He was good. How was Iqaluit?"

"Cold as hell," she says, then moans. "My poor grandpa. He's going to be so lonely."

We stay silent for a few moments. Amka gazes at the wall. Maybe I should go home and let her catch some sleep.

"Anything interesting happen while I was away?" she asks as I'm about to get up.

I sink back down. "Nope. Just a ton of schoolwork."

"It's going to be a pain to catch up."

Another lull, like we don't know each other anymore. Amka checks the bracelet on her wrist. From my vantage point, the mood stone looks muddy brown. A question burns on my lips, the same one that's been searing a hole in my mind throughout the week. I've got nothing to lose—I hope—so I let it fall out of my mouth.

"How was it in Mississauga?"

Her eyes flick to me, then away again.

"My mom turned Norma Bates on me the minute I got there," she says. "I spent most of my time at—at my friends."

She lowers her arm to rub her lips over the stone. And smiles—dreamily.

Is she thinking about one friend in particular? Someone with a name that starts with an A?

At least she came back. That's something. Maybe my curse-cancelling letter burning wasn't black magic—the threefold law also works for good deeds. I never had bad intentions. Why can't she just love it here? She has friends here, too, she's away from her mom, and she can have as much of me as she wants.

"Remember our plan to hike up the Devil's Tail?" I ask. "We'll be able to go soon."

Amka props herself up on her elbows. Her eyes sparkle, not with tears anymore but with interest.

"You and me camping in that old trapper's cabin, right?"

My stomach somersaults. "If we don't find it, there's always the tent."

"When?"

I'd pack my gear and leave right away, but the mountains will probably rumble with avalanches for a couple more weeks. "The long weekend in May should be safe enough."

"Safe from what? That corny old lynx?"

"Yeah." I roll me eyes. "But let's bring garlic, holy water, and a silver bullet just to be sure."

Chapter 10

Amka sits in the school lunchroom, alone at a table by the window. Her hair is parted in two tight French braids, and she hides her hands in the sleeve of the black hoodie I let her steal from me. This is the first time I've seen her today because she skipped class for counselling.

My heart urges me to cross the room and wrap her in my arms. I'd do it, too, but I have no idea what Amka actually wants. She's been really quiet—distant, even— these past three weeks. I suppose grief does that to you.

I've been giving her space, just enough that if she needs someone to fall back on, I'll be right there to catch her. That's me, nice and selfish.

Mickey bumps into my back with his lunch pack. "What's up?"

"Nothing's up." I bump him back and wince as my funny bone hits his ribs.

We playfully elbow each other as we scramble across the room to Amka's table. He reaches it first and slides onto the bench, right up against her, so I sit opposite.

"How was it?" Mickey asks. "I hope the counsellor didn't grill you too hard."

If I said anything like that, I'd probably sound like a jerk, but Mickey brims with gentle concern.

"It was fine," Amka says. Her mascara-free eyelashes stick together in little wet clumps.

He gives her a sympathetic hug. He knows what she's going through. His great-grandma, who lived at his house, passed away last year. I empathize with Amka, but it's like I'm the only one around here who hasn't lost someone precious to them, so how well can I understand what she's feeling?

Caden walks into the room, spots me, hesitates. Things are still a bit awkward between us. He's watching what will happen between Amka and me while I do the same for him and Chloe, like we take each other's happiness extremely to heart.

Mickey waves him over. Caden nods and heads our way. I scoot closer to the wall, as if there isn't enough room for at least three more people on the bench. He sits on my side, not too close, but not too far. No hug for me, though. Just brief eye contact and a lift of one side of his mouth. I'll take it.

I unpack my sandwich—ham and mustard, since I've become self-conscious about the PB-and-cheese combination. The guys talk about four-wheelers and muddy trails while I fill Amka in on what she missed in science class.

Her eyes glaze over, and she turns to the window. The tender-green fuzz of new leaves decks out the aspens in the foothills. Higher up, the mountain slopes are a deep emerald slashed with the occasional rusty arrow of a conifer that has fallen prey to bark beetles. The Poltergeist Tree is as dead as ever. Above the treeline, snow still covers the summits.

"The long weekend's coming up." Amka cracks her first genuine smile in weeks, one that creases her eyes and shows her dimples. "I dug out a backpack from the basement for our trip."

"What trip?" Mickey asks.

I drum my fingers on the table, waiting for him to return to his own conversation, but now we've got Caden's attention too.

"We're going camping on the Devil's Tail," Amka says. "You guys should come."

Damn.

Mickey side-eyes me and smirks. "Sorry. I doubt my mom will let me go. The aunties are coming over."

Amka pokes a baby carrot into his arm. "You always listen to your mommy?"

"Everybody listens to Mickey's mommy," I say. She's sweet, but she'll give you tough love if she thinks you need it and your parents aren't around to give it to you. It's all good, though. If Mickey doesn't come, Caden probably won't either. Problem solved.

Amka's bracelet clinks as she slaps her palms on the table. "So, who's in?"

"Who's in what?" Chloe drops her backpack beside Caden.

I want to bash my forehead against the window.

"Field trip," Amka says. "But sorry, the bus is full."

I love this girl.

Chapter 11

The Devil's Tail is looming, its snowy summit shining against the pure blue of the afternoon sky. Amka stands between the tangled willows, her thumbs jammed beneath the straps of her backpack. For once, she's appropriately dressed in cargo pants and a plaid shirt, like any true Fort-Castorite.

"Are you guys gonna stand there forever or what?" she asks.

Caden squares his jaw and hops across the ditch to join her. He's coming whether I like it or not. They both stare at me, as if they're waiting for me to make a choice. Again. But I've already made it. I chose Amka. And now, she doesn't want to go alone with me, and it sure as hell looks like Caden doesn't want me to go alone with her. I should beat them at their own game—spin around and go home. But there's no way I'm letting them go without me.

"Are you getting cold feet?" Amka asks me.

Caden sneers—a rare expression for him. It makes me feel kind of warm and fuzzy on the inside. He knows I don't ever back down.

"I don't get cold feet. I've got insulated boots and merino socks. Toasty warm down to the toes."

I cross the ditch, bump between the two of them, and keep walking. The warm spring air cools by several degrees as I dodge beneath the cover of the old-growth forest. Wildlife—moose and bears—must have been using the narrow trail because it's still fairly visible. The trees are gigantic—some of them two-huggers, at least. White-flowered queen's cups, tender ferns barely unfurled, and the crooked, spiny stalks of devil's clubs poke sparsely from a carpet of russet tree needles. Blue pees indiscriminately on the protruding roots of cedars, hemlocks, and Douglas firs.

"Wow," Amka says. "Can you believe those trees were already there when Lucifer Columbus '*discovered*' the Americas?"

"Can you believe climate change might kill them off in our lifetime?" Caden counters.

Sad but true, though the wildfires have missed the area so far.

I speed up, leaving them to their musings.

Whatever you do, stay away from that mountain.

My scalp prickles. Fantastic. I can't believe I'm letting Karine's pointless warning invade my mind right now.

"Wait up." Amka's feet come stomping behind me. She catches up and hangs onto my arm like a little kid, out of breath. "What's the rush?"

"No rush. This is my cruising speed."

"You look nervous."

I glance behind me. Caden lingers, but he's probably within earshot. I just hope she won't start blabbering about my "curse."

"Are you worried about the curse?"

Perfect. "No, I'm not worried."

"You can borrow my bracelet if you want." She twists it from her wrist. The stone glimmers a pretty turquoise with a blush of pink at the center.

"What's it gonna do?" I can't help but think it'll turn some mucky brown shade if I wear it.

"It's my protection charm. Kept me out of trouble more times than I could count on my fingers."

"Like that time you ripped open your knee on a cemetery fence?"

"Could've been worse. I didn't end up with gangrene, *and* the White Lady didn't show up to slit my throat."

"That's definitely a plus. Keep your bracelet." I wriggle the bear spray holster hanging off my hip. "I've got my own protection charm."

We chat a bit but save our breath for manoeuvring up steep terrain. The sky clouds over, low and oppressive. A steady drizzle starts as the afternoon draws to an end. Blue's enthusiasm isn't dampened. He spends his time between zooming into the trees and checking in on Amka.

Just now, his paws are pounding the ground behind us. He lopes past with something furry and limp in his mouth.

"Ew." Amka takes off after him. "Get back here!"

Five seconds later, Caden catches up with me. "Having fun?"

Meh. I'm not admitting that to him, though, since he's the party pooper and knows it too.

"Why did you decide to come with us, anyway?" I ask.

He shrugs. "Safety in numbers, right?"

"Safety from what? The chat-cornu?"

"Of course." The smile he throws me says he doesn't believe a word of the legend, and that he knows I don't believe it either. This should mellow me out, but it ruffles me instead. Makes me want not to be nice.

"You could have stayed in town instead and asked Chloe on a date," I say.

"Was *this* supposed to be a date?" His hand brushes against mine. Warm. He does nothing to break contact. "To me, Amka seems more like a party girl than a bush girl."

I shove my hands in my pockets. "Well, maybe you're wrong."

"Is the cabin much further?" Amka whines, up the trail. "I'm beat."

I stalk away from Caden and his vindicated smile.

"We might walk to the summit and down the other side without ever finding it," I tell her.

"I'm not made for climbing mountains."

One more thing to check off her "don't like" list of to-do things in Fort Cass.

"I hope you like camping out because we don't have time to go back down before sunset," Caden says.

On his own, he would be fast enough to make it down the mountain before full dark. I almost point it out, but safety in numbers *is* a thing. I would hate anything bad happening to him. Sprained ankle, bear encounter, or whatever. I'm not parting with my pepper spray, and Blue would stay with Amka, so Caden's safer here with us.

The rain doubles in intensity. The ferns and queen's cups on the forest floor glisten, and our clothes are getting soaked. Blue is the only one who seems unfazed by the worsening weather. He looks right at home on the mountain, his coyote-side wide awake.

"Should we set up camp?" Caden asks, looking at me like I'm the boss.

"Yeah." I spot an area that's fairly flat, a few steps off the path. "How about right here?"

No one objects. Amka sits on her folded rain jacket under a tree while Caden and I do all the work. I don't mind. I wouldn't even have minded setting up the tent alone for just me and her. The three of us in there, it's going to be awkward.

The clouds, the rain, and the denseness of the forest bring on an early twilight. We light a small, smoky fire for drying our sodden clothes, and Caden cooks canned chicken soup on his camp stove. Amka brought cookies she baked, and I pass around some elk jerky Dad and I made after last fall's hunt.

We talk about small stuff, until Amka's teeth chatter so much it's hard to follow what she's saying.

"Didn't you bring a warm jacket or anything?" I've already got all my layers on.

"I d-didn't think it'd be this c-cold," she says.

Before I can think of it myself, Caden pulls off his extra hoodie and hands it to her.

"Thanks, you're the best," Amka says, pulling it on. She hugs herself. "It was rainy like this the night we broke into the cemetery back in Mississauga."

Caden raises an eyebrow. "What were you doing in there?"

She launches into the tale. I try to pay attention, but

my eyes keep drifting to Blue, who's scanning the deepening shadows, his ears pricked up. Now and then he lifts his nose, catching whiffs of something. It could be anything. Bear, moose, wolverine. I shouldn't be too worried about those, but tension builds between my shoulder blades and I can't shrug it off. I wish my back was against a tree trunk instead of open space.

"What about you, Alex?" Amka asks.

"Um, yeah." No idea what she's talking about.

She stands and stretches, yawning. Looks like it's bedtime.

"I'll keep an eye on the fire for a bit," Caden says.

Thoughtful of him. Blue stays with him, still on watch.

Inside the tent, I turn on the light hanging from the dome. Amka pulls a small blanket from her backpack and folds it into a square. "Can you put this down for Blue?"

"You didn't bring any warm clothes for yourself but you packed a blanket for your dog?"

"What? I wanted him to be comfortable."

Shaking my head, I lay out the blanket in the tent's vestibule where we've agreed he will sleep, smoothing out the wrinkles. Then I zip up the door flap.

Caden's sleeping bag is tossed to one side, and Amka unrolls hers on the other side. Is she worried the chat-cornu will come to snatch me in the middle of the night? Fine. I don't mind being snug in the middle. I change into sweats. Amka goes inside her sleeping bag and tosses out her cargo pants. I leave the light on for Caden and lie on my back, listening.

Outside, Blue growls.

Caden's voice comes muted through the tent's walls. "It's all right, Blue. There's nothing there."

"I think he senses something," Amka whispers.

"Of course, he does. He's a dog." At least I think she's talking about Blue.

"Last time I was in Iqaluit, my grandfather told me the story of the *Ijiraat*."

"The e-rat?" I know that's not what she said, but I can't make that dry "r" sound in the back of my throat. Maybe I could have, if Karine had stuck around to teach me French. "What's that?"

"A creature that takes the shape of a caribou, but it can change into a human. It steals children and hides them away."

"Those darn shapeshifters." The chat-cornu is also said to be one, as so many creatures from all mythologies. "They sure love stealing loved ones."

"His grandfather told him the story, which he heard from his grandfather, and so on."

"So?"

"You can't say the *Ijiraat* doesn't exist because you haven't seen it."

"I never said it doesn't exist."

"And if you'd seen it, you'd probably have no memory of it."

Oh. I see where this is going. "The chat-cornu is not real. If I'd seen it, I'm sure I'd remember. It's just a story."

"How can you tell for sure? Your mother believed in it. That makes it real, in a way." She moves closer to me and lowers her tone. "I think I felt it earlier, when we were outside."

I turn onto my side to face her. Her eyes are glossy, and she has tucked her fists under her chin. She's scared. I reach over and rub her bracelet with my thumb. "You have your protection charm. Even if there were a chat-cornu, it wouldn't be able to steal you."

"I'm not worried about me. You're the one who's cursed."

I grit my teeth.

It's. A. Story.

"Don't worry about me," I say. "If that beast shows up and tries to touch me, I'll exorcise it with my bear spray."

I hold her gaze and let my thumb slide to the soft skin of her inner wrist. After a moment, the anxious line of her lips relaxes. My own body slackens. Amka is the moon, and I'm the tide. If I give in to the pull, I might lean toward her, slowly. Give her time to realize I'm about to kiss her. Time to show me whether she wants me to.

But Caden's boots stomp the ground, and the weak glow from the fire's embers dies down. He's at the door a moment later. Amka blinks and moves away, as distant as a star now.

"Can I come in?" he asks.

"We're decent," Amka says and chuckles.

"It's not locked," I make myself say lightly. I can't take my frustration out on him. He's not here to thwart me, even if he unknowingly did just that.

Caden is quick and efficient. He pulls off a few layers (I don't look so don't know which ones) and zips himself inside his sleeping bag. In no time, the light is turned off and we're lying side by side in the dark. Amka's bag rustles as she tosses and turns.

I lie quiet, taking in the strangeness of Caden beside me. We haven't slept in a tent together since we hit puberty. As per Dad's decree, whenever we'd camp at the lake, it would be the guys in one tent, and the girls in another—Chloe curled near me, my body and mind engaged in a confused battle I didn't quite understand yet.

The pitter-patter of rain on the tent should lull me, but I can't fall asleep. It might just be anxiety, but it's as if the mountain beneath me is a sleeping beast, its breathing a barely perceptible tremor.

There's something else, too. A *want*. It seeps through the tent floor, my sleeping bag, my clothes, my skin. It courses through my veins, begs me to bury my face into Amka's hair, to press my lips to the soft curl of her ear and whisper her name.

Caden takes a deep breath, then releases it slowly. Does he feel the want inside of him too? Sense mine? He turns his back to me.

I lie awake for a long time and eventually drift off, like an undertow is dragging me into deep water. But something pulls me back—a mouth kissing mine, soft as a feather. Those lips are all I feel. The rest of me is weightless. The peach aroma of Amka's shampoo bathes me, mixed with the woodsy scent of Caden's hoodie. A kernel of panic pops in my middle.

Who the hell's kissing me?

I jerk my head back and wake up. The darkness is dead

quiet, except for Caden's slow, steady breaths and Amka's light snores. Damn. It was so real my lips still tingle. I try to relax, feeling myself drift off again, but then I have to pee. The last thing I need is to fall asleep with a full bladder and have a going-to-the-bathroom dream.

I crawl out of my sleeping bag and unzip the tent. No one stirs, not even Blue curled up on his blanket in the vestibule. Not bothering with shoes, I step to the path, toes cooling within moments. The moon shines through the thinning clouds, giving me just enough light to navigate. I pull down my pants and crouch behind a large trunk. I manage to not spray my bare feet but realize my roll of toilet paper is tucked inside my backpack. A couple of leaves from a nearby shrub will do (a poor job but better than nothing), as long as it's not from a spiny devil's club.

As I toss the used leaves, a crack echoes through the forest. My pulse stutters. I spring up and yank my sweats back up.

"*Alexsssss,*" a voice rasps.

I whip around. Amka stands on the path, Caden's hoodie reaching mid-way down her bare thighs, her dark hair falling across her face like Samara in *The Ring.* I almost expect her to lunge at me at supernatural speed, but she hovers there, unsteady.

"That's not funny." I cringe at the unexpected loudness of my voice.

I wait for her laugh to break the chilling spell. She turns without a word and walks up the path.

"Wrong way," I say.

She doesn't pause or turn.

"What are you doing?" I tramp after her. The quicker I walk, the faster she evades me, even though between the two of us, I'm the fast walker. "You spooked me. Nice job. Can we go back to sleep now?"

She veers off the path and disappears from view. I hurry after her, stopping dead in my tracks as I enter a clearing. Amka's at the foot of an immense tree, awful in its decaying deadness. I don't need a clear view of its broken summit or a pinpoint on a GPS to know this is the Poltergeist Tree. I just know. Twisted strands of lichen droop from its lower limbs, and a gaping hollow between its roots looks like a mouth ready to swallow Amka.

"You're really creeping me out," I say. "Come on. Let's go back to the tent."

No reaction. I know she hasn't turned into some vengeful ghost, but something's off about the way she stands, head hung low and hair trailing across her face. Maybe the *want* that invaded me earlier called out to her, too, and she sleepwalked after it? I have no idea why you're not supposed to wake a sleepwalker, but I won't risk finding out. I'll take her hand and lead her back to the tent.

My body hums with dread as I approach. The clouds part, and the light of the moon tints her skin blue-white. She lifts a pale arm to clear her face. Her hair cascades behind her shoulders, and she smiles at me. I gasp. Amka is gone, and I'm staring at my own self, as if in a mirror. Like that time in Mickey's bathroom, it's me, but not quite me. The hair is silvery blond. The blue eyes lighter than mine.

"Dammit." I must be the one who's sleepwalking, and the sound of my voice does nothing to wake me.

"Alexia, sweetie."

That voice. I haven't heard it in years, but it's been lurking in some secret drawer of my mind. That smile. Always peeking through the aloe vera's spiky leaves from its dusty picture frame, easily ignored after years of practice. But my conscientiously trained willpower drains from me and pools at my feet. I can't ignore *her* now. This is Karine, and I can't tell if the swell of her stomach is only the bulk of the hoodie she's wearing or fetus-me curled up inside of her.

I swallow hard. Okay. This is a nightmare. I can deal with nightmares—been dealing with them my whole childhood.

"I'm Alex." My voice comes out strong and assured. "Only Dad can call me sweetie."

Karine arches a white-gold eyebrow. "Maybe so, but did he care enough to warn you to stay off the Devil's Tail?"

How strange that this girl who looks barely older than me is my mother. There's something hollow and strange beneath the softness of her voice—like water churning under ice. She takes a step toward me. I pretend to stand my ground, but my feet are frozen in place.

"You should have listened to your mommy," she says. "You loved me long ago, you know."

"I don't anymore." It's true.

Is it?

"I don't love you," I repeat, loud enough to believe myself. Confidently enough to hurt her.

"You ungrateful child." Instead of grief-stricken features, a widening grin. "I left to break the curse, but now that you've ignored my warning, you've cursed yourself all over again."

My brain rattles in my skull as I shake my head. "You're the curse. I don't need you."

Karine smiles like my words don't bother her at all. She walks—no, glides—toward me. Her shadow creeps along, horned and feline.

Well, shit.

This is the chat-cornu. But I should have known it the moment Amka turned into Karine, shouldn't I? It doesn't matter. I won't let that beast scare me.

"Who's dearest to your heart?" the Karine-thing asks, now amber-eyed and sharp-toothed.

"Get the hell away from me," I spit.

Her chin snaps up and her eyes flash darkly. The feline shadow stretches and swirls around my legs, intensely cold. I should have taken the bear spray with me. I can't move, can't swallow the lump blocking my throat.

A long, low growl floats from behind me, the most comforting sound I've heard in a long time. Blue pounces at my side, hackles raised.

Karine hisses like a damn cat, her face a blur of human and animal features. Moonlit hair and black horns.

Blue's sand-papery footpads scratch my bare toes. My body thaws. I spin around and sprint back toward the trail, panic sinking its fangs into every muscle. Little girl's cries bounce off tree trunks, echoing within the walls of my skull. Blue—or maybe it's the chat-cornu—is right on my heels.

Sticks and tree needles poke my soles as I pound down the trail. How far have I wandered from the tent? I can't stop. Won't stop until I stumble onto the road, until I've made it to my house and locked myself in.

Blue cuts in front of me. I stumble and stop. The pale glow of the tent's fabric beckons like a will-o'-wisp. I fall to my knees in the vestibule, nearly rip the zipper off the door, and dive inside. Blue jumps in right after me and burrows into the folds of Amka's sleeping bag. I seal us in—for what it's worth. This is a tent, not a fortress. My heart thrashes in my ribcage like a feral creature caught in a live trap as I scramble into my own sleeping bag.

Caden stirs. "What's going on?"

"Nothing. Just a bad dream."

He sits up, a comforting shape in the darkness. "Do you want to tell me about it?"

His voice is so filled with care that tears sting my eyes.

"No. It's fine." I take deep breaths, counting to ten. As far as I'm concerned, I went to pee, and now I'm going back to sleep. None of that shit in between, with Amka, Karine, or the chat-cornu happened.

We both lie down at the same time. Caden's hand gently squeezes my shoulder.

"It's fine," he whispers, as if I haven't just said so.

He gives me another squeeze, and as he starts to move away, something makes me reach for his hand and hold it in place. His palm ends up on the side of my neck, warm and comforting. My body relaxes, and my pulse slows, beating softly against his fingers curled on my throat. This should feel wrong—I'm not into love triangles—but I don't want to move. Amka unsettled me by bringing up her grandfather's story. Caden wouldn't fall for any of that, and his touch reminds me that I wouldn't either.

Amka has her bracelet for luck. I'm lucky to have Caden.

I drift between anxious dreams for the rest of the night—and at some point, away from Caden—until I wake to watery morning light. Amka has rolled into me in her sleep and cradled her face into my neck. She sits, wiping her eyes. The collar of my hoodie is wet with her tears.

"Are you okay?" I ask.

"I had the strangest dream," she says. "My grandma was here. She talked to me about my grandpa…"

She doesn't continue. I hope it was nothing as horrific as what happened in my own nightmare.

"I had some pretty wild dreams too," I say.

Blue crawls over Amka's legs and rolls onto his back between us. The tension in her face vanishes as she scratches his chest. "What are you doing in here, you silly goof?"

"I woke up in the night. He wanted to come in." Something like that, anyway.

"Did you have nightmares, too?" Amka coos to him.

I wish he could tell. I'm glad he can't.

Caden is the last to wake. He sits and rakes his fingers through his hair.

"What about you?" Amka asks. "Did you have any weird dreams?"

He flushes and takes a moment to answer. "Don't think so."

Man. I've had enough of this mountain. I grab my balled-up socks from the far corner and pull my feet out of the sleeping bag. Dirt and tree needles stick between my toes. Perfectly normal. That's what happens when you wander barefoot in the forest. Monsters and nightmares have nothing to do with it.

"Anybody want hot chocolate?" Caden asks. "I'll light the camp stove."

I need a cup of sugar with a dash of coffee.

"Can we just leave right away and never come back?" Amka's voice trembles like she's about to cry again.

Her suggestion sounds good to me. "I have some breakfast bars in my pack. We can eat on the way down."

We pack up quickly and head downhill under drizzling rain. I can't help looking over my shoulder every minute or two, trying to spot the Poltergeist Tree and make sure no ghosts are following us. Caden brings up the rear, so I force myself to stop doing that. I don't want him to know I'm unsettled, and his shifting eyes make me wonder what he's been dreaming about—though he claims he didn't dream.

Amka walks close to me, often slipping her fingers inside her sleeve, checking that her bracelet is still on her wrist. Last night, she said believing in something makes it real. If she thinks a silver bracelet can protect her, then I guess it'll do that for her.

I choose not to believe I've cursed myself again, as the Karine-thing said.

Chapter 12

"I'm so full." I push my chair away from the table to look at our little gathering.

Dad came home from his shift with a surprise—Melody, his now-official girlfriend. She has deep-umber skin, mahogany hair in a curly bob, and downturned eyes that make her look a little sad when she's not smiling. She smiles a lot, though, especially at Dad. She's not trying too hard to win me over, which sort of wins me over.

They're cute together. A refreshing sight after a week of nightmares of Karine clawing her way out of a Chatty costume that looked too much like a live chat-cornu for comfort. It seems silly in the daylight, but when waking in the dead of night—very creepy. I slept fine last night, so I guess the residual creepiness of my trek on the Devil's Tail is finally gone.

Back to the present, I wonder how things would be if it were her—the real, adult Karine—sitting there instead of Melody. What kind of mother she would be. Would we be like best friends or have screaming matches like Amka and her mom? Would she let me go kayaking on a school night? But why am I even wondering about this? Dad's okay with it, probably eager for some alone time with Melody. I check the clock and start piling up dishes.

"You can go," Dad says. "We'll clean up."

Melody wipes her mouth with her napkin, but I don't miss the crinkles at the corners of her eyes. I never knew washing dishes could sound so exciting. I set my stack of plates and utensils beside the sink and come to hug Dad's shoulders from behind, asserting my territory. Melody is a great person, but I'm still his Number One.

"I should be gone for a couple of hours," I say close to his ear, but loud enough. "Just so you know."

Our house must have been built before the invention of soundproofing. I have a fair idea of what's going on behind closed bedroom doors, but I don't really want to hear any of it.

Dad reaches back and tickles my neck. "Get out of here."

I escape his grasp and run for the door.

"Have fun," Melody says.

"Yeah. You, too."

Half an hour later, Amka and I launch our kayaks from the dock at Pecan Lake. The evening isn't especially warm, but she's in a pink tank top that makes her skin seem especially kissable.

We paddle along the shore where the water is so clear that light ripples on the sandy bottom. Amka keeps slightly ahead. Her ponytail brushes her back like frayed silk, and her bracelet slides up and down her wrist with each paddle stroke. The stone is leaden, like the sky and the mirror-smooth water. My chest tightens. I really want to believe that bracelet protects her because there must be a hundred ways I could lose her—if I were cursed, I mean. But if I were, I'm sure I'd feel it, like an itch that's out of reach or a constant tingle on the back of my neck.

She'll be fine. I'll be fine.

"Are you sure you've never kayaked before?" I ask. "You're a natural."

"Must be in my blood. My grandfather's a master builder, even now that his arthritis has gotten really bad."

In three robust strokes, I draw alongside her. "We can paddle all summer long if you want."

I mean it, but I'm also fishing for information. Amka hasn't mentioned her plans for the summer yet, hasn't said if she intends to stick around or hightail it back to Mississauga the minute school is over. Maybe I should ask, to avoid a repeat of our locker room fight, but I don't want to bring it up if she's not thinking about it. What else can I tempt her with that'll make her want to stay?

"We should apply for summer jobs at the Beaver Lodge." Because who doesn't love earning minimum wage cleaning up after tourists?

"I'm game for anything," she says, "as long as it doesn't involve ice-fishing, mountain climbing, or sleeping in a tent."

"That's too bad. Everybody will be camping here at the lake after the school year-end party."

She sets her paddle on top of her kayak. "I'd hate to miss a good party."

I stop paddling. Our momentum slows until we're near each other, drifting at the whim of the wavelets.

"We could sleep at my house afterward," I say. "I'm sure there'll be a designated driver around if we party a little too hard."

"That sounds lovely."

The party, or sleeping over at my house? Both sound perfectly fine to me.

The setting sun takes a last peek over the horizon, bathing us in gold. The uncertainty has lasted long enough now. After the party, when we go back to my house, I'll tell her how I feel about her. Tell her I wish she'd stay for the summer and for the next school year.

But what's keeping me from telling her this right now? How do I even say it? Hey, Amka, I'm in love with you. Too blunt? Her reply would probably be as direct. Sorry, Alex. I'm not into you that way.

The golden moment passes before I can say anything. Maybe I'm getting ahead of myself. There's still a month of grade eleven to go.

"We should head back before dark," I say.

"Race you?"

"Last one to the dock is a chicken with three legs."

We pick up our paddles and turn our backs to the wind. Amka is a strong paddler for someone who spends most of her time on her phone. I could win if I gave it my best, but tonight, I'll be a happy loser.

Chapter 13

The bonfire is down to embers in the stone ring. The last month of school passed in a blur, and so did the year-end party. Some parents came to feed us then packed up the barbeques and little kids and left. The booze came out, car stereos competed in loudness, someone got pranked and spent an hour locked in the stinky outhouse. A couple of lightweights were hurling in the bushes before dusk. Regular party stuff.

Only the toughest of us are still hanging out. Amka and me, Mickey and a couple of his cousins from out of town, Caden, and Chloe, who's wrapped in a wool blanket and cozied up against him.

A knot from the log I'm sitting on digs into my butt, but Amka's head is pleasantly heavy on my lap. She's been throwing me these long, indecipherable looks ever since I picked her up at her house this afternoon, and she's been increasingly cuddly as the evening progressed. Maybe it's the booze. Or maybe she's sensing that tonight's the night we come clean with each other. I run my fingers through her hair, teasing out tangles and wondering how things will unfold once we get back to my house.

Around the clearing, a dozen tents glow like radioactive

mushrooms. They blink off one by one. Caden studies his truck keys and casts me an occasional look. Unsurprisingly, he volunteered to be the designated driver in case someone needed a ride. Either he's tired of Chloe, or he's really into her and can't wait to get rid of Amka and me. I've had a couple of drinks, so I can't drive.

"Ready to go?" I ask Amka.

She stretches like a cat. "Yep."

Caden gets up. Chloe does, too, and clings to him like a burr.

"Are you coming back after?" she asks.

I can't help it—I'm all ears.

"Probably," he says.

"Can I crash in your tent? Mine's really crowded."

Ugh. She's so obvious.

"Yeah, sure," he says coolly.

She walks away with a silly smile on her face, her blanket sweeping the ground behind her. Caden watches her go, probably calculating his next move in his romantic life, just like I am calculating mine.

"I'll be waiting at my truck," he tells me.

"We'll be there in a minute." I stand and stretch the kinks out of my body.

"Crap," Amka cries.

"What?" I ask.

She lifts her sleeve to show me her bare wrist. "I left my bracelet on the dock."

I've been so focused on the after-party moment of truth that I hadn't even noticed her taking it off. "No worries, I'll get it for you."

She catches up when I step onto the planks.

"I mean that dock over there." She points toward the middle of the lake where a floating platform is anchored, currently invisible without a moon to light it. She unbuttons her shorts. "Shouldn't be too long a swim."

Wouldn't it be ironic if she drowned on her way to retrieve her protection charm?

"Stay here, I'll go."

"Alex, don't." Caden steps out of nowhere and stands between me and the dark expanse of the lake. "It's just a bracelet. We can get it in the morning."

It's not just any bracelet. And I'm supposedly cursed to lose someone I love. I still think it's bullshit, but I'd rather take no chances.

"If we leave it, the crows might get to it before we do," I say. I pull down my jeans and drop them into a pile with the rest of my clothes on a corner of the dock. Caden looks away. Not sure why. He's seen me in this bikini all afternoon and all summer last year.

"Let's use the raft, at least," he says.

"You mean the one I brought and never got to use because everybody kept stealing it?" I huff. "It's useless. Some genius let the paddle drift away."

"If you're not going, I'm going," Amka calls from the far end of the dock.

"I'll be right there," I tell her.

Caden gently grabs my wrist as I try to step around him. He still won't meet my gaze. "I get it. You like her a lot, but this is dangerous."

"You know I'm a good swimmer."

He licks his lips. "I'd never force you to do something like that."

Damn. Do I always have to be torn between the two of them?

"Of course, you wouldn't," I hiss. "You're too good and sensible. The voice of reason."

I sound like a total ass, though I'm saying the truth. He lets go of my wrist. Now I feel like an ass, too.

"Listen." I touch his forearm. "Just—keep an eye on me, okay?"

He only shakes his head and shrugs. I'll have to take that as a yes.

"Thanks," I say and walk over to Amka.

Amka hugs me. "You're the best."

"I know, right? Sit tight, I'll be right back."

I line up my toes at the edge of the planks. The dock bobs up and down as Caden comes to join us. An unpleasant itch pervades my throat, so sweet it's disgusting, like those pineapple Breezers I've been chugging all night. But I've raced to the floating dock so many times that I could swim there in a drunken stupor, in which I'm not. I stretch my arms and dive. The frigid water envelops my body. I swim underwater until my lungs scream for air, then break to the surface. I can't see anything, but I think I'm halfway there.

I'm a strong swimmer because everybody is one around here. We grew up with the lake as our playground, and I'm competitive as hell. Even so, I never liked being in the water. During the day, the shallow parts of Pecan Lake are clear. In this darkness, the whole lake might as well be bottomless.

My hand hits the platform, a wooden square fitted onto plastic barrels and anchored to the bottom by a cable. I catch my breath, holding on to the slimy planks.

A loon lets out a long, mournful call.

"You all right?" Amka yells in a shrill voice. She seems so very far.

"I made it," I shout.

The bracelet sits at the edge, somehow throwing a crimson gleam when I pick it up. I hesitate to put it on my arm. Now that I've got it, I'd hate to lose it, and I still don't think it would protect me from anything. Amka needs it. I tuck it into my top where it digs into my skin and should be snug until I get back to the shore.

I push myself off. All I can see is the white flash of my arms diving in and out of the dark water. The shore seems farther than it appears during the day. I'm losing steam fast, like in one of those dreams where you try to run but make no progress. Maybe I'm drunker than I thought I was. I twist onto my back and windmill with waning energy.

The sky is a starry ocean. Red auroras bleed down the horizon at the other end of the lake, loud enough to tint the snowy summit of the Devil's Tail in a pinkish, raw-meat hue. A cramp stabs me in the ribs. A distant alarm in my brain tells me this isn't good, but I'm incredibly calm about it.

If I drown and there's a Hell, I'm headed straight to it for being such a pawn. It'll be nice and warm there with Amka. Because she'll be joining me, no doubt, for sending me out on the lake like this.

I'm not sure what happens next. I'm not swimming

anymore—not even treading water. I breathe in and out, lake water swirling in my lungs as coolly as midnight air. The sky through the surface of the water is red, molten glass. Hell lies at the bottom of the lake, with the decaying vegetation, the snails, and the silt.

A silhouette bends over me, long hair veiling her face, tugging at a memory I don't want to face. I fight back, but everything goes black, until—

"Alex. Hey, ALEX."

As it turns out, Hell is packed sand and a lick of heat from the dying fire. Caden hunches over me, the sleeves of his hoodie dripping wet. The glow from the embers casts his scowl in gold, like he's a guardian angel.

Amka kneels on my other side, her long hair—as dry as the rest of her—shrouding her face. "You panicked. We've got you."

She nudges Caden. "Maybe we should give her mouth-to-mouth."

"She's breathing," he says.

Am I?

Amka huffs and bats his fingers off the wild pulse at my throat. "Never mind. I'll do it."

She leans down. My exhale catches as her shape eclipses the stars. Then her lips press down on mine, not giving me breath but taking it away. She tastes bitter and sweet, like the drinks we shared all night.

Heat blossoms in my belly. When she moves in again, I kiss her back. I'm no longer on the cold, hard ground but floating somewhere warm and wonderful. Amka's fingers slip into my top. She slides out her bracelet, whispers thank you against my ear, and pulls away.

A whiff of lake slime from the shore hits my nose. My stomach spasms. I roll onto my side, catching a glimpse of Caden's mortified expression before hurling an acrid brew onto his lap.

"Oh my god, ew!" Amka cries.

"Sorry." I struggle to sit up and lift a hand to wipe my mouth.

A beach towel lands on my head. I wrap it around my shoulders as Caden strides toward the lake to rinse off. I'm so glad the party's over and no one else got to witness my miraculous recovery.

Amka stuffs my bundle of clothes into my arms. "You should get dressed."

She stands by as I struggle to yank my jeans up my damp legs. This is eons away from how I imagined our first kiss would happen, but the night is not over yet, and all parties need not end with a disaster. All I need is a shower and a toothbrush.

I pull my hoodie over my top. Caden returns, pants wet from taking another dip in the lake to clean my mess off him. His jaw muscles clench in the rippling light from the fire. He's livid. At Amka or me? Both of us, probably.

"Come on," he says, hooking my arm as if I need assistance. "It's time to go."

Amka clutches my other elbow. I shake both of them off. "I can walk, you guys."

Pebbles bite into my bare soles as the three of us shuffle to the parked vehicles. I can't remember where I left my flip-flops. I'll have to come back for them tomorrow, and for my truck, too.

Caden opens the passenger door of his pickup.

"I need my house keys," I say.

"I'll get them." He walks away before I can argue. I go after him, and my heel lands on something sharp. Ow. A bottle cap, maybe. It's so dark I can't see a damn thing.

Caden returns. I turn my palm up for him to toss the keys. He steps close enough to drop them into it.

"Let's go," he says.

"You first," Amka says to me, stepping back to let me inside the truck. I shrug and clamber in, stuffing my legs on the passenger's side. The heat of the afternoon lingers in the cab, but I'm chilled to the bone.

Caden squeezes in beside me and starts the engine. The pickup's headlights slide across the cluster of tents, then through the forest surrounding the beach. The narrow track leading to the road is riddled with potholes. Amka bumps into me, pushing me into Caden. I hold myself stiff and try to avoid his elbow as he switches gears. He doesn't say a word all the way to Fort Cass but downshifts at the top of his road.

"We should get my mom to check you over," he says.

"What for?"

"You may have aspirated water into your lungs. It could be dangerous."

If she sees the state I'm in, she's sure to tell Dad. He told me to party reasonably. He'd probably be okay with me having a couple of drinks, but not about the drunk swimming. "I only swallowed a gulp and threw it right back up."

"On me."

"I said I was sorry."

I can't recall what happened in the water or him splashing in to save me. Doesn't matter. I'm here now, and I'm fine. "Keep going, please?"

He gives me a dead stare. "Sure. Whatever."

The stretch of road at the base of the Devil's Tail is pitch black. No fog outside, but the atmosphere in the truck is thick. I search for words to appease Caden. Nothing comes to mind. It seems that he and Amka mix no better than drinking and swimming. Why can't I have both of them on *my* terms? After tonight, though, I wouldn't blame him for giving up on me for good, but I'm sure he won't.

We reach my house. I forgot to leave a light on. He parks with the headlights aimed at the front porch.

I elbow Amka. "We're here."

She moans as if she'd fallen asleep, then struggles with the door handle. I undo my seatbelt and slide across the seat, getting out after her.

"Thanks for…everything," I tell Caden. Lousy, but it's the best I can manage right now.

"Anytime," he says without a smile.

As I move to shut the door, Amka hauls herself back inside the cab.

"Aren't you sleeping over?" I ask.

"I think I'd better go home." She wipes her mouth with the cuff of her sleeve. "I'm feeling gross."

What's that supposed to mean?

"Suit yourself," I say like I don't care.

I shut the door and wave without looking back. My shadow grows against the house as I walk in the path of the headlights. The yard is crushed shale. I'm used to walking barefoot over it, but my heel stings where I stepped on whatever sharp thing it was back at the lake.

Caden doesn't leave until I've let myself in. I watch the tail lights through the kitchen window, two red eyes glaring at me through the trees. Then, they're gone.

Chapter 14

It's past eleven when I drag my feet into the kitchen, feeling like pond scum. Bitterness clings to the inside of my mouth, the sweetness from Amka's kiss long gone. I fill the kettle and stare at her overnight bag sitting on the entrance mat. She went home because she was feeling *gross*.

Was kissing me so awful? Or did the sickly-sweet Breezers also wreck her stomach? I know I'd rather puke in my own toilet…or on my most trusted friend. If Caden and I are still that. He's the one who should be grossed out.

I carry my breakfast of champions to the table and slump into Dad's chair. The steam wafting from the French press perks me up. I drizzle some coffee over the heap of sugar cubes in my cup. They suck up the liquid, slowly turning brown before melting out of shape. I usually find this little ritual comforting, but this morning it reminds me of murky lake water seeping into lungs. I flood the sugar with more coffee and plenty of cream.

What the hell happened last night anyway? Did I pass out in the water? Maybe I got food poisoning from an undercooked burger.

I rake my fingers through my tangled hair. A dried piece of pondweed flutters down into my cup. Speaking of gross. Last night, I crawled out of my clothes and into bed after Caden dropped me off. I need a shower, then I'll have to bike to the lake to get my truck. Maybe stop at Amka's on the way back. We need to talk, obviously.

As the hot stream of the shower washes out the grime that clings to me, I rehearse what I'll say. About last night… If you want to be just friends, fine, but you can't keep touching and kissing and expecting me to pick you over Caden and then forget all about it the next day.

The phone rings. I throw a towel around myself and slip into the kitchen on dripping feet, hoping it's Amka but figuring it's going to be another scammer.

"Hello?"

Wait for it, someone spent $438.46 on the credit card I don't have.

"Hey, lovely," Amka says.

Ooh. She sounds upbeat. Maybe she's forgotten last night's rotten ending. "Hey."

"Wanna go to the lake?"

"Yeah. I need to get my truck." And to clarify things between us.

"I'll pick you up in a few. Bring your bathing suit."

I hang up and rush up to my room. Maybe I've been overthinking all this. My discarded bikini is still damp from last night, so I slip on board shorts and my spare top, throw on a shirt, grab a beach towel, and stuff my bare feet into beat-up sneakers.

The day is already hot, and a haze blurs the mountains. I sit on the porch steps and untangle my wet hair as I wait, distracting myself with the scenery. Up on the Devil's Tail, the Poltergeist Tree towers above the rest of the forest. It must have been magnificent once upon a time. If it really has a hollow heart like in the nightmare I had when we camped up there, it's bound to rot and fall someday soon.

Amka's silver Honda flashes through the trees at the end of the driveway. I rise as she coasts to a stop and waves out the open window. Her hair is up in a knot, and her eyes are hidden behind oversized, pink-lensed sunglasses. Blue sits shotgun, his adoring eyes glued to her like she's the goddess of dog treats.

"Hop in," she says.

I don't bother competing for the front seat. I climb into the back, and we drive off.

"How'd you sleep?" she asks.

"Fine. How about you?" I hesitate, then add lightly, to test the waters, "Feeling less gross?"

She chuckles. "Slept like a baby."

I think of what to say next. It seems a bit soon to broach the real talk, and the words I rehearsed in the shower have evaporated. But I need to know. Does she love me in a possibly girlfriend kind of way, or not?

Amka turns up the volume of her pop playlist and sings along. I watch tendrils of her hair dance on the nape of her neck, wondering how it would feel to brush my lips on the smooth, tan skin there. She tilts her chin up as if she's looking in the rear-view mirror, though I can't tell for sure because of her shades. The corner of her lip turns up. Not a real smile, but her dimple appears. I quickly turn to the window.

We drive across the village. Caden's truck is at the

Trading Post. I'll have to tell him I didn't drown in my sleep, sometime. As we get closer, I see Chloe in the passenger seat, texting on her phone, bare feet propped on the dashboard. Well, that time isn't now.

Goodbye, clamours the large sign at the end of town. *Thanks For Visiting Fort Castor.*

I pull my face between the seats, a nervous tickle in my belly. "If the Beaver Lodge doesn't call us in for work, we should go pick cherries in the Okanagan or go tree-planting or something."

Amka purses her lips.

Not a fan of road trips? Fine. Maybe Fort Cass has finally grown on her. "Or we could stay here and spend our days at the lake."

She nods, but I'm not sure if it's to what I'm saying or to the music. She stretches her arm and pets Blue's head. What's bugging her? Could it be the same thing that's killing me right now? I'll find out soon enough.

She turns onto the dirt track leading to the lake, driving too fast over the potholes, then parks crookedly a short distance from my truck. The tents are gone. Perfect. We have the lake all to ourselves.

We step out and survey the aftermath of the party. Not a bottle, can, or empty bag of chips anywhere, and my flip-flops are parked side by side on the hood of my truck. I almost expect to read *Caden was here* written on the dusty door panel.

While I trade my sneakers for the flip-flops, Amka opens the tailgate and pulls out the inflatable raft we never got to use at the party because everybody kept stealing it.

"We should bring the kayaks tomorrow and look for the lost paddle," I say.

"Yeah, maybe," Amka says.

"I thought you liked kayaking."

"I do, but right now..." Amka links her hands and stretches her arms. "I just want to relax."

Fair enough.

Blue leads us to the dock, tail swinging. Halfway between the shore and the ashes from the bonfire, a patch of sand has been swept with the edge of a foot. Caden, the gentleman, has hidden the evidence of my vomit.

I dump my shirt and beach towel on the planks and lower the raft onto the water while Amka slathers herself with sunscreen.

"Do my back?" She hands me the bottle with a contrived smile.

"Sure, I don't mind." Like, at all.

I spread the coconut-smelling cream on her skin, watching my fingers glide over the soft hollow of her spine. My skin tingles all over, like when I watch a movie and know something wild is about to happen.

"Make sure you don't miss a spot," she teases.

I work a little faster, cheeks flushing.

"There." I wipe my hands on my towel.

"Need any?"

"I put some on before leaving."

"Ah." She tosses the bottle and stands.

Why the hell did I say that? It's not even true. I do want her hands all over me. Why not give her a chance to show me what *she* wants instead of asking outright?

"Good boy, Blue. Stay right here," she says. As if he'd wander anywhere without her.

I climb into the raft and hold it steady against the dock. Amka tumbles in beside me, accidentally driving a knee into my ribs and scratching me with her bracelet. The stone is violet. I looked it up—violet means sensual. Or cheeky. Or mysterious. I can't remember really, but Amka is all that.

Once she's settled, I push us away from the dock. If we drift too far, we'll have to swim back. I don't love the idea of the water closing in around me in a cold grip again, but it's daytime. Safe enough.

The drifting raft draws concentric circles on the calm water. Amka's hip is cradled in the curve of my waist, her head propped on the bulging bow. I close my eyes and try to loosen up. The sun tints the inside of my lids the colour of amber. Amber means tense, unsettled, or nervous. I'm all that.

Because if she doesn't bring up last night's kiss soon, I'll have to ask.

I open my eyes and gaze at her parted lips. Her head lolls to the side. Through the rosy lenses of her sunglasses, her long lashes cast spidery shadows on her cheekbones. A sweet kind of pain twists my insides. What would we be doing right now if last night hadn't gone wrong?

Goosebumps appear on her belly as a cool breeze blows down from the mountains. I have the urge to smooth them down with my palm. My question doesn't necessarily have to be asked in words.

The corners of her lips twitch with a smile. Feeling caught in the act though I haven't moved a muscle, I quickly lace my fingers over my stomach. She nestles her sunglasses into her hair and peers at me with narrowed eyes. "You know Caden has a massive crush on you, right?"

"Who cares." The words fly out of my mouth before I realize I'm saying them. I do care about him, just not that way, just not right now.

She nudges me with her elbow. "Did you see the look on his face when I kissed you?"

The mouth-to-mouth thing was just to provoke him?

Before I can ask, Blue barks at the empty dirt road. A red pickup cruises into the clearing a moment later.

"Speak of the devil." Amka raises an arm and waves.

Caden idles by our vehicles. Please, leave. I can't handle him and Amka at the same time.

He drives in a slow arc as if he's not staying. I exhale. But then he reverses and parks between my truck and Amka's car. At least he got rid of Chloe. Blue struts out to greet him and escorts him back to the dock. Caden looks down at us while Amka attempts to paddle us closer with one hand. She only sends us in circles.

"Hey," I tell him. My face feels stiff as a plastic mask. "What's up?"

"You didn't answer the phone."

"Were you worried I drowned in my own bed?"

"I just thought I'd make sure you got a lift to come get your truck."

"As you see, I did, but thanks." I ratchet up a smile. "Nice job with the cleanup, by the way. We could've helped."

"No sweat. Chloe gave me a hand."

"Ooh." Amka says, confirming my suspicions they did more than pick up trash.

Caden and Chloe. Fair enough. She's been after him forever. He deserves someone who's fully committed.

"Come to swim or what?" Amka asks.

"Yeah, come on." I splash him with water.

He drops his frown and pulls off his T-shirt, showing his modest six-pack and farmer's tan. He cannonballs, splashing beside the raft. Amka squeals and throws herself overboard. The empty side lifts into the air. I barely have time to hold my breath before belly-flopping into the water. Cold shock, a flash of panic.

I emerge into the trapped air beneath the overturned raft, breathing noisily, my feet sinking into the muddy bottom. Something thin-edged wedges between my toes. Not Amka's damn bracelet, I hope.

A shadow glides underwater toward me. My chest tightens but then releases as Caden breaks through the surface and joins me under the raft.

"Sorry about capsizing you." He smirks.

Who knew Caden could play dirty?

"Sorry, my ass." I shove my palm into his shoulder, smiling too. This feels almost normal, like before Amka. I was strong back then. Now, I don't know.

"Seriously, you could have drowned last night," he says.

Our voices sound weird in this dim, little space.

"I'm sorry. I—I'm not sure what happened. But thanks for…you know. Saving me?"

"I don't want you to get hurt," he says.

He's the one who looks hurt. My infatuation with

Amka must have turned me into a monster last night. Where is she, anyway?

Water churns around my legs. Air bubbles up between us, followed by Amka's head. With her dark hair plastered to her scalp, she looks like Sedna, the goddess of the sea. The three of us are now treading water and bumping against each other in our rubbery floating cave.

"Can I join the party?" She drapes an arm around our necks, pulling us provocatively close.

I pull back, looking for a way out. "I was just about to drown Caden for making us capsize. Wanna help?"

"You bet," Amka says.

I make a lunge for his shoulder and Amka grabs at an arm. Caden flips the raft over in an attempt to escape, but we converge on him and wrestle in the water. Even Blue joins in, yipping from the dock and jumping around. My secret agenda slides away, and for a while, I'm actually having fun. But fingers skim my body in the scuffle, and I don't know who they belong to. I kick away a few metres. Now my feet can't touch the bottom. They just dangle above a cold, black void. I imagine slimy hands reaching up from the deep to grab my ankles.

I breaststroke toward the shore, tempering my speed so it doesn't look like I'm swimming for my life, then haul myself onto the dock. My instinct tells me to tuck my legs safely beneath me, but I stubbornly let them dangle into the water, shins and feet shining fish-belly white. Light slithers on the clear bottom, and silver minnows dance around Amka's sunken shades. I yank on my towel to wipe my face. Her bracelet rolls out of the folds. I catch it a moment before it dives into the lake. Disaster averted. I lay it onto her beach bag.

Out on the water, Amka clings to Caden like a baby sea otter. She's safe without her bracelet. He wouldn't let anything happen to her.

I look away from them. Minnows swirl around my toes. Their silvery dance is soothing—almost hypnotic. I should be the one keeping Amka safe. I could dive back into the lake and go steal her from Caden, like she once stole me from him. It shouldn't be a tough choice for her—she doesn't like guys. And she liked me enough to kiss *me*, whatever her reason.

"Caden?" Amka yells at the top of her lungs.

I jerk my chin up. Amka is alone, way out near the floating platform. The deserted raft drifts toward me, faster than it should in the faint breeze. Caden pops up behind it.

"You asshole," Amka shouts in the distance.

He pushes the raft toward the shore and treads water at my feet. Sunshine catches the gold flecks in his eyes. If we existed in an alternate universe where Amka was nowhere near, I would slide into the water to meet him without trepidation. I would feel safe.

"I'm the asshole," I say.

"Don't say that. It's not true." He pushes himself out of the water and sits beside me. His gaze is as clear as the sandy lake bottom.

"I—" I twine my fingers and grip until my knuckles hurt. I wish I had a magic stone—a crystal ball or whatever—to show me the right words. "You were right last night. I do like Amka a lot."

Holding his gaze is hard, but I want him to see that I like him too—that he's important to me.

"I know. You don't have to be sorry for that." His gaze turns challenging. "Do you see me apologizing for making out with Chloe last night?"

Ouch.

"Anyway." He breaks eye contact and stands. "I have to go to work."

"See you around, then."

"Yeah. See you."

He walks away. I yearn for a stronger sense that we've patched things up, but let's say that's a work in progress. On the other hand, it's finally time to ask Amka to cut the crap and tell me what's what.

I jump as fingers close around my ankle.

"I survived our shipwreck, if anybody cares," she says with a cheeky smile. "Thanks to no one."

Water droplets pearl on her face, her shoulders, and the tops of her breasts. Those curved eyelashes split into little bunches. Her eyes are blacker than those bottomless parts of the lake. It all crushes me into a ball so tight my thoughts are a jumble.

She wades into shallower water and steps onto the dock. Once she's walked back to the end where I'm sitting, she tosses her bent sunglasses onto her straw bag and slips on her bracelet. Blue flashes a dog grin and wags his tail. She scratches his ruff and coos at him, then spreads out her beach towel.

"Everything good between you and Caden?"

"Yeah, why?"

"Just asking." She pats the space beside her.

I flop down like a mollusk. She lies on her back, and I'm on my stomach. I inhale warm summer air and let the breath flow out, long and slow. "Hey, Amka?"

"Yeah?"

"About last night…"

"Um…yeah."

Her eyes are soft as she props herself onto one elbow and leans toward me like she's considering kissing me again. Now's the time to take the plunge. I lift my hand to the back of her neck and gently pull her down. When she lets me, I lift my head to meet her halfway.

Her lips are chapped and taste like sunscreen, but her tongue is soft and warm. And kissing me back. I've been dreaming of this for such a long time, but I haven't dreamed sweetly enough. This is so much more real and perfect. The back of my head thumps on the planks. Amka follows me down, her belly pressed on my hip, her mouth letting me kiss her some more.

Until she pushes away. "Alex?"

My throat feels dry. "What?"

She slips one finger beneath the shoulder strap of my top and pulls it aside. Her purple fingernail traces a line untouched by the sun, bright white against the fiery skin on each side. This is going to hurt later, but for now, I'm drowning right here on the dock.

"This was good," she says in a husky voice. "Really good, actually. But…I need to tell you something."

My heart hovers. "Yes?"

She bites the corner of her bottom lip, then says, "I'm going back to live with my mom."

"W-what?" I brush her hand off my shoulder and sit up, sliding the bikini strap back into place. "Why?"

She kneels facing me. "I got my act together. That was the point of me coming here, remember?"

"You had a bunch of drinks just last night!"

"I had two in, like, five hours." She waves this off like she'd shoo a fly.

"It was something. You nearly sent me to my drowning death."

"You were fine. Caden panicked, and then you panicked when he grabbed you."

I struggle to wrap my head around this, but I just can't.

"Sorry, Alex. I told you I'd go back home as soon as I could."

So much sorry-ness floating about today, like some foul fog shrouding everything.

I find my voice. "Well, you do you."

"Aw, Alex. Don't be like that."

"Like what?"

The next logical action would be to get up and leave. The real Alex would, without a backward glance. But I'm a messed-up version of myself, duller than a butter knife. I pick up the bent sunglasses and straighten them out. There must still be time to change her mind.

"When are you leaving?"

She plucks at a leg hair that escaped waxing. "On Saturday."

"This Saturday?" That's in three days. My sunburn

sinks beneath my skin, turning my blood to molten glass. "Why didn't you tell me earlier?"

"I swear to you, I only knew for sure yesterday morning. I didn't want to ruin the party for you."

"Right. Because the party was a big success, with me almost dying for you." I stand and drop the warped shades into her lap.

"Where're you going?"

"Home." I shove my arms through my shirt sleeves, grab my towel, and drag the raft across the grass.

Amka catches up as I tie it into the truck bed. I slam the tailgate shut.

"Alex, please." She clutches my arm and turns me to face her. She makes a concerned pout at my sunburns and brushes gentle fingers along my collarbone. "Come to my house. I'll put some cooling gel on that."

My body wants to soften. I don't let it. "Never mind my sunburns. *Vera* will take care of them."

"Will you at least come over to my house tonight? We could watch a movie."

"Sorry, I have plans. But thanks for the consolation kiss." I stride to the driver's door. "By the way, Blue will hate living in the city."

I start the engine, reverse, and idle for a few seconds. If she really cared, she'd try to stop me. She could plant herself in front of the truck and beg me to stay. Maybe I would. But she steps back and lets me go.

So, though I never asked the question, I have my answer.

Chapter 15

I don't pick up the phone when Amka calls the next morning. Too busy. I've been skimping on my chores, and Dad's coming back this Sunday. I lovingly wash my stack of dishes and vacuum the floors, the rugs, under the rugs, and even dust Vera, who's now missing a limb. The aloe isn't doing a thing to ease the tentacles of negative energies wrapped around me, but it worked wonders on my sunburns.

I focus on the pain of clothes rubbing on my scorched skin to stop Amka's last voicemail from looping in my mind: "Fine. We don't have to talk ever again if that's what you want," her voice breaking at the last word.

Yes, that is what I want. If she cares at all, why isn't she driving over here? Why isn't she kicking down my door to wrap me in her arms and tell me she loves me at least a little?

She's no better than Karine, who abandoned Dad and broke his heart. I'm not heartbroken—I'm angry. But at least Amka didn't come up with some cheap excuse about curses or other nonsense. I have to give her that.

She leaves another message late Friday night. "Alex, listen. I'm leaving early tomorrow. I need to see you. Please. I'll come to your house before I go." I'm curious as to why she'd need me now that she's going back to her fabulous life in the city.

On Saturday morning, I get up before sunrise and splash fresh-brewed coffee into a cup—no cream, no sugar to fit the mournful tone of the day ahead. The kitchen is dim and my eyes aren't ready for harsh lights, so I step outside and sit on the damp porch steps. Robins hop across the grass, hunting for worms. The snow-bare summit of the Devil's Tail is a rotten grey tooth against the tender pink sky.

You don't win, chat-cornu. You didn't steal her from me. If I loved her so much, I'd be melting in tears instead of searing on the inside. I gulp some black coffee and spit it right back into the cup. Gross. That's what battery acid must taste like. I toss the brew on the driveway, but the bitterness clings.

Chin cupped in my hands, I contemplate my bare feet. A bottle-cap-shaped scab has formed on the arch of my foot. It will leave a scar. One more for my collection. No problem, scars don't hurt.

Tires crunch on gravel as the silver panels of the Honda flash through the bushes. I picture Amka at the wheel, Blue riding shotgun. Me hopping into the back seat, and we're off on a road trip to anywhere.

But nope. Not gonna happen. The car rolls to a stop. Amka's dad is driving. The passenger door pops open, and she steps out, adorable in light-wash jeans with torn knees and a dusty-rose sweater sliding down one smooth shoulder. A pair of white, rhinestone sunglasses shield her eyes even though the sun is still hiding in the mountains.

The anger I've been holding onto melts, turning into something that tastes a lot like defeat. Or despair. What was I thinking, shutting her out those precious last three days instead of spending every possible minute with her?

I stride barefoot across the yard, barely feeling the sharpness of the crushed shale. She opens the rear door. Blue hops out. He looks up at her quizzically as she clips a leash onto his collar. She flips her shades to the top of her head and walks up to me. Her eyes are carefully made up, but the puffiness underneath them can't be disguised. Blue stands beside her, ears laid back and tail between his legs.

"Hey," I say, purposefully cool.

She wraps me in a tight squeeze. My hands are fists at my sides. Part of me longs to return the embrace, but like that night I almost drowned, I'm split in two. My mind is severed from my body.

"I'll miss you," Amka says against my shoulder. "You're a really great girl, Alex."

Right. I'm so great that she's leaving.

My resistance crumbles anyway. I hug her so hard she might pass out and miss her flight. Her dad gives a short blast of the horn. Blue pulls on the leash, jerking her out of my grip. Her eyes are shiny with tears. My own are dirt dry.

She hands me the leash.

"You're dumping your dog on me?"

"Please? My dad's taking a job out of town, and my mom won't let me take him home. You know he wouldn't be happy in the city. You said so yourself."

I hoped she would love me, but I know she loves Blue. She could have offered him back to Caden, and she chose to give him to me. That's worth something. But whatever she's going back to is worth more than him and me combined. I take the leash.

"Promise you'll take good care of him?" she asks.

"Of course. I have a heart."

She kneels on the gravel and buries her face in his ruff. "You be a good boy for Alex."

Blue paws at her, leaving pale claw marks on her forearm. She rises, sniffling and red-eyed, and pecks me on the cheek. "Be nice to Caden, eh? That's all he's waiting for."

How dare she? She didn't care about his feelings when she kissed me right in front of him. I bite the inside of my bottom lip hard to keep my renewed anger from hurtling out of my mouth. I don't need her advice on my love life.

"Amka, let's go," Mr. Tanuyak says. He waves at me. "Have a nice day, Alex. Thanks for taking the dog."

His words taste like déjà-vu.

"Let's keep in touch, okay?" Amka flashes her dimples one last time, then swivels on her feet and jogs to the car.

Blue strains against the leash as her dad takes her away. I need both hands to hold him.

The car disappears, and Amka is gone. For good this time. Blue is frantic. I'm something like a robot, stiff and mechanical.

"Come on. Let's go inside."

I tug on the leash, but he digs in his claws. A silver loop shines in the dirt. I nudge it with the tip of my foot. It's Amka's precious mood bracelet. Do I have time to jump into my truck and catch up to her dad? Probably. Do I want to? Hey, I never claimed I was a nice person. She keeps misplacing it when she's around me, anyway. Fate has spoken, I'm keeping it.

I pick it up and drag Blue inside the house. He pants and whimpers. I lean against the closed door, my skin hot and cold at the same time. The edge of the bracelet cuts into my palm. I should crush it into something misshapen and useless. Tempted, I run my thumb on the inside face. The silver is slightly rough where letters are engraved. I tip it to catch some light.

They spell "soul."

Oh, I get it. Back in grade two, Chloe gave me a split-heart necklace that spelled BFF when joined with the half she wore on a chain herself. I bet this bracelet has a twin that spells "mate." Amka hadn't been talking about soulmates for nothing, that day I took her ice-fishing.

How could I have been so dense? Her soulmate is obviously not me—I was just something to relieve the boredom until her mother agreed to take her back.

Who has the other half? Someone else she ditched? Nah. It's someone she's going back to. Someone whose name she once whispered in my ear while her hand glided all over me.

I don't care. I toss the bracelet into Vera's jungle of spiky leaves and raid the kitchen cupboards for a treat for poor Blue. There's none, so I bake cookies to pass the time: peanut butter for him, and chocolate chip for me—lots of chocolate chips, in a chocolate dough.

Blue drags me to the end of the driveway when I take him out for a bathroom break. He sits facing the direction

Amka went. With the sun high overhead, the gravel road is a dusty, bleached ribbon. Empty.

"Get her out of your head, Blue. She's not coming back."

That hard truth chokes me up.

Would the chat-cornu curse dogs as well as people? Blue came with us on the mountain, and he just lost the person he loved the most.

Midnight, sleepless. I invite Blue onto my bed, but we both know it should be Amka sharing the space with him, not me. At three in the morning, I take him for a walk, then crash on the couch with the leash wrapped around my wrist to stop him from wandering. At last, he lies down and whimpers in his dog dreams. He's breaking my bitter heart.

I watch movies with him all day on Sunday, both of us huddled on the loveseat. Nothing scary, just car chases and explosions. Dad's on his way home. I wonder what he'll say about us having a dog.

At dinner time, the rumble of his truck vibrates through the walls. Blue beats me to the entrance mat. I pull him out of the way because I'm sure he'll run out if he has a chance.

"Well, hey." Dad shuts the door and dumps his duffle bag. Looks around for Amka. Takes in the table I've set for two people only. "Are we dog-sitting again?"

I release Blue and fall into his arms.

He wraps me in a bear hug. "What's wrong, sweetie?"

"Amka's gone." I lay my head into his two-week stubble

and breathe in his comforting dad-smell of machine grease and road dust.

"When's she coming back?"

I can only shake my head.

"Ah, I see." He sighs and pats my back. "Looks like we've become a family of three."

On Monday, Dad settles on the couch with Book One of *The Trickster* trilogy, which he's been meaning to read for months. I alternate between baking stuff that doesn't turn out quite right and taking Blue on unhappy strolls. We leave him in the house while we take out the kayaks to go fishing on Tuesday. He chews the door jamb to splinters. He wants to leave so bad.

The week crawls by. I wish he'd start getting over Amka. Then, maybe I'd have an easier time forgetting about her myself. I also wish he'd sleep through the night. Dad says he's almost as restless as me when I was a newborn.

"Did you ever feel like sending me back where I came from?" I ask as we're having breakfast.

"A bunch of times." He smiles, and I know he means never.

He feeds Blue a crust of his toast. "I do need my sleep, though, now that I'm an old man."

"It's not my fault he won't settle."

"How about we build him a doghouse? He might be more comfortable outside."

"And keep him tied? That wouldn't be fair."

"We can build a fence, too."

"Sounds like a plan," I say, trying to sound enthused, even though the plan involves getting lumber from Caden's family's sawmill.

"Coming for a ride, Coydog?" Dad says.

I jam a baseball cap over my unwashed hair. We pile into the truck, Blue in the middle, and drive to Caden's. Dad rolls down his window.

"Don't open it too much. Blue might try to jump out."

"Someone's got bad breath, and it's not me."

Instinctively, I run my tongue over my teeth. Did I forget to brush? Blue turns to me, panting. Ew. Dog-breath. I crank the air conditioning and aim the vent on my face.

Caden steps out the door when we pull up in front of the house. He walks up to the truck, gloves in hand and an ease in his step. He's in love with Chloe and flaunting it.

"Coffee's on," he tells Dad. His brow creases as he notices Blue, then his gaze lands on me. "Alex and I will load the lumber?"

I shrug. "Sure."

"Thanks, Caden." Dad gets out and slaps him on the shoulder.

"Meet you out back." I scoot around Blue to sit behind the wheel and cruise past a stand of aspen toward the vast timber-frame shed, back up to the door, and kill the engine.

Blue crowds me when I open the door. "No, Blue."

"You can let him out," Caden says as he joins me.

"I can't." I roll the windows down a bit, step down, and shut the door behind me. "He'll run away."

"Poor guy." Caden taps on the window. "You miss your human, don't you?"

"He's my dog, now." I pull the brim of my cap lower over my eyes. "So, where's that lumber?"

"In there." He points inside the shed where planks and beams are stacked by size. "That pile by the door should do."

I grab a stack of four planks.

"You don't have gloves?" he asks. He starts pulling off one of his.

"I'm good." I wave him off. Who cares about me having soft hands?

We load the wood in silence. The buzz of a cicada rises from the trees. After a few back-and-forth solo trips from the shed to the truck bed, we team up and move thicker stacks of planks, me leading the way. Our efforts synchronize, and I take comfort in the mindless work.

After we slide in the last stack, I sit on the free corner of the tailgate to examine my hand. A splinter has pushed deep into my palm, but my nails are trimmed too short to pull it out.

"Can I see?" Caden pulls out his pocket knife and unfolds the blade.

It's been a long while since we played paramedics. I'm pretty sure I'd trust him with my life if it came down to it, so why not? I place my hand face up in his waiting palm. His fingers curl to hold me while he scratches at the splinter with care.

The sharp end of the splinter must poke a nerve. Each time the knife blade touches it, a needle of pain stabs me in the heart. That traitor. I had promised myself not to let anyone under my skin. Amka wedged herself there so smoothly, then ripped everything on her way out.

Caden's warm aura calls to me. I could lay my forehead on his shoulder and let him try to make things better for me, but he's so damn gentle that tears prick my eyes. I don't want to fall apart in front of him.

"Gimme that." I steal the blade and shear layers of skin until the tiny, offending piece of wood slides out.

"Thanks." I fold the blade and hand it back.

Caden pockets it and stands there, trapping me in my narrow spot on the tailgate. My eyes are wet. I keep the shield of my cap's brim between us.

"I should probably go before Blue gets too hot in there."

He rocks on his feet but doesn't move back yet. "If you need me, you know where to find me, right?"

"Won't Chloe mind? I thought you two were dating now." I give him a view of the shadowed bags under my eyes.

"Not sure I'd call it dating…"

Meaning I can fall back on him? I was tempted just minutes ago, but as Chloe once said, with me, it's always all or nothing. Right now, I'm in a nothing sort of mood, which is probably the best for everyone around me.

"I shouldn't mess up things for you." I push past him, get into the truck, and start driving toward the house to pick up Dad.

I wave to Dad as he leaves for another shift. We've built a pretty fancy doghouse, fully insulated because winter will be back sooner than we think, and fenced a large area for Blue to roam in.

When his truck disappears behind the trees, I walk to the backyard to check on Blue. He's already worn a dirt path in the grass along the fence.

"Wanna come inside?"

He sits and gazes at me, one eye ice-blue, the other an unsettling yellow. I'll take that as a yes. I slip through the gate and snap on his leash before leading him out of the pen. He pulls me along, focused on the road.

"In here, Blue." I tug, and he reluctantly follows me inside.

The house feels empty. So do I. It should be better now that I have Blue to talk to, but he curls up on the mat and goes to sleep.

I go to my room and wipe the dust from my laptop, unused since my last school assignment. Maybe I can find some toys to order for Blue. Three emails, not counting spam, sit in my inbox.

Saturday last week: *Made it home!! (Had to text Caden for your email.) How's Blue?*

Monday: *Have you seen my bracelet by any chance?*

Tuesday: *Ever check your emails? Why don't you have a cell phone like normal people?*

"What's wrong with the landline?" I say out loud. And who sends emails anymore except people who want your money?

I type, *Blue's fine. How are you?*

She replies within minutes. *Mom's already turned into Norma Bates LOL. Follow me on Insta*

I open a new tab and find her account. It seems new, with only a handful of pictures. Photos of her with, presumably, her old friends. I zoom in on their faces. They seem okay enough, and Amka looks happy.

Then, a selfie with the dusty taxidermized black bear at the Prince George airport, taken the day she left. *#solong.*

My mind jumps right in and adds "suckers" to the hashtag. Because Fort Cass is a hole in the middle of nowhere, and we're all a bunch of backwoods hillbillies over here. For a few moments, Amka suckered me into believing I mattered to her.

Another email comes in. *You should get an account. Post pictures of Blue.*

The hell I will. I'm not getting on social media for her or anyone else. Amka made her choice to go back to her old life, so I'm gonna go back to mine. I was fine before she came, and I will be fine again.

Don't hold your breath, I type, ignoring the voice that tells me not to hit send.

Amka doesn't reply, so I guess she got the message. We don't live in the same world anymore.

Part II

Devil by the Horns

Chapter 16

Once upon a time

The cursor blinks, taunting. My first English assignment of grade twelve is due in two days, and I have writer's block. I wish the subject was "Describe Your Summer Break." Then, my laptop's blank screen would paint an accurate picture.

I got the room-cleaning job at the Beaver Lodge—free lunch included, served on those paper placemats telling the legend of the chat-cornu. Nothing exciting to report about making beds and cleaning toilets. I worked hard at believing the curse didn't make Amka leave. She was here less than five months. Hardly long enough for her to become "dearest to my heart," as the legend says.

And she wasn't stolen. She left—just like Karine—because there was nothing and no one good enough for her here.

Blue stretches at the other end of my bed. He's fully grown now, compact like a heeler, and slant-eyed like a coyote. His paws spasm as if he's still dreaming of running away. If it weren't for him, I could have forgotten Amka by now, but his presence and his longing keep reminding me of how easily she abandoned us.

I, on the other hand, have become a model dog owner. I give Blue treats, but not too many. We go for long walks every day, always on a leash to make sure he doesn't run into any kind of trouble.

He's a good dog, too. He wags his tail when I talk to him, follows me from room to room, and shares the loveseat and a bowl of popcorn with me when we watch a movie. He doesn't love me like he loved Amka, though. He looked at her like she was a goddess. I'm a petting and feeding machine. But fair's fair.

As for Caden, his summer fling with Chloe is apparently over. I haven't seen her bare feet propped on his dashboard for weeks. He's being cautiously friendly with me but keeps a wider distance between us than he used to before Amka. But then again, fair's fair.

That's it—my summer in a nutshell. Not the stuff that would fill the word quota, but the actual task is to retell a myth. Half the class, me included, picked Fort Cass's very own legend. I don't know what I was thinking. Maybe I wanted to prove how silly this story is and to dissociate myself from it once and for all. In the end, Ms. Bakker had us rock-paper-scissor it, and I was the unlucky winner. So, I'd better get on with it. Let's see.

Once upon a time, an inept trapper named Gabriel wanted to prove his worth to a girl.

Blue lets out a big sigh.

"Boring, I know."

I need to clear my head. Blue jumps as I snap my laptop shut.

"Let's go for a walk."

We jog downstairs, and I poke my head into the living room. Dad is on the loveseat, texting like there's no tomorrow, a smile on his lips. Melody, no doubt. At least one of us has a love life.

"People these days," I say. "Always on their phones. If you don't watch it, your brain will turn to mush."

He sets his phone face-down on his thigh. "How's the homework going?"

"It's going. I'm taking Blue on a walk before dark."

"Keep an eye out for bears."

"As always."

I step into my shoes, throw on a jacket, and clip on Blue's leash. Amka's soul bracelet, still hanging in Vera's serrated leaves like some worthless trophy, glares at me with an olive-green eye. I should send it back to her, but I relish the idea of having it and Amka not knowing where it is. She hasn't asked me about it again. Maybe her "soulmate," whoever they are, got her a new one. We haven't been in contact at all since those emails we fired at each other, and I've been good at ignoring her social media too.

"Say hi to Melody for me," I shout before stepping out the door.

The evening air is crisp. The leaves haven't begun turning, but fall is in the air. White veins of snow crisscross the highest mountaintops.

Blue and I head down the gravel road, not even pausing at the top of the hill. We're one fearless team—at least for a few moments. My guts clench as the thin fog at the bottom laps at my feet, but I think this is just what I need. A dash of spookiness to get my creative juices flowing.

I stop near the ditch. On the other side, the bleached branches of the dead willows glow quietly against the deep-green forest. Blue sits, leaning against my leg, ears cocked at the trail. All is silent. No leaves rustling—or little girls crying, as in my episode when my sled broke in this very spot. Still, I shudder.

I try to imagine I'm Gabriel, ill-equipped for a winter on the mountain that used to be called *Tsa*. Would the chat-cornu have already been waiting for him up there, or would it have followed him, waiting for the perfect opportunity to strike?

Whichever it is, I know how he was feeling. I felt it myself when I had that weird nightmare during the mountain trek with Caden and Amka last spring. As I remember facing the chat-cornu posing as Karine beneath the Poltergeist Tree, my body buzzes with something like dread, but I'd rather call it inspiration.

"I've got it, Blue. Come on. We have a story to write."

"Alexia," Ms. Bakker says the following Monday. "You've done an excellent job with Fort Castor's very own legend."

I prefer Alex, but I don't correct her because a smug smile spreads on my lips. I got this baby written from scratch and polished to a shine in forty-eight hours. It was cathartic work.

"I would like you to read it to the class."

A few faces turn to me, and my smugness melts away.

"Um, really?"

"Really." Ms. Bakker pushes her glasses back up the

ridge of her freckled nose. "You did have a few grammatical errors. Tell you what, class. Five extra points to anyone who wants to share the story they've written."

Ms. Bakker waves a sheaf of paper at me like bait. How cruel. She knows I can't say no to a perfect grade.

"Come on, Alex," Mickey says. "You can do it."

Well. Presentations aren't all that bad, considering most of the class usually spaces out within the first few minutes.

I make my way to the front, grab my story, and clear my throat. "The Devil by the Tail. Eighteen-eighty-six. Gabriel was the youngest son of a family of thirteen, born in Quebec on a piece of land where rocks grew faster than potatoes."

I pause for effect, more than a little bit proud of this line. A few gazes turn toward the windows where the Devil's Tail is well visible. Caden's eyes are on me. A flush creeps up my neck. Unfortunately, he will listen to each and every word because he always pays attention in class.

"Alexia?"

"Yep," I say like this is roll call.

I take a deep breath and resume reading.

"On the eve of his eighteenth birthday, the call to adventure whispered in Gabriel's ear. The next day, he heaved his pack onto his skinny shoulders and canoed west on the fur trading routes with twelve seasoned *voyageurs* as companions.

"However, adventure had made a mistake and summoned up the wrong person. Gabriel got sick and weak along the way. Daunted by the burden he had become, his companions dumped him in Fort Castor before continuing their journey.

"A son of French-Canada, he barely spoke any English, but he met Atwanet, a Métis girl who was fluent in French. He was charmed by her lilting voice and her skills on the land. And by some miracle, she responded to his flirtation with a smile and a blush."

I pause to gauge the class. Half the gazes have glazed over already, but a few are still alert and aimed at me, including Caden's.

"Anyway," I say, though this word is not actually on paper. "As winter set in, Gabriel prepared to go trapping for the season. He loaded a toboggan with supplies to last the whole season: warm clothes, smoked fish, dried berries, and the bannock Atwanet had baked.

"She wanted to go along—the trapline and cabin he was headed to had belonged to her father before the pox took him—but it would be a sacrilege. They weren't married yet. Gabriel had asked for Atwanet's hand, but he wanted to prove he could provide for a wife first.

"So, Atwanet lent him the bewitched snowshoes that had been in her family for generations, saying they would help him make good time on the arduous trek. Then she made him promise to return before the catkins bloomed in the willows.

"After teary goodbyes, Gabriel stomped down Fort Castor's snow-packed main street and past homesteads and fallow fields. At the end of the road, round-topped *Tsa* Mountain squatted like a fat beaver in the shade of its sharp-toothed sisters. He strapped on the bewitched snowshoes and passed through the tangles of willows that grew on each side of the trailhead.

"The snowshoes lent a surprising ease to his steps, but Gabriel couldn't shake off the feeling that God must frown upon such unholy contraptions. He kept looking over his shoulder, worried Satan himself would open up the earth with a tap of his pitchfork and cast him into the fires of Hell, but what he glimpsed instead was an ungodly creature with the body of a lynx and the black, hooked horns of a chamois.

"He dismissed the sighting as a trick of his imagination but couldn't quite forget about it. It reminded him of one feverish night of paddling the Peace River during his westward journey. Tremblay, the crew's *raconteur*, had claimed that the first settlers hadn't only brought the smallpox and the Devil with them across the ocean. Creatures far older had also followed. He told the tale of a cunning shapeshifter and warned that 'those who see the beast are cursed, for it will steal from them someone dearest to their heart.'"

A frisson passes through me as I finish reading this line. I copied it from the Beaver Lodge's placemat. Karine used similar words in her letter, too.

I lick my lips and continue.

"Gabriel set up his traps but didn't catch a single fox, marten, or ermine for weeks. Only lynx tracks dotted the snow, larger than any he'd seen before. This is how he realized he had really seen the chat-cornu, and that the beast had cursed him. For if he went home to Atwanet without a single animal pelt come spring, she would see him as a failure and close her heart to him for good.

"Another fruitless month passed. By the full moon, the catkins would bloom. Gabriel couldn't bear losing Atwanet, so he had to find a way to break the curse. He continued his unsuccessful trapping, all the while studying the chat-cornu's tracks until he discovered its lair, a gigantic, hollow hemlock higher up on the mountain.

"He would bind the beast to this wretched place, just like God cast wicked souls in Hell. He set a snare—a loop of rusted wire nearly invisible against the dark opening of the tree's hollow. By God's grace, the next evening his snare held the dead horned lynx. He rejoiced, for with the beast dead, the curse must be broken.

"How magnificent Atwanet would look in a parka trimmed with this russet-flecked, creamy-white fur. Gabriel skinned the beast right then and there, tossed the naked carcass inside the tree hollow, and stuffed the rolled-up pelt inside his parka.

"He trekked down the mountain on Atwanet's bewitched snowshoes, a spring in his step. Around the last bend at the trailhead, the boughs of the willows shimmered a vibrant green in the twilight. Thank the Lord, his lonely winter was over.

"Suddenly, a vicious roar shook the entire mountain— the snarl of the foiled beast, so powerful it set off an avalanche of stone and snow. Gabriel quickened his pace. The chat-cornu's pelt pulsed against his chest as though hungering for a heart. The willows were near. If only he could pass through their gateway, he thought he'd be safe.

"'You thief.' The chat-cornu appeared in front of him, now a patchy-furred shadow of its former self.

"Freaked out, Gabriel yanked the beast's pelt out of his parka and tossed it at the insubstantial creature. He didn't care about furs anymore. All he wanted was to behold his sweet Atwanet again, even if for one last time.

"'This belongs with my body in the tree hollow,' the chat-cornu spat. 'Pick it up. Now.'

"Gabriel's body obeyed against his will. He lifted the pelt and set into motion, the bewitched snowshoes heavy as lead, as though they were now cursed. The dead hemlock towered above the other trees, beckoning. Higher still, the rounded back of *Tsa* had crumbled away, replaced by a peak as sharp as one of the beast's fangs.

"When he reached the tree, night had fallen and the chat-cornu waited under the glare of auroras as red as sin. As Gabriel bent to toss the pelt inside the hollow, the chat-cornu slashed his neck with razor-claws, then butted him in the ribs with its horns.

"The impact threw Gabriel's body into the black maw of the tree. As he lay bleeding on his grave of moss and twigs, the chat-cornu tried to crawl back into its stolen pelt, but it had already frozen stiff.

"'Well played, Gabriel,' it hissed. 'You think you've tethered me to this mountain, but I'll find my way out.' Under Gabriel's gaze, the beast transformed into his own image.

"'Sorry to leave so soon,' it said with Gabriel's voice. 'When I don't show up in the village, my beloved Atwanet will come find me at the cabin.'

"The curse had come true—the chat-cornu would steal Atwanet from him. Gabriel moaned, powerless with his legs tangled in the damned snowshoes. He prayed, in the slim hope God would listen, that Atwanet would recognize the beast for the fraud that it was."

Someone starts clapping, and a few others join in. I snap out of my story and blink under the fluorescent lights, feeling like I've been yanked out of a bad dream.

"That was wonderful, Alexia," Ms. Bakker says.

"It's Alex," I mutter, walking back to my desk, not feeling my legs as if I'm having an out-of-body experience. As soon as I sit, the bell rings. I beeline for the door as Caden approaches, but he catches up and falls into step with me in the hallway.

"Great story," he says. "I didn't know there was that much to it."

I land back into my body. It's been a while since the last time we traded anything more than hellos. It feels good. I want to make it last.

"I had to summon the chat-cornu to get the full scoop," I say.

"No shit. Did it try to steal your soul?"

"Didn't want it. My dark soul is not 'dearest' to anyone."

We're at the glass door that leads outside. Caden swivels as if he's going to open it with his shoulder, but he doesn't. I stop, just short of bumping into him. In the muted light, his eyes are the same olive colour as the mood stone the night I went on my writer's block-busting walk with Blue.

"You don't believe what you're saying, do you?" he says.

I shrug, but he's right. I know he cares about me, and that I'm important to a few other people as well. Nothing will change that, not even the darkness of my soul.

Chapter 17

Fall flows by in yellows and golds as I ease back into my old life; the good life that contains only the people I actually need around me, plus Blue as a perk. But today, I'm not feeling it. The sky is heavy, and the last leaves in the trees have turned brittle and brown.

I haul my feet up on my kitchen chair and hug my knees. School starts in fifteen minutes, and I'm still in my ugly pyjama-sweatpants. This time of the year always has me in a funk. I know I'm not the only one to get those late autumn blues. I'm sure they'll go away when the snow flies and makes everything shiny and bright.

There's something else, too. A detail my brain picked up and tossed into my mind's junk drawer. When I woke up this morning, that drawer had slid open. The corner of a letter stuck out, with today's date handwritten in purple ink on it. November first, the anniversary of Karine's desertion.

This anniversary doesn't deserve celebrating, but the fact that I've been doing perfectly fine all these years is worth something. I slide one foot off the chair and nudge Blue's tail with my toes.

"How about a lazy day, Blue?"

My grades are good, and I haven't missed any classes so

far this year. I can afford to skip school this once. I'll bake a chocolate cake with a ton of icing and have it for breakfast, lunch, and dinner—maybe with a side of something healthy.

Blue shakes himself and trots to the door. I throw on a jacket, clip on his leash, and we head out into the blustery morning. We go for a short walk, and when I lead him back toward the front steps, he pulls on the leash.

"You want to go into your pen?"

He wags his tail. Force of habit, I guess. He trots in and hops onto the flat roof of his doghouse.

"I'll come get you in a little bit, okay?"

He lifts his nose to the wind, eyes narrowed. Something's in the air. It swirls around me along with dead leaves, cold and gripping. I shake it off. It's just the funk. I jog back to the house, hoping to leave it outside. A chocolate cake is guaranteed to chase away any dark clouds still hanging over my head.

The phone rings at quarter past ten. It must be the school checking on my absence. I don't pick up. Dad won't learn about this until he reads his messages at the end of his twelve-hour shift. I'll email him about it, too, so he doesn't have to worry about me. I turn on my laptop and look for a recipe since we're out of boxed mixes. A few messes later, I pour the batter into two round pans and open the oven, expecting a wave of hot air to hit my face. It doesn't come. Crap. I forgot to preheat it. I slide the pans on the rack and turn on the heat. An extra ten minutes on the timer should do the trick.

Meanwhile, I sit with my laptop and the mixing bowl,

scooping out the leftover batter. I know it's not recommended with the raw-flour germs and all, but if I can stomach microbe-laden lake water, I can stomach anything.

I email Dad, delete a string of spam, and then I can't find another valid reason to be online.

Sometimes, I do things for no good reason. Things I know will be bad for me, like swimming drunk in the middle of the night. Or opening a letter that's been mouldering for fifteen years at the bottom of a box of wool socks on a basement shelf. I lick a smear of chocolate batter off my finger, as if a cleanish fingertip will make what I'm about to do any smarter. It won't, and I'm strongly aware of that as I click on Amka's Instagram URL.

Pictures appear three to a row. For the briefest instant, I glimpse my face in one of them, but my brain quickly catches up to my eyes. That isn't me sitting with her on concrete steps littered with maple leaves and old gum. We never sat together on any such steps. She never even took a picture of us together.

I click on the photo to get a better view. The other girl is tall and lean like me. Long, honey-smooth hair, sharp cheekbones like mine, but beautiful. Alex 2.0, new and improved.

Amka's face is cradled in the curve of 2.0's neck, and her index finger is hooked beneath a silver mood bracelet on the slim, creamy-white wrist. I don't need to see it up close to know that letters are engraved on the inside, and I know they spell "*mate*."

The chocolate batter turns gross on my tongue. I spit the mouthful back into the bowl. This isn't Alex 2.0. This is The Original, whatever her name is. It starts with an A, whispered in my neck while Amka's hands explored my body in search of someone who wasn't me.

I slam the laptop lid shut, but in my mind's eye, the girl's hand still clutches the back of Amka's neck, her acid-blue gaze still holds mine and tells me that Amka belongs to her—has always belonged to her.

Well, I don't care.

I. Don't. Care.

The back of my chair hits the counter as I stand and march out of the house. My legs rush me over to Blue's pen, who Amka discarded like trash. And, still, he'd try to run back to her if I gave him a chance.

My dark soul takes hold. Why should I care when he doesn't love me either? I've always been fine on my own. I throw the gate open. Blue stands on the roof of his doghouse.

"You can leave if you want." My voice is dead calm. He'll just run to that yellow house in town and wait for Amka to open the door for him, but she never will. No one will come to that door. Mr. Tanuyak vacated shortly after taking his out-of-town job, and the house sits empty. Some passerby will see Blue, and they'll realize Alex isn't good enough for this dog. They'll find him a good forever home with people worth loving.

Finally believing his luck, Blue hops down to the ground and dashes out of the pen, like I knew he would. But then, he stops beside me, his face lifted to mine, asking, *where to?*

My knees buckle, and I sink to the ground, throwing

my arms around him. Why do I have to be such an awful person?

I bawl so hard I can't make myself stop. I hadn't shed a single tear for Amka before this. Why now? Just *why*? I don't even know what I feel, and even less what I *should* be feeling. I'm burning and freezing at the same time, from the inside out.

Blue only has so much patience. After several minutes, he slinks out of my grasp and lies down, chin on his front paws. I cry even harder. When I'm emptied out, I'm half-frozen because it's November and I'm outside in a tank top.

The drone of a familiar engine cuts through the wind. Shit. It's Caden. I spring up to my feet and wipe tears and snot on the hem of my top. He cruises into the yard and parks in front of the house, his green-gold gaze finding me the instant he steps out of his truck. Blue trots over to him and leads him back to me. I shoot Caden a warning glance, and he pauses, far enough that maybe he won't notice my raw nose and eyes.

"Why aren't you at school?" I ask.

"It's lunch break."

As if this explains anything.

"I thought I'd check on you. I just wanted to make sure you were all right."

"Why wouldn't I be all right?"

He shoves his hands in his pockets and shrugs. "You're always miserable around this time of the year, because of... you know."

Everybody around here knows my mother abandoned

me, but he's been noticing my funk every year? Tears want to rise again, but I smother them down.

"I'm not miserable," I say, and, damn, my voice sounds as if there's a wad of soggy cotton balls jammed down my throat. "You can leave. I'm fine."

He half swivels around but then changes his mind and strides right up to me. What's wrong with him?

He studies my exposed skin reddened by the cold. "You should go inside. You look like you're freezing."

"Yeah." I step toward the house, but he's standing in my way. I could go around him, I suppose, but the edges of his unbuttoned jacket flap in the wind, and the flannel lining looks so warm and inviting. So, I plow straight into him, sliding my arms inside the jacket and around him.

He wavers from the impact, or perhaps from the surprise, but his arms wrap me up and hold me tight. I go soft and lay my forehead on his shoulder, breathing in the clean warmth of his skin. He doesn't ask anything, doesn't say it's all right, because Caden gets me, and he knows I'm not all right.

He keeps holding me while the dust settles in my mind. I wish I never let Amka steal me away from him. But I shouldn't be this upset. She's been gone for months.

Amka was intoxicating and dangerous, like a drunken swim in a lake at night. On the other hand, Caden is safe and good, like a warm blanket. When she touched me, I was drowning in want. Standing like this with Caden, I can feel his deep caring flow into me and fill me up. This is what I was looking for, until Amka collided with my life and sent me out of orbit.

"Sorry for the meltdown," I say, pulling away.

"No worries." Cautiously as if I might bite, he moves a strand of hair stuck to my chin. "I'll give you a ride to school if you want."

I look down at my ugly sweatpants smeared with flour and my chocolate-stained tank top, appalled he's seeing me like this. "I think I'll stay home the rest of the day."

"You'd better get out of the cold, then."

If I could pick anyone in the world for a soulmate, it should be him. My dark soul sends out feelers for the old flutter his closeness sometimes gave me, before Amka. There it is, lurking in a hollow in my core. I want it to burst into flames and burn up all traces of her.

I grasp a handful of his shirt, look him in the eyes, then at his lips. "Caden."

His Adam's apple bobs as he realizes what I'm thinking of doing. I give him a moment to run. He doesn't. I move in too fast, and our lips connect, hard and sudden. He kisses me back with a hunger that might be even stronger than mine. For about three seconds. And then, he pulls away.

"What's that about?" he says.

A blast of wind cuts between us. We stare at each other. His face reflects the shock I'm sure is plainly written on my own face. I can't believe what I just did.

"I—" I start, evading his gaze. "I need—" The words escape me. What I need is a shovel so I can hit myself on the head. I never imagined our first kiss, if it ever came, would happen this way. I never thought he would want none of it.

"You need *time* to think about this?" he asks—not

harshly, but I catch his dismayed headshake. Still, he's throwing me a lifeline I don't deserve, saving me from drowning—again—in the mire of my embarrassment.

Caden: pure gold.

"Yeah." I press the heel of my palm against my forehead and squeeze my eyes shut.

"I have to go back to school," he says.

By the time I open my eyes, he's striding away, not even bending to scratch Blue's head as he passes him by.

Inside the house, the smoke alarm goes off.

The day after I turned my chocolate cake to charcoal, I arrive at school as tense as a loaded rat trap. Did Caden spend all night thinking about what I did? Is he still as appalled by it as I am now? Yet, I can't quite bring myself to regret kissing him.

There's an open parking spot near his truck. I've parked beside him a hundred times without thinking twice, but today I don't want to announce my feelings before I understand his, so I park further away, in a puddle the size of a lake. Thin ice cracks under my boots, and hard frost coats every surface in white, like chalk dust on a blank slate.

Things could go down either of two ways. Either we pretend yesterday never happened, or we pretend Amka never sidetracked us and resume right where we were the day before she showed up. I don't know which option would be best. I'll wait for Caden's cue. I owe that to him, given I'm the one who messed up, as usual.

Inside the school, I find him leaning with his shoulder

against the lockers, his back to me and listening to something Mickey's saying.

"Hey, Alex," Mickey says as I approach.

"Hey."

Caden turns, poker-faced.

I don't know how to act. I drop my backpack. "Can you two move? I need to get into my locker."

"Sure." Caden gives Mickey a friendly slap on the arm and walks away.

"What's up?" Mickey asks.

"Nothing much," I say a little fast. Heat flushes up my cheeks. "Kind of chilly this morning, eh?"

I open my locker door between us and root in there until he leaves. Textbook in hand, I head to Physics and sit in my regular spot beside Caden. He usually greets me in some way, but today his eyes are riveted to the pristine whiteboard.

Mr. Brar starts a lecture about the differences between electrostatic and gravitational forces.

A) Gravitational forces are always attractive.

B) Electrostatic forces may be either attractive or repulsive.

C) Something-something about dependence and medium.

I can't live with not knowing where I stand with Caden.

I nudge his arm, attentive to any clue. "Can I borrow a pencil?"

He rifles inside his backpack, slides a pen across the table, and returns his attention to the front.

I doodle in the margin of my notebook in red ink. Is

that colour a code for something? Love? Anger? Or maybe, *you surprised the heck out of me yesterday but now that I've had time to think about it, I'm not buying your bullshit?*

First period ends. He's up and headed for the door before I can return the pen. We have different electives for period two, and he spends lunch outside shooting hoops with Mickey while I feign to read in the library and watch them through the window.

It looks like we're pretending yesterday never happened. Okay, fine. I'll have to corner him somewhere and ask—just to be sure.

He's as elusive all afternoon and whizzes past our lockers right after the last bell. His truck is gone by the time I get to the parking lot. It must be some kind of punishment—if not directly from him then from the universe.

I drive home, ruminating. The frost is gone, and everything is darkest-green, grey, or brown. If Caden was waiting for me to decide what will happen next, I'd say, I'm not taking back what happened yesterday. Are you? He was kissing me pretty damn hotly before his thinking brain kicked in.

I reach home before this scenario finishes playing out. Blue crawls out of his doghouse.

"Hey, Blue," I shout. "Be there in a minute."

I change into old jeans and a hoodie and walk to the backyard. Even after yesterday's milestone, I hold my breath as I open the gate. He pads out and sits, grinning at me.

"You silly dog," I say, though I'm the silly one. Blue was wise enough to move on from Amka long before I was.

"What do you think, Blue? Am I a bad girl for kissing Caden?"

He wags his tail.

"Yes? I think so too." And I want to be bad again.

I eat spaghetti in front of the TV, then sit at the kitchen table to do my physics homework. I open my laptop, which I never shut down after the burned cake incident. The screen blinks to life, still on Amka's Instagram. I brace myself and study that picture again. The girl's possessive blue eyes. Her hand on the back of Amka's neck. Amka's smile is soft, but her gaze seems melancholic. Maybe Mississauga isn't as great as she thought it was. Maybe the soulmate isn't living up to her expectations.

Well, we all have to live with our choices. Goodbye, Amka. I click off the tab and clear my search history, then look up physics stuff to complete my sparse notes. Caden's red pen rolls out of my textbook when I open it. Are we going to go on forever acting as if nothing happened? Lingering questions are a major pain, so I should at least clear the air.

If only I could text him. But I can't, so I dial his cell. The call goes to voicemail. I try his landline, hoping his mom won't answer.

She does. "Hello, Alex. Feeling better today?"

Caden told her about my episode? I hope he kept it vague.

"Yeah, thanks. Um… Can I speak to Caden?"

"Just a minute."

"Hey." His voice startles me. That was the quickest minute ever.

"Hey. I stole your pen by accident. Could you come over and get it?"

His sigh whistles in the earpiece. The next few seconds of silence stretch on like days. It's just a pen. I know he couldn't care less about it. I can hand it back to him tomorrow or never and he won't miss it much.

"Sure. I'll be there in a bit." He's not thrilled, I can tell.

"Okay." My legs are wobbly even though I'm sitting, and I don't know if it's with tension or relief.

I hurry to change back into my good jeans. I brush my teeth—just in case—and comb my staticky hair, until there's a knock at the door and Blue barks. I rush to open it. Caden stands there, golden-haloed by the porch light.

We're both frozen. What now? His eyes sparkle, but again, that might only be an effect of the light.

"Thanks for coming," I say. Damn. I should have rehearsed what I was going to say. I run my thumb against one of Vera's fat leaves. "Look. About yesterday…"

"It was an accident?" he says, an edge in his voice.

"Yes. No! I meant it, but…"

I shoot him an imploring look. I need help with this, but he just waits. I had it coming, I guess. You break it, you fix it, right?

Here goes. "I won't do it again if you don't want me to."

It's dark outside, but I sense the Devil's Tail looming. That damn chat-cornu might as well be watching too, waiting for Caden to whip around and walk away.

"Just so you know," he says, "I'm not just some doormat you can roll up and put away when you don't need it."

Shit, oh. "I know. I know. I never wanted to make you feel like this. I'm sorry."

He nods, maybe not believing me yet but taking it in, at least.

I need to do something. Anything. I step on the cold door sill, levelling our gazes, and stare him down, like I did way back in our staring contest days. "Maybe, we could just…try and see what happens?"

He nods, but he's not saying yes just yet.

The wait is unbearable. I could slip my hand onto his neck, entice him with gentle pressure from my fingertips, but I want the choice to be his, so I keep waiting.

He makes a face like he's about to rip a band-aid from his skin and knows it will hurt. Like he knows this is a bad idea but there's no way around it. He releases a breath and leans in. I close my eyes and meet him halfway. The kiss is cautious, but oh-so-soft, like our first kiss should have been.

I teeter on the doorsill and step down before I lose my balance.

"This felt so nice," I say.

Caden still stands outside, but he smiles a little. "So, can I get my red pen back now?"

"I'll give it back to you if you come in and help me with physics homework."

I tug on the cuff of his sleeve and step backward. He follows me. We're all right. More than that, we're made for each other. If I really was cursed to lose someone dearest to me, Caden would have been the one. Yet, after all my BS, here he is, for me, like he's always been.

I reach around him and shut the door in the chat-cornu's face.

Chapter 18

Caden and I are having a secret foot conversation under his dining room table. So, when we smile, it's not necessarily because the corny dad jokes (his or mine) are all that funny.

All week at school, we have perfected the art of pretending we're still regular friends in front of everyone. Caden lets me kiss him in stolen moments only, as if he's still unsure about us being together. I'm eager to make up for the wasted months.

"A skeleton walks into the Beaver Lodge Pub," Caden's dad starts. He tugs at his braided beard, chuckling at the punch line before even saying it. He's older than Dad—like, regular-parent-old—and would have the right look to play a Viking in a movie.

I miss the joke's ending but laugh anyway because Caden has caught my foot and tickles it. Melody leans into Dad, her brown palm on his forearm, stars in her eyes.

"Wanna watch a movie?" Caden asks when the laughter dies down.

The happiness going around makes me warm on the inside, but it will be short-lived if I stick around for the planned game of Monopoly. This game I can't ever seem to win turns me into the most horrible loser.

"Sure," I say, faux-casual. I've got better plans than passing go and collecting a fake two hundred bucks.

"No popcorn?" Tina asks.

She makes the best from scratch. I pat my belly. "Thanks, but that cheesecake did me in."

We head toward the basement stairs.

"What did Baby Corn say to Mommy Corn?" Dad calls after us.

Oh my god, Dad.

"Get me out of here," I whisper to Caden. He gestures me down the stairs and shuts the door behind us, which might look suspicious, but who cares? We won't always be a secret. He'll eventually cast aside his doubts—maybe no later than tonight—and realize I'm fully invested in us. I really am.

Down in the outdated but cozy wood-panelled entertainment room, Caden turns the TV on and hands me the remote. "Your pick."

I snuggle in beside him on the sagging floral couch. The last time we watched television alone together, it was cartoons. He's not into horror (but still a keeper), and I doubt we need a romcom to incite whatever's going to happen down here, so I settle on a movie about a plane crash in the wilderness.

The opening sequence shows the shadow of a plane racing across a mountain glacier. Dramatic cello and violin music crescendos. Caden stretches out his arm on the backrest, his fingers hovering just above my shoulder. It will slide down eventually, so why not right now? My belly flutters as I pull his hand down, and flutters even more when

Caden draws me close as casually as if he'd done it a thousand times.

On the TV screen, turbulence shakes the Twin Otter. As expected, the plane crashes, trees snap, and snow flies everywhere. A dazed man and equally dazed woman crawl out of the wreck.

"So predictable," I say. "Give them fifteen minutes and they'll be at each other's throats."

If I were to survive a plane crash in an ocean of trees, I would want it to be with Caden. To begin with, we wouldn't be underdressed and freezing our asses off like these city people. But I'm fine being right here, too, with his fingers lazily tracing the line of my collarbone.

I twist to face him. "So…are we watching this whole thing or what?"

"I don't know." One corner of his lips turns up. "What else could we do?"

This time around, I don't miss the occasion to kiss that little smirk right off his face. He seems to like the suggestion and evens the score. Before long, the saggy old couch swallows us in its cushions. The movie and the laughs upstairs fade to a background drone.

Being with Caden is easy and good. And kinda hot. I kiss him hard, and in the pauses between kisses, the only name on his lips is mine. Me, Alex. When we come up for air a long time later, the sun rises over the movie couple, worse for wear but alive. The end credits roll.

Caden stretches. His arms come back down and wrap around me, hugging me tight. "Best movie I ever seen."

"You'll have to come check out my fabulous DVD collection sometime. We could watch them all."

Chairs scrape the floor upstairs. I cuddle closer to him. I'm not ready to go. But then footsteps come close to the stairs' door.

"I guess that's my cue." I stand and straighten my T-shirt and my hair.

The door clicks open. "Melody and your dad are ready to go, Alex," Tina calls.

We head upstairs to the crowded entrance. I'm flushed, and my over-kissed lips feel like they're pulsing neon lights. Everybody exchanges thanks and goodnights, and I wave nonchalantly at Caden, who stands halfway down the stairs, hands in his pockets and a neutral expression on his face. We deserve an Oscar.

"See you at school," I say and exit into the crisp night.

"How was the movie?" Dad asks as we step toward the truck on the frost-hardened driveway.

"It was okay," I say.

Melody makes a sound in the back of her throat—a chuckle, perhaps—and bumps me lightly with her shoulder. I meet her gaze and her mouth turns up into a conspiratorial smile. She sits beside Dad for the drive home. I look out the passenger window. Under the dim stars and a bright moon, the road, the bare trees—everything sparkles with frost. I smile at all of it.

The following weekend, I find myself with Caden in his lumber shed, ready to tackle a trailer full of boards that need to be sorted and stacked. The inside is dim, the only light coming in from the large doors thrown wide open.

"Have you got your gloves?" Caden asks. Steam rises on his breath. Snow hasn't fallen yet, but it was minus ten Celsius overnight.

"Why? If I get a splinter, we could play doctor." I wriggle an eyebrow, but I still pull my gloves from my back pocket.

He smiles, so handsome in that same grey wool sweater of his.

"Let's get that heart pumping first." He points to the pile of lumber. "Then maybe I'll take a listen."

He gives me a kiss-and-squeeze on his way to the trailer. My pulse does a little dance. Requited love is fabulous. We set to work, careful not to trip over Blue, who's poking in and around the shed.

"Are you going to get a new cell phone eventually?" Caden asks. "We could text at night—you know, if we miss each other."

"Sorry to be so old-fashioned, but Dad's not buying me another one until college. He's teaching me a lesson, I guess." I've been too stubborn to beg for one, but I'd love some late-night texting with Caden. "I've got some money saved up from scrubbing toilets at the Beaver Lodge all last summer, though. Maybe he'll change his mind if I pitch in."

"Until then, I could come throw pebbles at your window at midnight."

"Bring a ladder. There's no big tree for me to climb down."

"Plenty of lumber around here to build one."

He lifts the front of a beam, and I grab the back end. As we're halfway toward the stack of one-by-eights, he turns his head and asks, "Have you heard from Amka lately?"

"No." I barely stumble. Why is he asking? "You?"

"Not really, but I saw she's on Instagram."

"Yeah. She wanted me to follow her not long after she left. But you know I'm not into social media."

Translation: Don't worry. She's not a threat anymore.

I wish I had the nerve to say it out loud. It wouldn't be a lie, but what if he hears something else in my voice? I can't say that I *don't* care about her—even though I've told myself that many times. We had some nice moments together, but she wasn't being real with me, so the person I miss might not even exist, so to speak.

He doesn't say anything more, so I let it drop. We move lumber in silence until our old ease at working together returns and the moment of tension falls away. After we lift the last beam into place, he sits on the stack.

I stand between his knees and lean a bit so our faces are level. "Are you going to examine my heart now?"

"Let's see." He pulls off his gloves and tilts my chin up. First, he checks the pulse at my throat with two fingers, then with his lips. "Yes, I feel it. It's beating very fast. Have you been walking your ten thousand steps a day?"

"I'm sure I just did for today," I say, breathless.

"Been sleeping eight hours per night?" He kisses my neck again.

I shiver all over. Then, a fleeting thought passes through my mind. Was he this gentle and nice with Chloe when they had their fling last summer? Selfish, I know, but I want him to only ever have been like this with me.

Dammit. I'm jealous. How could I blame him for inquiring about Amka?

"Any dark thoughts?" he asks.

"Yes. Very bad ones."

He pulls me up onto him. I straddle his thighs, and he laces his fingers at the small of my back. We kiss in the joined clouds of our breath, and I feel the thrill of falling into deep, endless space. It's almost dark when we walk out of the shed some time later. Dad and Melody are leaving for work at the mine tomorrow, and we're supposed to cook dinner together.

"Will you have more lumber to unload next weekend?" I ask. "This is my kind of date."

"No, but I want to get started on that trail at the back of our woodlot."

"Am I invited?"

"For sure. My parents will be heading to Prince George for the day, too," he says, smiling.

Exciting.

"I'll come. With Blue as a chaperone, of course, me being old-fashioned and all."

The longest school week ever is finally over. I lie in my cold bed, unable to fall asleep. Caden and I didn't get much alone time. He still seems kind of cautious in front of everyone at school, not quite trusting me yet. It's okay for now, especially since most of the things I yearn to happen between us require some privacy.

My mind wings back to last weekend, with the two of us bundled up in too many layers of clothing. I slide my palm down my belly and imagine it isn't my own hand but that of someone I love and who loves me right back. I hold Caden in my thoughts and eventually drift off to sleep.

The phone downstairs blares like an alarm. I swim up from a dream, unsure of which world the rings belong to. Probably a wrong number, but I jump out of bed and race to the kitchen, missing a couple of steps on the way down the stairs. Somehow, I land on my feet and don't break anything.

"Hello?" I croak.

Breathing on the line. Then, "Hey, Alex."

"Amka?"

"It's so good to hear your voice," she says. The roar of vehicle engines rises and falls in the background.

The microwave clock reads three a.m.

"You needed to hear my voice in the middle of the night?"

I climb back up the stairs with the cordless phone and sit at the edge of my bed.

"Sorry," she says. "I lost track of time. How are you? How's Blue and everyone?"

Blue—*my* dog—is sitting up in front of me, head cocked. I wrap a throw blanket around my shoulders. "I'm good. Everybody's good."

A buzz rises in my ears. I don't know if it's anxiety or anger or…longing? No, not longing. I was doing fine with her gone. I pull the blanket tighter around me. "Anyway, what's this about?"

"Can I ask you something?"

I stick my thumb and index finger over my closed eyes, pretending to myself I'm doing her a favour, but I'm all ears. "Ask away."

"If I make it to Fort Cass, do you think I could crash at your place for a couple of days?"

"Why would you come here?"

"I'm thinking of going to my dad's."

"In Dease Lake? You know he moved, right?"

"Duh. I was going with Ari, but then her car broke, and then things got kind of messed up and, um…we parted ways."

Ari. Starts with an A but isn't Alex. The soulmate.

I huff in the mouthpiece. Is she hoping to come here and wreck everything between Caden and me? Or does she think she can just have Blue back and take off with him? That'd be a sneaky way for the curse to come back and bite me in the ass.

"I'm not a hotel." I'm aware of how cold this sounds, but it's necessary. If she comes here… I don't want Caden's doubts about me to be justified. Can't let that happen.

"I know but—ugh, never mind."

In the background, traffic wheezes by.

"Wait. Where the hell are you? Tell me you're not hitchhiking."

"I'm not." She trails off, as if she's purposefully withholding the word *yet*.

A vise squeezes the back of my neck. I want her to stay

away from me, but I don't want her to take that kind of risk. Good job at being a soulmate, *Ari*.

"Does your mom know about this?"

"You know we don't get along. Alex, I—"

"You don't need me, Amka. You never did, and I'm fine with it." That fist of annoyance in my gut threatens to turn into a deeper ache that I don't want to feel again. "You have a mother. Work it out with her."

"You have a mother too," she says. "Why don't *you* work things out with her?"

I gasp as if she's just brass-knuckled me in the face. How dare she say something like this to me? "I don't need her. I don't need YOU."

"Right. I just wanted you to know that—"

"Amka, wherever you are, just go home, okay? Are you able to do that?"

There isn't even a click as she hangs up, but the dead air is loud in my ear.

Chapter 19

The overcast sky hangs like a concrete ceiling. I'm running on not enough sleep and too much coffee as I buzz to Caden's backyard, where he's strapping axes, bucksaws, and a lunch pack to the front rack of his quad.

"You look tired," he says when I come within touching distance. His eyebrows squeeze together. "Is everything all right?"

"Yeah. Just insomnia." I couldn't fall asleep again after Amka hung up on me. Caden doesn't need to know this. It would change nothing.

He walks around the quad and wraps his arms around my waist. "I won't make you work too hard."

He kisses my nose, my lips, and lets me go, but I hold on, resting my forehead on his shoulder. There is something comforting in hugging someone bigger than me.

"Ready?" he asks when I finally pull away.

"Let's do this," I say, mustering some enthusiasm and hopping onto the quad's rear rack.

We ride slowly past the lumber shed and onto the main trail through the woods. Blue trots along, sniffing around bushes and clawing at burrows. He really would have hated living in the city, being either leashed or stuck in an apartment all the time. Where would he be right now if Amka had kept him? Hitchhiking and protecting her from any creeps she might encounter?

But he's here with me, living his best life.

I slide into Caden as we descend a steep trail lined with spruce and fir. My arms wrap around him, and my cheek lays itself on his shoulder. My body knows better than my distracted brain that I am living the life that was meant for me.

His great-grandpa began logging this plot selectively ages ago, and Caden and his dad are still at it now. Here and there, a tree stump pokes from the ground, ranging from barely greying to covered with rich green moss. There are old trees, but none as big as those on the Devil's Tail. I look over my shoulder, but we're hidden from the mountain's view. Somehow, for no reason at all, I'm relieved.

We coast to a stop beside a fir tree flagged with orange tape. Caden kills the engine. The trail we're clearing will help the family access more trees for their sawmill. Blue is rolling in something I can't see from here but that's undoubtedly smelly and disgusting.

We get to work. No big tree needs to be cut, only saplings and brush. The sounds of our axes fill the chilly air, echoed by a woodpecker. As my muscles warm up, the ghost of Amka's phone call loses its power over me.

By lunchtime, lazy snowflakes begin drifting to the ground.

"You hungry?" Caden asks.

"Yeah. Let's make a fire."

We pile up birch bark, broken twigs, and bigger dead sticks. I dig the lighter from my pocket and touch the flame to a curl of bark. After much smoking, the fire crackles to life. Caden hands me a PB-and-cheese sandwich and a thermos of hot chocolate. My favourites. How sweet of him. He's my feel-good talisman, my good luck charm.

Blue lies down and watches, hypnotized by the food.

Caden's cheeks are flushed from the work and the chill. He picks sunflower seeds off his bread crust and studies them before tossing them away.

"My mom suspects something's going on between us," he says.

"Okay." Were we keeping this a secret because he thought *I* wanted to keep it that way? I'll admit that keeping it under wraps makes me feel safe, though safe from what I'm not sure. Not from the curse. Maybe if things don't work out between us and we're the only ones to know, breaking up will hurt less. But why wouldn't they work out? Amka's not even coming.

Caden pokes the fire with a stick, side-eyeing me. Waiting for me to say something.

"You can tell your mom about us. It's fine." My answer hangs on the smoke between us. "But maybe keep the juicy details to ourselves?"

Caden throws me a horrified look. "You bet."

I have to laugh, but I stop when he doesn't so much as chuckle. Did I say something wrong? I'd lean over and kiss him to dispel whatever's bugging him, but damn peanut butter breath.

"Let's get back to work," I say.

We resume hacking and tossing brush out of the way. The falling snowflakes turn into heavy, wet clusters. If Amka was around, I bet she'd be in jeans and a hoodie, no hat, no gloves, and complaining about how cold it is. I hope she listened to me and went back to her mom's.

"Hey, slacker." Caden stands before me, frowning.

"Um…hey." How long have I been standing doing nothing?

"You look kinda lost." He shifts his body to shield me from the big wet snowflakes falling sideways. "What's on your mind?"

Why can't he just let it drop, whatever it is?

I choose to ignore the question.

"Me, lost in the woods?" I shake my head. "Never."

But I've had enough of the forest for now. Even the best work clothes are no match for this kind of weather. Everything is sodden and weighs a ton. I wring out one of my gloves with numb fingers.

"Should we call it a day?" Caden says.

"Yeah."

We pack our gear onto the quad.

"Wanna drive?" Caden asks.

"Sure."

He hoists Blue up onto the rear rack beside him and we ride out of the forest. When we get to his house, the snow in the yard is pristine. The windows are dark.

"When are your parents getting back?"

"Sometime this evening." Caden opens the basement door.

"Will your mom mind if Blue comes in?"

"Course not. Come on, bud."

Blue trots in, and I shut the door against the gathering gloom. We're in the unfinished part of the basement, which serves as a storage and laundry room.

The wood stove hisses as Blue shakes snow off his coat. He flops down in the warm orange glow as if he owns the place, and he did, in fact, grow up here. The first time he left was with Amka, and tonight he'll happily go with me, his true forever person. I dump my waterlogged outer layers—gloves, jacket, sweater, snow pants—in a pile on the floor. The legs of my jeans are soaked.

"I should lend you some sweatpants," Caden says.

"Dry clothes would feel wonderful."

We wash our hands, then cross the rec room to his bedroom. A remnant of light still filters in from the ground-level window. Caden roots in his dresser drawer while I peel off my clammy jeans.

"There." He turns around but pauses midway into handing me a pair of sweats.

"What?" I tug my shirt down over my thighs.

"Nothing."

It's not the first time I've undressed in front of him. There isn't much difference between underwear and a bathing suit…technically. But this isn't the same. We're not at the lake but alone in his room. Alone in the whole house.

The dusky light wraps us in a wired silence. The secret I'm keeping hovers between us like a foul hex. I need to banish it once and for all. Holding my breath, I unbutton my shirt and toss it aside, too, standing in front of him in just my bra and underwear.

Caden drops the sweatpants and steps over to me. His hands slide down my ribs and come to rest on my hips. I lift his T-shirt and help him pull it off, which doesn't quite even things out, but his skin is so warm.

We kiss standing, slowly inching toward the bed. When I pull him down on the mattress with me, I burn and chill simultaneously—not cold but trembling. I'm excited, and maybe a little bit scared, but I'm ready for this.

He brushes my hair from my face. "You okay?"

"Yeah." But the more I burn, the more careful he becomes. Shouldn't he be fighting with the clasps of my bra by now? Kissing me where he's never kissed me before?

The room has become almost completely dark, but I see the gleam in his eyes as I move on top of him. "Let's go all the way," I whisper in his ear and fumble with the button of his jeans. Caden finds my hand like he wants to help me, but instead, he stills my fingers.

"Are you sure about this?" he asks.

What the hell? "Don't try to tell me you're not into it."

"Yeah, well." He cradles my hips with his hands and moves me off him.

What's happening? I kneel in the middle of the mattress, feeling oddly alone. "I thought you liked me."

He turns on the lamp and sits at the edge of the bed, ruffling his hair. "I more than *like* you, Alex."

"Then what's the problem?"

He sighs heavily. "She called you, didn't she?"

I shove my bra straps back into place. "How'd you know that?"

He grabs his phone from the dresser, fiddles with the screen, and hands it to me.

Can u give me Alex's number? I'm coming to Ft Cass

He replied with my number, but not a single word.

I scroll down to the next bubble. *Tx calling her now*

"So what?" I say. "I'm not allowed to talk to a friend?"

"Just a friend? I've been waiting all day for you to tell me about it, but you kept it to yourself. That's kinda telling, actually."

"I said you could tell your mom about us. Isn't that telling you something?"

"Look. I'm just trying to figure out what you want from me." He puts his T-shirt back on. As his mussed-up hair emerges from the collar, he adds, "I wouldn't want you to regret having slept with me when Amka shows up and you ditch me again."

I open my mouth to say words I haven't figured out yet, but Blue howls in the other room, cutting me off. A moment later, the front door bangs closed and feet stomp on the entrance mat.

"Shit, my parents," Caden says.

I fly off the bed and wriggle into my soppy jeans.

"We're back," Tina calls from the top of the stairs.

"Hey, Mom." Caden tosses me my shirt.

Tina flips the rec room light switch. We rush to stand by the coffee table, probably looking like deer in the headlights as she thumps down the stairs, arms loaded with bags of food for the deep freezer. Her snow-damp hair is frizzed into tight curls, and her glasses are fogged.

Caden jumps into action, taking the bags from her. "I got it."

Tina looks at my soaked jeans. "Did you just get back from the bush?"

I hide the top of one bare foot with the sole of the other, feeling too naked. "Yeah, just a while ago."

"Caden! You could have lent her some sweats."

I shake my head. "It's okay. I was just about to go home."

"Really?" She removes her glasses and wipes them with a tissue she grabs from the coffee table. Her golden-brown eyes are warm but inquisitive. "You're welcome to stay for dinner."

Blue howls again. I feel like howling myself.

"I don't know what's up with my dog. I'd better get going."

Tina reaches for my hand but changes her mind and squeezes my shoulder instead. "Can I lend you some dry clothes?"

"It's fine. I'll be there in five minutes." Or ten, but so what? The heater in my truck works fine.

She pinches her lips but doesn't insist. "Take it easy on the road, at least. It's awful out there."

"I'll be careful."

I pull on my wet everything while Caden stands by, watching. Tina hangs around, reorganizing the stuff Caden dumped in the laundry room deep freezer, so we can't talk. I wouldn't know what to say anyway.

"Well, so…" is all I can manage. I open the door, step out into the blizzard and look back. "See you later?"

Caden stuffs his hands in his pockets and nods. "Drive safe."

"Okay."

Nothing's okay, but I shut the door and walk away.

The hood of my truck is covered with snow, but I don't bother clearing it. I sit behind the wheel, waiting for the cab to warm up. Each swipe of the wipers on the frosted windshield grates directly on my nerves.

Why couldn't Amka stay gone instead of wrecking things between Caden and me? I wanted to love her, and she didn't let me. I should hate her now, but I hate myself more. My bad for sucking at relationships. I'm my own curse.

I shift into gear and drive off into the snowstorm, face close to the steering wheel and eyes squinting. Beyond the reach of the headlights, the white strip of road seems to fall off the edge of the world. My house will be cold, dark, and lonely while I could be warm and cozy at Caden's right now. There would have been plenty of time to patch things up before dinner. In the heat of the moment, I didn't get a chance to tell him Amka's not coming. That this time around, I picked him over her, like I should have done a long time ago.

What I'll do is feed Blue, shower and change, and then I'll drive right back to Caden's and fix the mess I've made. If curses can be cast, they can also be undone.

I can barely see a thing, but I know I'm getting close to my least favourite part of the road. Blue whines and paces on the seat. The tip of his tail brushes my cheek at each of his turns.

"Sit, Blue."

One moment I'm pushing his butt away from my face, and the next, the back end of a vehicle materializes on the road. I jerk the wheel and swerve, stopping short of hitting the opposite ditch.

"What the—"

I twist toward the back window. A beige SUV went halfway off the road. Hunters from out of town, I bet—the mule deer season is still on. There's only one way out of Fort Cass, and this isn't it. I should check if someone is stuck inside. I grab the flashlight from the glovebox and pop the door open. Blue wants to follow me out, but I block him and close the door. One of us out in this weather is enough.

"I'll be right back." Unless Michael Myers is hiding in there, kitchen knife at the ready. Would I be savvy enough to save myself? I wish I had my axe.

The wind is brutal. I lower my face against the hurtling snow and sweep the ground with the light beam. No hint of footprints. The SUV's engine isn't running, and there's no light inside the cab.

I swipe the snow off the driver's window. It falls at once like a curtain. My heart stutters as I expect a face to be pressed against the glass, but—whew—no one's in there. The backseat is filled with stuff. Duffel bags and hunting gear, probably. The hunter must have walked back to town for help. Good for them. Time to get back on track with my own plan.

I shuffle back to the truck and open the door. Blue flies

out like a jack-in-the-box. He runs in circles in the beams of the headlights, sniffing the snow, the air.

"Get back here, you silly dog."

He trots down the hill. But he's not running away. He's running home. Good call, Blue.

I jump inside the truck and drive after him. When my headlights sweep the bottom of the hill, he's facing the old trail between the willows, head cocked. His shadow stretches on the road, transforming him into a leggy creature of nightmares.

"Dammit." I park in the middle of the road, engage the parking brake, and step outside, freezing instantly in my soaked jeans. Blue stands, still intent on whatever he's hearing. My guts churn, but to my ears, there's only the growl of the wind and the rumble of my truck's engine.

"Come on, let's go."

Blue bolts across the ditch and disappears into the trees.

"Shit."

I race back to the truck, grab the flashlight, and jump across the ditch. The dead willow branches click in the wind like old bones. A clump of snow falls on my head and melts down my neck as I pass beneath the brittle branches.

"Blue!"

The forest rises darkly on each side of the trail, veiled with thickly falling snow like static on an old TV screen. Blue is a grey shadow at the farthest reach of my flashlight beam. He darts out of sight. There are indents beside his tracks, too filled with snow to let me identify them. A moose, perhaps, or a bear that hasn't gone to bed for the winter yet. Whichever it is, it must've passed a while ago, but to Blue's nose, it would smell fresh. What a time for his coyote instincts to kick in. Please don't let him come across a grouchy grizzly.

I sway on my feet, my upper body half-turned toward the road. The truck's high beams point the way home, where I should be heading this instant. I'm in a hoodie, no toque, no gloves.

The wind carries the echoes of a cry. A dog whimper. I'm not leaving Blue behind.

I slip and slide in calf-deep snow, spurred on by his whines. The cold bites my hands, and I'm sweating inside my damp clothes. I slow to a walk because I'm out of breath. How long have I been going uphill? Five minutes? Fifteen? Blood pounds behind my eardrums. Dammit. This chase is ridiculous. No one knows I'm out here. I picture Dad coming home next week and finding the truck on the roadside, the driver's door open. No Alex.

Blue has his thick coat of hair to keep him warm and a powerful nose to show him the way back. I don't have any of that.

"Fine," I yell. My voice quakes. I'm just so cold. "Scratch at the door when you're ready to come in."

I turn around and half-jog, half-slide downhill, head bent against the storm. The slope is steep, and gravity forces me to run, the beam of my flashlight jumping around wildly. Running makes me feel like I'm fleeing, and fleeing makes me believe something's after me. I slip to a stop as a shadow slinks across the outer reach of the flashlight. It was quick, but I had time to take in the silhouette of a lynx, to imagine the hooked horns on its head.

How could I see the beast's shadow but not the beast itself?

Simple. It's because I saw nothing but the play of snowflakes falling hard. I resume jogging toward the truck, calling Blue every half-minute, hoping the tingling across my scalp is me sensing his presence behind me.

I hear his whine again. No, it's a laugh. Amka's. A shot of adrenaline whirls me around. I'm expecting to see some nightmarish version of her, but all I see is Blue, sitting only a few paces away.

"Oh." I dismiss what I thought I heard. "There you are."

How crappy of me to have considered leaving him behind.

"Come on, Blue. It's time to go home."

He doesn't come. His shadow, feline and horned, rises a second before he actually does. He turns to face uphill, looks back at me, and trots away into the darkness. And once he's out of sight, he whines again, like he wants me to follow him.

My blood freezes in my veins—impossible, but that's how it feels. I'm having a freaking hallucination. I must be going into hypothermia. Or whatever went awry in Karine's mind when she was my age is now happening to me.

The whoop of a coyote pierces the night. A scalding shiver runs over my skin. A few more pack members join in, and the howls are closer, more daring. Coyotes don't attack people. Not in the wild where they're wise enough to stay away from humans. But they might not have qualms about hurting a dog, even a coydog.

"Blue," I yell.

I swipe my flashlight beam uphill. The coyotes are coming. What if they've become rabid? Doesn't make sense. But what if? I turn around and dash down the trail. Except the trail seems to have vanished, along with my tracks. I keep stumbling downhill, blasts of pain blinding me as I bash into trees.

At my heels, claws skitter on patches of ice. I hope it's Blue. Whatever the creature, it's not leaping to sink its teeth into the back of my neck, so it must be him. A red tail light blinks through the branches. My truck. We're saved. I burst out of the forest and fall on all fours into the ditch. We made it. But when I turn, Blue is not there.

I stumble out of the ditch as the pack's howls fill my ears, mingled with what I'm sure are Blue's yelps. They've got him, and I can't do anything about it. I run to the truck, lunge inside, and slam the door.

"Shit, shit, shit!" My face is wet with snow and tears. Outside, the coyotes shout bloody victory. I grasp the wheel with shaking hands and somehow take myself home. When I arrive and lock myself inside, the house is so silent even the fridge is quiet.

A horrific knowledge sits like a boulder in my stomach.

I loved Blue.

And now, Blue's gone.

Stolen.

Chapter 20

There he is.

Blue sits on the windswept surface of the frozen lake. I skid and slip toward him, but I never seem to get any closer. Yet, I see every detail as if I stood right beside him—his twitching nose lifted to the wind, his eyes half-closed, the ripple of the fur at his throat as he emits a low growl. Then, the high-pitched howl of a coyote slices through the air. He stands and turns to face me. Both his eyes are yellow.

I startle awake, heart racing. Blinking in the muted daylight, I roll out of bed and step to the window. A thick coat of snow covers the shed's roof, the trees, the doghouse.

In another lifetime, AKA last night, I was going to drive back to Caden's house and make things right between us. It would have taken only a few words: Amka doesn't matter to me anymore.

Instead, I ran away like a coward and let Blue meet his death.

I could never face Amka, now. And I can't face Caden today. I throw myself back into bed and pull the blankets over my head.

. . .

Life resumes on Monday—a life in which I've pretty much lost everyone I love. Except for Dad, but then, he's a thousand kilometres away right now because I wouldn't let him quit his well-paying job and move us away from Fort Cass.

I wish he were here.

The road has been plowed, but I drive slowly. In the shadowed hollow where that evil trail begins, the snow is pristine—no coyote tracks, torn dog flesh, or blood. Not that I expected to see any, with the load of snow that has fallen.

Ahead, brightness returns to the road as the forest thins. The empty SUV still sits in the ditch, enclosed in a white, frozen shell. Another cold reminder that Saturday was something other than just a nightmare. I'm tempted to turn around and go home, but I have to pick up the broken pieces of Caden and me and see if any will fit back together again.

I make it to school and shuffle into Physics as the bell rings. Chloe gawks at me from her desk, as if she somehow knows I've jinxed myself once again. I ignore her.

Caden's eyes probe my face, no smile in them. There's no loathing either, which somehow makes it worse. How awful it would be if I lost him but still had to sit beside him every day. A sense of loss grips me, almost unbearable. Caden was always in my life. I can't let him go. I set my binder on the table and push my stool closer to him—relieved he doesn't move away—before sitting.

"Hey," I say.

"Hey." Almost a sigh.

I don't know what to say next. Bringing up Amka, even if to say I told her to stay away, would be like picking the scab off an unhealed wound. Thankfully, the bell rings and Mr. Brar launches into his lecture.

Caden's pencil sits on the table between our binders like a barrier. I grab it and write in the margin of his notebook: *Can we talk at lunch?* It's uninspired, but it's a start. He reaches for the pencil in my hand and squeezes my fingers before gently pulling it away. He's saying okay—to talk, at least.

The tension slides off me like a wet, heavy blanket. I'll tell him everything. How Amka messed me up. How I lost Blue. How I've known all along he was the best person for me. Tentatively, I lay my palm on his leg. He covers it with his hand. I'm so relieved I could cry.

When class is over, Chloe swings by our table, twisting a faded-pink strand of hair around her index finger and studying our arms disappearing beneath the table. She considers me like I'm some mouldy leftover she just found at the bottom of the fridge. But she's here for a reason. The sooner I know, the sooner she'll leave.

"What do you want?" I ask.

"Have you heard from Amka lately?"

"Why?"

She shoves her phone screen into my face, showing me an Instagram post of Amka, standing in some fog-hazy parking lot flipping the bird with both hands, a contemptuous half-smile dimpling her cheek.

"F*** YOU A..." the caption reads.

Alex? Ari? Whatever. We both deserves this.

"What's she up to?" Chloe looks from me to Caden and back, like we solely exist to update her on the status of Amka's life.

"Why don't you ask her if you care so much? I'm not her mom or anything," I say.

"You're not talking anymore?" She flips her pink hair behind her shoulders. "What a surprise."

Caden scrolls on his phone and opens the Instagram app.

"Don't bother," Chloe says, waving her phone at us again. "It's a screenshot. She deleted her account." She twirls around and ambles away.

Oh, crap.

My hand goes limp and slides from beneath Caden's. Amka *is* hitchhiking. And I didn't try hard enough to convince her to stay put, wherever she was calling from. I'm no better than Ari. I was never Amka's soulmate, but I haven't even been a friend. She asked for help, and I basically told her to go to hell.

Caden becomes a blur. He might be saying something, but I can't hear through the rush in my ears. If something bad happened to her, it's on me.

"Alex?"

I blink and focus on his concerned face. His grip on my elbow is the only thing that keeps me standing.

"Maybe you should try calling her?" he says.

I go through his contacts and hit her number. She might not want to talk to me, but maybe she'll answer if she thinks it's Caden. The call goes straight to voicemail. I send her a text, still letting it look like it's from Caden. *Where r u? Are u ok?*

I wait for "delivered" to appear under the blue bubble. It doesn't. And no reply comes. Maybe her phone's battery is dead. Maybe someone took her by force and tossed her phone out the window.

I grab my coat from the back of my chair and rush outside. Caden comes after me in his short sleeves across the parking lot.

"Alex, where are you going?"

I don't know what's coming over me, but I have the urge to run away. "I'm not feeling good. I'm going home."

His fingers close over mine. "I'll drive you there."

I should allow him to stop me, but I'm too antsy to stand still.

"I have my truck."

"Alex, stop."

I do, and turn to face him. His cheeks are red, and his brow is creased the same way it was the morning he patiently waited for me to tell him I'd spoken to Amka.

"I know you're still in love with her, but will you at least let me be a friend?"

The last word hits like a snowball in the face. Friend. That's all we are?

"I wasn't going to ditch you for Amka again, okay?" I say, almost a yell. But I'm nobody's friend, obviously. "Blue's gone too."

"What?"

"He ran off on the Devil's Tail when I went home

Saturday night." I focus on building a little mound of snow with my foot to avoid looking him in the eye. "I lost him."

"Shit, Alex." He throws his arms up. "I would have helped you look for him if you'd asked."

"The coyotes got him. There's nothing you could have done."

His eyes, usually golden-warm, turn iron-cold. "Sometimes, Alex, you amaze me."

There I go disappointing him again. But this is how I am. He should be used to it by now. Why is he even sticking around? I grit my teeth to keep myself from saying that out loud. He doesn't deserve those words, and I wouldn't be able to take them back.

"I need to be alone for a bit." I rub my cold cheeks with even colder palms. "Maybe you can come over tonight?"

He shoves his hands in his jeans pockets, already turning away from me. "Yeah, maybe."

He's saying no without saying no, I guess.

"Well, have a good one." I swivel on my feet and walk away from him so I don't have to watch him walk away from me.

I steer my truck toward home, numb from head to toe. Burning Karine's letter didn't break any curse. I'm the poisoned apple that fell right under the rotten tree. Cursed, like Karine, to lose the people dearest to my heart by my own fault.

Ahead on the road, a coal-grey jacked-up truck I saw parked at the Beaver Lodge the other day is dragging the SUV out of the ditch. I pull over at a safe distance while two men take their time to clear the road. Once they've dragged the vehicle onto the shoulder, one guy steps out of the SUV and waves me past. The other one walks around his truck and fusses with the tow line.

I drive by at a crawl because there isn't much room to spare. The guys, both dressed in fancy camo hunting gear stop what they're doing to leer as I squeeze through. One is even skinnier than Mickey and missing a front tooth, and the other one looks polished like the models in my Cabela's catalogue. I'm not sure which one of the two creeps me out the most. They look like the type who would pick up a girl hitchhiker, do god-knows-what to her, and then dump her on some isolated roadside.

Maybe I've watched too many horror movies, or maybe I'm paranoid because of Amka. True horrors are much more likely to happen to an obviously Indigenous girl like her than to a white girl like me. Shit, now my head is full of even worse thoughts.

Well, here's something else for my morbid imagination to chew on: up ahead is the spot where Blue disappeared.

I slow down and crane my neck to peer at the trail, knowing that even if my head could do a three-sixty like that girl in *The Exorcist*, I wouldn't see Blue anywhere because he's dead. But there are tracks where the trail begins. Too shallow for a moose and not round like a lynx's. Coyote?

Or dog.

Shit. What if Blue's alive?

And I didn't even try to go back and look for him.

Chapter 21

My boots dump snow on the kitchen floor. I turn on my laptop, then unzip my coat and toss it on the floor. I look up Amka's Insta, but it's really gone. If she took off from Mississauga without warning, someone would have reported her missing, I'm sure. Her mom is white—the police wouldn't dismiss Amka as just another Indigenous runaway. They'd really look for her.

I search the web for "missing" pages. My heart skips as I see a photo that vaguely resembles her, but it's someone else—a Two-Spirit kid who's been gone for three weeks. Some asshole troll asked in the comments if they've checked all the ditches. What's wrong with people?

And what's wrong with me? Awesome Alex, all right.

Caden is right. I'm a shitty girlfriend, a shitty friend, and an even shittier dog owner. He would never say anything like this to me, but he must be thinking it.

Well. Shittiness isn't a life sentence. I need to write a self-improvement list and work at it until I turn into a reasonably non-shitty person.

First item: look for Blue.

I pull on my snow pants and parka. When I kneel on the entrance mat to tie my bootlaces, Amka's bracelet gleams in the aloe plant. Beyond it, Karine peers at me from her dusty picture frame on the wall.

"This is all your fault."

The accusation doesn't make me feel any better, but it's still true. If she hadn't planted the idea of a curse into my mind, I wouldn't have messed up everything so badly. I stand, grab the bracelet, and slide it into my pocket. For luck—or at least as a reminder to not be so self-focused all the time. When Amka turns up somewhere—anywhere—I'll find a way to return it to her and apologize for my damn shittiness.

I step out into the rapidly cooling afternoon. The sun has already disappeared behind the mountains, but I've still got a few hours of daylight. Zwing sits under the lean-to, tuned up and inspected from nose to tail for the sledding season, which for me starts right now. I strap a wooden box to the back of the seat and fill it with some essentials: snowshoes (of the not-bewitched variety), my axe, and a spare canister of mixed gas.

At the third pull of the starter rope, the engine coughs like a cat with a hairball. I climb aboard, and we're off to a crawling start. Above the snow-shrouded forest, the Devil's Tail hunkers like a predator. I pause at the bottom of the hill and step off Zwing to inspect the tracks I saw earlier. They loop on the road a couple of times—definitely canine, but too small to belong to a wolf, too big for a fox. Maybe Blue came looking for me and realized I abandoned him.

I follow the pattern with my eyes like it's a connect-the-dots drawing in a kids' activity book. Dread weighs down my stomach as the tracks cross the ditch and wander back into the forest. I really don't want to go there again, but I'm going anyway. Amka did say believing in something makes it real. I've got to believe I'll find Blue alive.

Bare branches claw at my sleeves as I ride through the willows. I'm like Gabriel a couple of centuries ago, except he was incompetent despite his girlfriend's bewitched snowshoes. I'm on my not-so-bewitched sled, but I know what I'm doing.

I duck beneath conifer boughs to enter the forest where barely any daylight penetrates the canopy. The trail is a gloomy blue tunnel between mossy trunks. The prints follow the trail for a short distance then disappear where Zwing rattles over a patch of bare, frozen ground. They just vanish, as if whatever made them sprouted wings and flew away.

I forge ahead, scanning the snow for fresher tracks and peering through the trees for a patch of mottled fur. Zwing struggles up an incline, the worn rubber track grasping for traction. On top where the slope levels for a short distance, new animal tracks meander across the trail and disappear into the trees. Round paw prints, no claw marks. Lynx.

Goosebumps rise all over my skin. What for? I've been seeing lynx tracks all my life, some of them even crossing my yard. There might be a lynx watching me right now, crouched under a bush heavy with snow, waiting for me and my awfully noisy machine to get the hell away from its hunting ground.

I won't let myself think about the chat-cornu. I'll be outta here before dark, before my nightmares come back to haunt me.

Though the snowed-under forest looks different than last spring, I'm pretty sure I'm passing the spot where Amka caught up to me and offered me her bracelet for protection. Her teasing smile appears in my mind, a sparkle in her deep, dark eyes. A knife slices across my heart. Oh, Amka. Wherever you are now, please be safe.

A shape slinks into view, way up where the trail veers out of sight.

I can't believe it! My dog stands right there, his blue right eye strikingly sharp despite the distance. I stand on the sideboards to get a better look. No ripped flesh, no bone sticking out, no blood staining the snow. He'd only been spooked.

"Stay, Blue. I'll be right there," I shout over the engine noise.

The throttle is maxed out, but Zwing isn't gaining any speed. Come on. Brand new spark plugs and that's all you can do?

I cover half the distance separating us. Maybe thirty metres left to go. Blue turns around, showing me his yellow coyote eye. Just like in the dream I had this morning, he whips around and lopes beyond the bend, tail held high as if he's happily leading the way on a fun outing.

How about leading the way *down* the mountain?

"Blue! Come back!"

When I make it around the bend, he's out of sight. Tracks still dot the trail. Round. Clawless. Another wave of goosebumps ripples across my skin. A dog's paws cannot stamp lynx tracks. I grasp for a logical explanation.

Is that what he's been up to since Saturday night?

Chasing after a big cat? I twist around to see if I've missed him veering off the trail. When I turn forward again, he's standing only a few paces away.

I brake and throw my weight backward, bracing for the impact. This is the moment my life should flash before my eyes, but instead, time slows to a drip thicker than tar. Trees lazily glide by, and the engine drones like a faraway cicada. Through the scratched lens of Zwing's windshield, Blue shifts from mottled and coyote-like to lanky and—

Holy hell.

This isn't Blue standing right there but a lynx. And not *Lynx canadensis*, either. It's bigger than any lynx I ever saw, and covered in mangy, russet fur. It's the Eurasian *Lynx lynx*, but not quite. Because black, hooked horns stick out of its skull.

As I try to wrap my head around the reality of this creature, the chat-cornu sits and yawns, showing its sharp, yellow fangs. Its roadkill breath wafts across the narrow distance between us. I clench my teeth to suppress a gag. I should squeeze the brake—I want to—but the command from my brain is bogged down somewhere along my sluggish nerves.

The beast's mouth stretches into a jagged grin. *Well, well,* it says in my head. *Hello again, Alexia.*

I'm Alex. We've never met. But, crap. Just like that, I *know* in my flesh, bones, and guts that the chat-cornu, the curse, the stories are all real, even if only for me and Karine.

The trickle of time shatters. Unable to release the throttle, I sink deeper into my seat. There's a thud, then an explosion of light. No shriek, no sound of tearing skin and cracking bones. Just a rush of air and then, absolute whiteness.

I float in a fuzzy in-between, warmish like shallow lake water. The vision, or whatever this is, starts with Amka hanging up on me after I tell her she's not welcome at my house. She's standing on the side of a four-lane highway, the wet asphalt shimmering in the grey dawn.

"I'll make you change your mind, Alex." She shoves her phone in the pocket of her leather jacket, faces the oncoming traffic, and sticks out her thumb. She's going west.

A big rig slows down. Amka jogs to it and gauges the man's jolly Santa Claus appearance before climbing in. Endless prairies, then the Rockies. Thank god for kind-souled, long-haul truck drivers.

"You sure someone's picking you up?" the burly trucker asks when he stops at the turnoff to Fort Castor. His two angelic-looking daughters smile from the picture taped to his dashboard.

"Of course." Amka eyes a string of vehicles in front of the corner gas station. She'll find someone. "Thank you so much for the ride, sir."

She asks around. The only guy headed to Fort Cass is a hunter, white, skeleton-thin, and missing a front tooth. Don't judge a book by its cover, they say. But she keeps her fingers on the pepper spray in her jacket pocket just in case.

The snowstorm hits soon after they leave, and the drive through mountains and forests feels endless. Everything but the Beaver Lodge is closed when they finally make it into town, and Alex isn't picking up the phone.

"No prob," the guy says. "I'll drive you to your little girlfriend's house."

Amka hugs her backpack to her chest. He's been leering for the past two hours.

The way to Alex's is empty and dark, and the snowplow hasn't been out. Slush drums the SUV's chassis. Skinny-guy swears and jerks the steering wheel. The vehicle lurches left, then right. They hit the ditch almost softly.

"Shit, you all right?" he asks.

"Yeah, just a bit shaken," Amka says.

They crawl out through the driver's door. No injuries. Also, no cell signal—she knows this already so no point in taking out her phone.

"I'm renting a room with a buddy at the Beaver Lodge," Skinny says. "I'll call him as soon as we're in range. You can stay with us until I find a tow truck in the morning."

"It's fine, I'm almost at my friend's. I'll walk." Creep.

Amka struts away and down the hill, pretending she's not freezing her ass off in her yellow dress and leather jacket. Then, she's at the foot of the Devil's Tail. And the mountain is calling out to her. Not in words, but in dog whimpers. Blue. What's he doing up there?

He's not there, Alex screams in her mind, but it's like yelling at the girl about to go down the basement steps in a horror movie.

Amka's hand goes to her bare wrist where her protection charm used to dangle. It's long gone, but she's taking the risk.

"Blue?" she calls.

He whimpers again as if he's stuck nearby.

She nods to herself and strides between the willows. The falling snow cloaks her as if in feathers, and Blue coaxes her along. Why isn't he coming to her? And what has Alex done to him? Her muscles ache and her skin is burning with the cold, but she'll catch up soon, she will.

Finally, she sees him waiting at the edge of a clearing.

"It's okay, Blue. I'm here."

Amka walks into the open space where the Poltergeist Tree towers. Blue cowers in the depths of the hollow trunk. She drops onto all fours and crawls inside. The black mouth of the Poltergeist Tree swallows her whole.

I come to with a gasp and the dazzling clarity that Amka is on the mountain. That night I found that SUV in the ditch, Blue ran from me to go after her. And now the chat-cornu has them both.

I'm lying flat on my back, blinking at looming treetops and shredded clouds in a cobalt sky. Zwing drones by my feet. I move my head from side to side and bend my fingers and toes. Besides the lancing pain in my left ribs, every part of me seems to be working. I roll onto my right side, push myself up, then stand on wobbly legs.

The forest spins. Deep breaths. Ow, my ribs. Small breaths, then.

It appears that I flew overboard when I hit the chat-cornu, but the beast is nowhere. I totter over to Zwing. The hood is unscathed and free of blood or hair. No animal tracks of any kind mar the snow either. I'm not fooled, though. If the chat-cornu bothered to send me this vision, it must mean Amka and Blue are still alive, huddling for warmth inside the hollow tree. I can play that game. It stole them. I'll steal them back. Awesome Alex to the rescue.

I don't know how long I was out, but the blue shadows tell me there's maybe an hour of daylight left. It should be enough. I climb on and rev the engine. Zwing roars but doesn't move. What now? Broken drive belt? No problem. I have a spare one. It'll take a few minutes to replace, and then I'll be on my way to rescue Amka and Blue.

I unlatch the hood and lean over the engine. The belt looks fine. Crap. It's the drive chain, which means I'm not sledding anywhere anytime soon.

You want my crappy snowmobile too, you devil-beast? You can have it.

I climb down and reach for my snowshoes. Shit. There's only one. The trail winds a long way downhill. No lost shoe in the snow. Maybe the dead willows snagged it right after I crossed the ditch. It doesn't matter. The snow only reaches halfway up my calves. I've hiked in deeper stuff before. And I might not have my bear spray, but I'm not unprotected. I grab my axe, Axcalibur, as Mickey named it, and start the steep climb. The sun is long gone, and the forest is painted in shades of snow, bark, and greens so deep they're almost black.

The throbbing in my ribs matches my quickening pulse, but as I warm up, the pain slips to the back of my mind. When I reach a bend in the trail, I turn around.

Zwing looks like a discarded toy beneath the crushing hand of the forest.

I grit my teeth and stamp forward, focussing on the powder tamping beneath my steps and the swish of my snow pants. The shadows are still, but the chat-cornu is watching. Or I imagine that it is.

Now, where's that Poltergeist Tree?

I pause to catch my breath. I happen to be wearing Karine's unlucky wool socks, and they're bunching up at the bottom of my boots. I lean against a tree to pull them up. There's a small clearing across the trail, somehow familiar. This might be the spot where we set up the tent last spring, which means the old hemlock is close and Amka could be within earshot. I cup my gloved hands around my mouth and call her name.

The forest absorbs my voice, then echoes it back as a sort of yowl. I lift my toque off my head to better hear. The sound is high-pitched, like…a snowmobile going full throttle. Did I kill Zwing's engine before leaving? But he's out of commission. And who would be trying to ride it, anyway?

The whine keeps coming closer. Instead of ripping the air as a sled's two-stroke engine would, it morphs into a feral shriek, and it's coming my way. I have to make it to the Poltergeist Tree. To Amka and Blue.

I bolt, panic powering my muscles. Somehow, I must've left the trail because branches whip my face, and roots trip me. Blood roars in my ears, and so does the entire mountain as if it's starting to crumble.

Is the chat-cornu triggering another landslide? Does it

even have that power? I don't want to be buried alive. I trip and sprawl on my hands and knees.

A long, cold wind sweeps the ground. Tufts of lichen roll past like miniature tumbleweeds. This isn't a landslide but a windstorm. Tall trees bend like blades of grass in a pasture. Their mantles of snow scatter and swirl around me like a smothering curtain. I struggle against the gale to pull on my hood and curl into a ball, arms shielding my head while the storm rages. Eyes squeezed shut, I wait for the killing blow. If it's not the disintegrating mountain coming down on me, a falling tree will crush me to death.

Neither happens. After a nerve-wracking eternity, the wind abates like someone hit the pause button. I lie motionless, my forehead buried in my crossed arms, my breath warming up the small snow cave enclosing my face.

When I'm sure the storm has blown away, I break out of my snowy shell. My barbed-wire ribs shift and wrench a grunt out of me. I take small gulps of air until the queasiness fades and the world settles around me.

"Well, that was freaky," I mumble.

My voice sounds loud in the renewed silence. The snow is as dark as powdered coal, and the forest melts into the inky sky. I find myself standing in a new world, as if I'd dropped from a passing airplane. The trail is nowhere within sight, and my tracks are erased. Impossible to tell which way I came from or what direction I was headed. How am I going to find Amka now?

I am fucked.

Chapter 22

Turning a slow circle, I look for options in the lighter spaces between dark tree trunks. I have no idea where the Poltergeist Tree is, and I can't run around the mountain all night hoping to find Amka and Blue. The smart thing would be to head downhill, find my way home, and call Search & Rescue. Yes, sir. Amka Tanuyak. Seventeen years old, last seen wearing a yellow dress and a black leather jacket. She's lost on the Devil's Tail. How do I know? I had a vision, duh.

Right. They won't come with a search team for Amka but with antipsychotic meds for me.

As I complete my turn, a whiff of smoke tickles my nostrils, pungent with a hint of sweetness to it, like wood smoke. Now, that's real. And it's too strong to be wafting from the town below. Could I have underestimated Amka? I've been so intent on saving her before she freezes to death that I never considered she might manage to save herself.

In my mind, the golden glow of a campfire lights up the hollow in the Poltergeist Tree. Two shadows stretch outside on the dusky snow, a girl and a dog. They're safe, the flames keeping away both wild and unnatural beasts.

I follow the ribbon of aroma with renewed energy and

emerge into a clearing faster than I can break a sweat. Wrong clearing—there's no giant, dead tree in it—but I'll be damned. A log cabin sits in the middle of the space, roof sagging, chimney smoking. Gabriel's trapping cabin is still standing? My legs have taken me halfway there before I notice I'm moving.

There aren't any tracks in the clearing, but the windstorm would have erased them. Amka's in there. I just know it. As incredible as this is, who else could it be? The big bad wolf in a grandma nightgown? The three little pigs? My stomach growls like a wolf. I haven't had anything since breakfast, and I'm starving.

Pale light glows through a tiny frost-obscured window. I thud on the door with my gloved knuckles and wait. When nothing happens, I press my lips to a crack in the warped planks.

"Amka? Open up. It's me, Alex."

The door flies open, and I tumble into embracing arms.

"Oh my god, you came." Amka hugs me hard. I gasp as pain explodes in my ribs. Axcalibur falls from my grip and clatters to the floor.

"Are you okay?" she asks.

"Yeah, just give me a minute." I crash-land on a bench, nearly knocking over the candle stuck in a pool of hardened wax on the nearby table. Silver pinpoints dance before my eyes, and my ears are ringing.

Amka shoves the door closed and stands before me, fingering the rumpled folds of her yellow dress. So achingly beautiful, like a dream that could vanish any moment. It must've been one cold trek for her. She could have ended up so dead.

I spring up to my feet. "What's wrong with you? Are you aware you might be just about to be reported *missing*? People must be looking for you. Your parents. The police."

She shakes her head. "I'm not missing. My mom watched me walk out with my stuff."

"I tried to call you. You didn't answer."

"I lost my phone. I'm sorry." She looks at the floor and steps backward. The cabin's shadows suck the colour from her dress. For a heart-clenching moment, I fear she'll fade and disappear.

"Is Blue with you?" she asks in a small voice.

Blue. I'd forgotten about him for a minute. I sweep the cabin with my eyes, taking in the wood stove in one corner, and the narrow bed pushed against the opposite wall. He's not here, obviously, or she wouldn't be asking.

"I—" I pull off my toque and scrunch it in my hands.

"He's dead, isn't he?" Her eyes gleam in the candlelight.

I look down at the snow-covered tips of my boots. The answer is likely yes. I haven't seen any sure sign of him besides the chat-cornu's dirty trick.

"You promised you'd take care of him," she cries.

I don't even brace myself when she comes at me, hands raised to push me. But she steps into my arms instead, and I teeter back against the door.

"I'm sorry, I'm sorry," I whisper into her hair. "He must have known you were on the mountain and he tried to find you."

I hold her tight, and for once, we share the same

feeling. Sorrow for Blue. After she left, I was so hurt and angry I never stopped to consider how hard it might have been for her to leave him behind.

After a long moment, she sniffles and pulls back. "At least you found me."

"Yeah. I'm so glad I did." Suddenly, I'm exhausted beyond words. I could collapse here on the floor, but I want to sleep on that bed over there, to forget my encounter with the beast, and to wake up in the morning with Amka snuggled against me.

As if she's reading my thoughts, she unzips my parka and pulls off my gloves, tossing them aside.

"Come on, sit," she says, pointing to the bench.

I step out of my snow pants and plunk myself down, finger-combing my tangled hair. Amka retrieves two tin mugs from a shelf, wipes off the dust, and sets them on the table. A pot hisses on the wood stove.

She carries it over and fills the cups. "Fir needle tea."

"Who would have thought we'd ever play tea party together," I say, blowing into my cup.

"In the cabin you said was a rotten pile, no less." One dimple appears with her lopsided smile.

"I said it *probably* was."

"Well, I don't know how, but I found it. Looks like I'm not as useless as you thought I was."

An impish smile still lights her face. I'm not ready to see it go, so I say, "But where's the rabbit stew? I'm starving."

I sip the weak tea. My belly cramps, begging for something more substantial.

"I had Cheetos in my backpack," she said. "I'd have saved you some if I'd known you were coming."

"You're lucky I came, too. What were you thinking hiking up a mountain dressed like this?" As if I was any smarter a couple of nights ago. "You should have come straight to my house."

Now, she's serious. "I called you and you didn't answer."

"With the phone you lost?"

She blinks quickly and licks her lips. "Long story, but the guy who gave me a lift let me use his phone. He was going to drive me to your place, but then we went into a ditch and I continued on foot and—" The more she talks, the wider her eyes become as if she's reliving the awful experience. "When I got near the trail, I heard Blue, I'm sure I did, and then—"

"Amka, stop." I lower my voice. "You were right about the chat-cornu. It exists, and now it has lured both of us here."

The tea sloshes in her cup as her hand jerks. "Does that mean one of us is going to die?"

It does. And it's going to be her because I'm the one it cursed to lose someone I love.

"Of course not," I say, "but we'd better spend the night here." I stand, gritting my teeth, and push the heavy bench against the door, for what it's worth. If the chat-cornu had anything to do with the freak windstorm, I'm sure it could easily huff and puff and blow the cabin down. But inside must still be safer than outside, at least while it's dark. "We'll leave as soon as the sun comes up."

The candle flame shines brighter, then shrinks to almost nothing. Amka rubs her bare arms. I suppress a shiver myself. The wooden walls of the cabin sparkle with frost, and there isn't any spare wood to stoke the fire.

"We should try to stay warm, then." Amka steps to the bed and crawls under the covers. She pats the spot next to her. "How about sharing some body heat?"

"Good idea." I lie down. My body is heavier than a truckload of wet sand, and pain washes across my ribs in muted waves. Amka pulls the musty blankets over us. We breathe together in the tense silence as the weight of this wild day settles over us.

"Can you believe we finally get to spend our night in this cabin?" Amka asks.

Our night? I remember very clearly that she didn't want to spend the night alone in a tent with me the last time we came up here. I turn onto my side to face her. The candlelight barely touches her features.

"I'm not sure I believe it," I say. Maybe I'm still passed out on the trail, enveloped in a cloud of Zwing's exhaust fumes, and all that's happened is a massive hallucination.

She reaches across the space and slides her fingers down my neck, along my arm, then settles at my waist where my sweater has ridden up.

"Believe it now?" she asks.

I hold my breath and wait to see if the moment will switch to something unlikely and unrelated as in a dream, but her fingers keep drawing small circles on my skin, giving me shivers.

"I'm sorry I left the way I did," she says. "No wonder

you didn't want to talk to me anymore after that. But… maybe I'd gotten this soulmate thing all wrong."

I feel a stab, nowhere near my ribs where the real pain should be. "I wish you'd figured that out earlier."

"Why? Are you with Caden now?"

Two days ago—or maybe even this morning—I would have said yes, but now? Our relationship crashed soon after takeoff. "I guess not."

"I'm sorry I messed with your feelings. I was a bit messed up myself." She scoots closer. "You can do whatever you want to me, Alex. I won't stop you this time."

I close my eyes as her forehead touches mine, but I'm not kidding myself. Tomorrow, we'll hike down to my house, and I'll make her call her parents. I know she won't stick around Fort Cass and love me forever after. And I know watching her leave again will hurt all the same. But since there's no escaping it, to hell with the chat-cornu. I'm embracing the curse for now.

Maybe we only have one night, but we have all night.

I slide my hand on the back of her neck and twine my fingers into her hair, kissing her temple, her cheekbone, the corner of her mouth. Slowly. Amka whispers my name over and over and speaks to my body with her fingers. This is as sweet as last summer on the dock at Pecan Lake, before she stabbed me with the news she was leaving.

As I move in to kiss her more deeply, a thud rattles the cabin's door. Amka gasps and shoves herself off me with such force that a grenade explodes in my ribs. A feral scream tears out of my throat.

"Alex?" Caden shouts. The bench we pushed against

the door crashes over, and the door flies open, blowing out the candle.

Eyes squeezed shut against the pain, I feel Amka sit up on the mattress.

"What are you doing here?" she spits at Caden.

"What are *you* doing here?" he echoes.

I blink, but his headlamp blinds me as he crosses the cabin in three strides, bringing in a wave of cold air.

"And you?" he asks me.

"Why are you here?" I croak. This seems to be the question of the day.

"I went to see you after school. Like you asked. Saw Zwing's tracks crossing the ditch. I'm sure you can figure out the rest."

"You came on your sled?" I glance toward the gaping door but only see darkness out there.

"Yeah, I thought we could have ridden to the lake or something. Talked. But I tracked you up here instead and crashed into a fallen tree when the windstorm hit."

That whine I heard. It was his snowmobile, not some blood-thirsty beast. If I hadn't panicked and run, he'd have found me. And I'd never have found Amka. My guilt slides off. I did the right thing.

Amka gets off the bed, closes the door, and relights the candle. When she returns, she says, "Alex is hurt."

"Where?" Caden asks me without sparing her a glance.

"It's just a bruise," I say, trying to get up, but Amka pushes my shoulder, and I have no choice but to lie down.

"Show us," she says. Before I can do anything, she lifts

my sweater and tank top. The rub of the fabric burns as if there were fire ants frenzying across my skin.

Caden whistles. "Shit. What happened?"

I crane my neck to look. In the beam of his headlamp, a sprawling purple bruise covers my left side. In its center rises a ring of swollen flesh the exact shape and size of Amka's mood bracelet. It's like the sheriff's star that takes the bullet and saves his life, except this is making my life so much harder.

"Zwing's gear chain broke. I must've bumped into the handlebars." I tug my clothes down, but hiding the damage doesn't make it go away.

"I'm getting you out of here right now," Caden says. "You probably need X-rays."

"No! Not 'til morning. The chat-cornu—it's real, Caden. Not just a story."

He frowns at me like he thinks I must have hit my head too, then looks at Amka for confirmation. She gives him a little shrug and a little smile. What the hell?

"The creature messed with me, I swear." I swing my legs off the bed, but a torrent of pain knocks me down. The cabin spins and I retch, but nothing comes out.

Caden rubs my back. "Just breathe."

I rest my forehead against his stomach and take shallow breaths through my nose until the nausea subsides.

"How far is your sled?" Amka asks him. "I should help you move the tree that fell on it, then we'll come get Alex."

"Hell, no." I try to stand, but my legs are too weak. "Haven't you guys ever watched horror movies? Splitting up is like the oldest no-no in the book. I'm not letting you leave without me."

"You might have some broken ribs," Caden says. "It won't help if you puncture a lung."

I look from him to Amka and back. It used to be me having to choose one over the other, and now they're choosing to leave me behind?

"If I'd broken any bones, I would know." I clamp my lips shut so no moan will come out as I try to stand again.

Caden holds me down and exhales forcefully. "Why do you have to be so damn hard-headed all the time? Can't you just shut up and let me help you for once?"

I gasp like a fish fresh out of the lake. I wouldn't be more shocked if he'd backhanded me across the face. Despite all my shit, Caden has never spoken to me like this.

"Sorry." He yanks off his aviator hat and rakes his fingers through his hair as if he can't quite believe it either. When he speaks next, he's the Caden I know. "You have nothing to prove, Alex. You're strong, everybody knows that. Let us help. Just this once."

To-do list for becoming a less shitty person, item number two: allow Caden to save me. I owe that to him. We haven't even discussed the state of things between us. If he'd decided we were done, he wouldn't be here.

Then I remember where things were going with Amka before he arrived. The taste of her lips is still on mine. I fuss with imaginary dirt beneath my thumbnail, loathing to show him the guilt oozing through every pore on my face. "Fine. I'll stay put."

"Mind if I borrow your winter clothes?" Amka asks.

"We'll figure something out when we all ride down later on."

"Be my guest," I say without enthusiasm. I may have agreed to stay behind, but I won't pretend I'm thrilled about it.

Caden opens the door. Cold air creeps across the floor, freezing my toes through my wool socks.

"We'll be right back," he says and steps out.

"Hey, Amka?" I say.

She zips up my parka. "Yeah?"

"Look in that side pocket. I've got something for you."

She pulls out her bracelet. "You had it all along?"

"Yeah. I meant to give it back..."

She slides it onto her wrist and adjusts it so the stone gleams in the candlelight. "No need to worry now. The chat-cornu won't touch us."

"Be careful."

She winks at me, steps out, and shuts the door behind her.

I'm left alone with the ticking of the chimney, the thrum of my heart, and my rambling thoughts.

What if something happens to them and they never come back? If there's any truth to the legend, Amka's lucky bracelet will protect her no more than Atwanet's bewitched snowshoes protected Gabriel. That fool. If he loved Atwanet so much, he should have seen through the chat-cornu's disguise and known it for what it was.

The chimney still ticks, like impatient fingernails tapping on a tabletop. I feel like I'm missing some crucial detail. Finally, it hits like the moose guard on an eighteen-wheeler.

"Shit!" A lightning bolt of adrenaline zaps me up to my feet. No wonder Caden wasn't being himself when he lashed out at me. The real Caden isn't here.

The chat-cornu has taken his shape. And now, it has stolen Amka again.

Chapter 23

I nearly forget the pain in my haste to find my parka and snow pants. But crap. Amka has them. I look around the cabin. The blankets. I take the woollen one to the bench, slice a hole in the middle with my axe, and put it on like a poncho. At least she left me my winter boots.

Axe in hand, I rush outside, blinking against the snow-lit darkness. The sky is awash with crimson auroras, like the night I almost drowned. I don't like it, but I couldn't drown on this frozen mountain even if I tried.

The fake Caden and Amka's tracks are plain to see. My breath hitches as I set off following them, puffing in short bursts of white. The air seems much colder than it was earlier. It must be close to minus twenty Celsius. The snap of a frozen branch echoes across the chill. No sound of Amka's voice.

Is the chat-cornu already done with her? I walk as fast as I can until I reach a barren patch. A huge tree looms in the middle, the opening at the base of its trunk gaping darkly. The Poltergeist Tree, as dead as ever—the curse's ground zero, the place where Gabriel tried to double-cross the chat-cornu.

I should keep going, but I'm rooted to the spot. Scraps

hang from the tree's boughs. Last spring I assumed they were lichens, but I now see they're animal pelts, limp and slimy with rot. There's something else, too. A scarf, purple and green like my unlucky socks, the colours eerily vivid. But Karine didn't die. She left. So, what's the scarf doing here?

"Alex. You're supposed to be at the cabin!"

I nearly jump out of my poncho. Amka stands at the opposite end of the clearing, fists on her hips.

"Get over here," I whisper-yell. "Caden's not real. It's a trick."

She frowns and turns to the forest like she's planning to tell on me. "Hey, Caden," she shouts.

Damn. She is.

"What?" he replies from a short distance.

"I need to pee. I'll catch up in a minute."

Smart girl.

She jogs across the clearing, eyes wide. I catch her and pull her into me with my free arm, the axe still gripped in the other.

"What are we gonna do?" she asks, voice trembling and hiding her face in my shoulder. "You'll freeze for sure in that rotten blanket."

I'm already freezing. "We have to go back to the cabin. Block the door with everything we can use. I think we'll be fine if we can keep the chat-cornu out until morning."

At least, that's how it works in the movies.

"Okay, sweetie," Amka says.

"Let's g—"

Um, *sweetie?* Amka would never call me that. I pull away from her fast.

She smiles like she just told a good joke, her dimples on full display. But then, they disappear though the smile doesn't, and it isn't Amka anymore standing in front of me but Karine, looking a lot like me dressed as she is in my stolen winter outfit. Her blue eyes sparkle with malice. The red auroras flare so bright they cast her shadow on the snow—and, of course, it's the chat-cornu's sinister horned lynx shadow.

My legs itch to turn tail and run, but I stand my ground. "What do you want?"

"You." Karine smirks. "Alexia."

The chat-cornu wants to steal me? "Hey. That's not what the curse says. How would I be the person dearest to *me?*"

Or am I that selfish? I did a lousy job at loving Caden. I shut the door in Amka's face when she called to ask for help—the real Amka, I mean, because the thing I kissed in the cabin's bed wasn't her. I wipe my mouth with the back of my hand, feeling freakishly soiled.

"You people have got this curse all wrong." Karine steps closer, her roadkill breath hot on my face. "*You* were supposed to be my way out."

That night we camped up here—it wasn't a nightmare, then. But Blue came to save me. This time around, I'm on my own.

"You're the one who should be dead," I yell, swinging my axe.

Karine jumps aside with wild cat litheness, and my

blade embeds itself in the tree trunk. The impact rattles my whole body. It takes me a moment to realize the atrocious shriek that rips my eardrums is coming from my own mouth.

Karine's voice laughs behind me. "I've wanted you for much longer than you think, Alexia."

I turn around but lose my balance and stumble back against the tree. The intensity of the pain blurs my vision. The thing that looks like Karine places her palms on my cheeks. I haven't felt my mother's touch in ages, but my skin remembers it. This isn't my mother, though. I scoot aside. Now, a void gapes at my back—the tree's hollow.

"Gabriel tethered me to this mountain," Karine hisses. "Atwanet saw through me when she came to look for that pathetic man, but you are a fool, Alex, and so is your little boyfriend." Her face blurs and rearranges itself slightly. The eyes turn from clear to blue-grey, and the dishevelled white-gold hair darkens to ash-blond. "*You* are my way out."

My own face looks back at me, the smugness of the smile no match for the horror choking the breath out of me.

Where's Caden? I try to scream his name, but my jaw is locked. From the cold, or fear, or shock.

"Don't you worry. Caden *loves* Alex, and I'll love him right back, as he deserves. Meanwhile, why don't you spend what's left of your miserable life in Gabriel's company?"

I'm dizzy. Sluggish. The monster with my face gives my shoulder the merest little shove. That's all it takes. I stagger backward, and the wind is knocked out of me as I hit the ground. The darkness of the hollow closes in on me.

"Caden, wait for me," the new Alex screams outside. "Don't trust Amka. It's a trick!"

A moment later, the soul bracelet I gave back to who I thought was Amka bounces off my chest and clinks somewhere in the dark. My ribs throb so fiercely I'm about to pass out. If I do, I'll freeze to death in here.

And the chat-cornu said I wasn't the cursed one?

If I die, I'll lose *everyone* I love.

I'm crying—or I think I am, but my voice isn't quite mine—more like a little girl's, the one I heard up the Devil's Tail that cold February night my sled quit on me. The cries pull me into a dark, watery place.

A suffocating weight crushes me. Then, I realize I'm in a seated position, held down by—

Oh, sweet. I'm back to being a toddler, tightly strapped into my car seat. Tears scald my cheeks, and my throat is raw from having the tantrum of the century. The tragedy is that I wanted to stay at Tina's and keep playing with Caden and his new puppy, Floof.

"Shit." Karine stops in the middle of the road and smacks the steering wheel with her palm. I swallow a big, snotty sob, and my despair turns to hope. She'll turn the car around and go back to Tina's.

But no. She pops the door and steps outside. "Sit tight, Alexia. I'll be right back."

She swings the door shut as she walks away, but a roaring wind blows it open again. Brittle leaves swirl inside the cab and nip at my cheeks. Beyond the cracked windshield, she struggles with the branches of a broken tree blocking the road. She's in skinny jeans and a hoodie, my own outfit of choice. If it weren't for her luminous hair tangling with the purple-and-green scarf around her neck, I could believe I was looking at myself. Except I'd be hacking at the fallen aspen with my axe instead of wrangling it with my bare hands, dispatching it in no time at all.

Little me wants to help, too—for all the good it would do. I'd just be getting in the way. Just then, a russet-brown fluffball crawls out of the forest—Floof. He crouches, butt in the air and tail wagging.

My pudgy hands rattle the buckle of the car seat and fumble with the red switch Mommy and Daddy push when they let me out. I get pinched a couple of times, but I'm a tough, determined little girl. At last, I break free, cross to the front seat, and climb out, just as Karine's scarf flies from her neck and lands in the bushes across the ditch, Devil's Tail-side.

The puppy pounces and catches it. I toddle around the back of the car and chase after him in my squeaky pink gumboots. Every time I bend to grab the scarf, Floof drags it out of my reach. I stick out my tongue and follow it past prickly bushes and leafless trees that look like giant spiders.

We enter the forest. The wind growls like a monster, and the treetops sway ominously. The puppy trots along the overgrown path for a while then veers off around a massive tree, the scarf slithering out of sight.

I trip after it in the underbrush and find the scarf floating in a pond that formed at the base of an uprooted tree. I yell at the scarf—like that's going to help. Of course, it stays right there, floating on a waterbed of fallen leaves. I take one step at the shallow edge, then another, the mud sucking at my boots.

The pup appears at the periphery of my vision. My guts twist as it transforms into a kitty, bigger than any I've seen in my short life. Its fur is matted and black horns come out of its head.

This is my very first encounter with the beast. No wonder Chatty the mascot has been scaring me shitless ever after. How dare it go after a baby? But it doesn't do a thing. It only sits on its haunches to watch as little Alex wobbles and falls.

Cold shock. I wave my arms around, trying to grab onto something. Murky pond water is getting into my mouth and eyes.

A dark shape hovers above the surface, like Dad when he used to dunk me in Pecan Lake. But I'm not laughing this time—I'm freaking drowning. Until strong hands grip my body.

"Alexia!" Karine pulls me out and clutches me to her heart. "*Ça va, Alexia. Maman est là.*"

Amazingly, I understand her French. "You're okay," she repeats over and over. "Mommy's here." I cough, unable to breathe. And then I can, and gulp in air in painful sobs. Karine takes off her coat and wraps me in its soft warmth. I'm a deadweight as she stumbles out of the forest. She climbs out of the ditch, and the wind pushes us toward the car's headlights. It's almost night.

Over her shoulder, I spot the damn horned lynx slinking in the shadows. As it passes us, it blurs and changes, like that werewolf I saw on TV when I was supposed to be asleep in my crib. It stands on two legs and grows tall. The patchy fur turns into a camo hunting outfit, and the whiskered face flattens to human form—the spitting image of Dad, looking barely older than Caden is right now.

But we're at the car. We'll be fine. At least I want us to be, though I know we won't.

"Karine."

She stops and turns at Dad's voice. He stands between the tangles of dead, spidery trees, the barrel of his .410 shotgun resting on his shoulder. I scream and claw at Karine's neck with one hand, but she doesn't understand a damn word I'm trying to say.

"What the hell is wrong with you?" he shouts, spit shooting out of his mouth. Dad *never* yells like this.

"I'm sorry," Karine says. "There was a tree on the road. I only turned my back one minute, and then—"

He points a finger at her face and it feels as lethal as the business end of a gun. "She could have died."

"She's all right. I've got her," Karine says in a shaking voice.

"You let her go on the Tail. She saw the chat-cornu. It saw her. Now she's cursed."

"But—"

"She will lose someone she loves, like in that damn legend that gives you nightmares all the time." He steps closer, stopping at the edge of the ditch. Of course. The beast cannot cross it, bound as it is to the mountain.

If Karine knows the legend so well, she should know

she's being tricked. Why is she even listening to this garbage?

"You're a lousy mother, Karine. Who do you think Alex should lose, between you and me?" he continues while all she does is gape. "Go home and pack your stuff. I'll come home to take care of *my* daughter as soon as you get the hell out of town."

Karine transfers me to her hip and stands taller. "Maybe I'm not a good mom, but I know you're not Steven. He'd never tell me to leave our baby alone in the house."

Yay, Karine. But what the hell? She knew and still left?

"Very well." Dad's face changes. His teeth are pointier, and his eyes flash.

"Your *Steven* is trespassing on my hunting grounds as we speak. I'll take his skin and leave his carcass to rot in the woods. Then I'll come *home* and expose you for the useless mother that you are. Who'll believe you? You're a nobody around here. You'll have to leave with your shame, and your precious Alexia will be mine to do whatever I want with."

"You leave her alone," Karine yells, but I hear the defeat in her voice—feel it in the slumping of her shoulders.

Wake up, Karine. Call out to Dad. The sun has set. He must be on his way back from hunting, with an actual shotgun.

"You know what you have to do." The monster smiles, showing its yellow teeth. The camo clothes and the gun melt and disappear. The horned lynx pushes out a raspy purr then stalks on soft paws into the trees.

Karine looks too stunned to cry. The beast's words have slithered into her mind and wrapped around the vulnerable part of her that believes she's a useless mother and that I'd be better off without her.

She drives us home. Gives me a warm bath and dresses me in pink unicorn pyjamas. Sits me on her lap at the kitchen table with a sippy cup of milk.

I watch her write the words in purple ink on a piece of paper I won't read until many years later. *Dear Alexia,* the letter starts. I know the rest by heart. When she's done, she writes on another sheet of paper. I've never seen that one. A letter to Dad, perhaps. I squint mentally, but I couldn't read back then so I can't make sense of the words now.

I doze off until she sets me in the crib I've been able to break out of for months. I don't want to let go of her hoodie, but sleep is like a hand pulling me underwater.

This time, there's no one to pull me out—no Karine, and no Caden. I may hate being in the water, but I hate the chat-cornu a hundred times more. I fight to the surface.

It's payback time.

Chapter 24

I'm back inside the tree hollow. Burning tears stream down my face as this long-supressed memory pools in my mind. *You've been cursed,* Karine wrote that fateful night while I sat on her knees, clueless. *The chat-cornu was going to steal from you a person you loved. Your daddy deserved you more than I did, so I had to leave.*

For years, I've been forcing myself not to care—worse, to loathe Karine. I double over. This realization hurts like hell. It crushes my heart as if all of my ribs have caved in.

My mother didn't leave to be rid of me or to escape life in Fort Cass. She was duped, too, at least for a time. What other choice did she have? The chat-cornu was going to get me one way or another. If I'd drowned back when I was little, the chat-cornu would have stolen my shape and gotten off the mountain in Karine's arms. And then what? Taken back his original shape and skipped town? Lived the rest of my life for me?

Maybe he's snuggling up to Caden right now, posing as me and smiling at its own cunning.

Well, I didn't die the first time, and I'm not dead now.

I only feel like I've been beaten to a pulp with a sledge-hammer.

I flex my stiff hand to wipe my tears, then open my eyes. The tree hollow isn't as pitch-dark as I'd thought. Refraction from the snow dimly lights the opening. Old bones, grey and mossy, lie on a lush, creamy-white pelt between me and the outside world. Tibias, fibulas, the many small bones of two feet. Snowshoes are still strapped to them, impossibly untouched by rot, as is the pelt.

These are Gabriel's bones. I have no desire to see his grinning skull nor whatever remnants of the chat-cornu he trapped and skinned, so I don't search the rest of the hollow. I need to get out of here before hypothermia sets in, or I'll be sharing this grave with him forever.

I kneel, releasing a string of swear words to keep in check the wildfire in my ribs. I don't know what a punctured lung would feel like, but if it were a ten, this is a twelve for sure.

My bare palm lands on the tail of one snowshoe as I crawl out. A tingle swims up my arm, and maybe—just maybe—softens the pain a little. Could the snowshoes really be bewitched? I've seen enough weird shit in one night that I'm willing to believe anything.

Feeling like a grave robber, I shake the bones off the snowshoes, toss them outside, and scramble after them. The red auroras are gone, and wind-driven snow drops heavily. Some coyotes sing in the distance.

As I fasten the snowshoes to my feet, the fire fades to almost nothing—magically so. But I have no time to revel in my awe. The snowfall has erased all traces of my struggle with the chat-cornu, and Caden's tracks as well.

I reach up into the tree's boughs and retrieve Karine's purple-and-green scarf, claiming it for myself at long last. Reunited with the matching socks on my feet, maybe it'll bring me luck. Last, I yank the handle of my axe still embedded in the tree trunk, but if the bewitched snowshoes spirit away my pain, they don't give me superhuman strength. The axe doesn't budge. I leave it there with regret. I have to find Caden before he and the chat-cornu sled off the mountain. Or else I—or more likely, my ghost—will be bound to it. Hell. In a generation or two, kids might even try to summon me for a thrill. Awful Alex, not in a flowy dress like Amka's White Lady but in a motheaten, threadbare poncho.

Not if I can help it.

I stride across the clearing in the direction I think Caden was headed earlier, not daring to call out his name. Then, yet another strange thing happens. Even as the snowshoes kick up powder with each of my steps, my mind expands beyond the boundaries of my body and soars skyward.

The Devil's Tail unfurls below me. I can even see the hidden slope that's not visible from down in Fort Cass, made up of a treeless jumble of boulders cocooned under snow and ice. Down the forested side of the mountain, Fort Cass's handful of streetlights glows like a lonely constellation.

The lights are on at Caden's. With everything that has happened, it feels like I've been on the Tail for days, but apparently, it's still too early for his parents to realize something's amiss. Their vehicles are in the yard, both dusted white. They must believe Caden and I are safe at my house. Little do they know.

I shift my attention back to the mountain. A pack of five or six coyotes is on the prowl, fast-moving shadows weaving beneath the multitude of trees.

Then I spot Caden's Polaris sled on the trail, a few hundred metres down from the cabin and the Poltergeist Tree. The fake-me stands hugging her ribs while Caden does all the work of moving the fallen tree out of the way.

I huff—this fallen-tree trick is getting a little old.

My mind slams back into my body. I'm not floating in the sky anymore but pushing through a wall of tight-growing fir saplings.

"Get away from him, you trickster," I yell, pointing at the other me.

The thick branch Caden just lifted off his sled's hood drops from his hand. He pales a couple of shades and gapes from me to fake-Alex.

"Don't listen to her," she says, sidling close to him and wincing as if in pain. "It's the chat-cornu again. Look. It doesn't even bother to act like it's hurting."

Caden nods, never taking his eyes off me. He opens and closes his fists, probably freaking the hell out and trying hard to not let it show.

"Let's go," he says, and fake-Alex climbs onto the sled's seat, smirking at me behind his back.

"Caden, please." I step forward, and he steps backward.

"The snowshoes take away the pain. They're bewitched, like in the legend."

"Um, sure?" he says, taking another step back.

"Yeah," fake-Alex says. "I read the story in English class, remember?"

Oh, shit. I've just fallen into some clone-themed comedy in which I must prove I'm the real Alex before it's too late. How fun. But I can't think of another way to convince Caden than by finding some detail only he and I would know.

"I got Blue from Amka, who got him from you," I blurt. "He's a coydog."

The other Alex doesn't miss a beat. "I'm so sorry I didn't tell you I lost him. I should have, but you know me, I'm—"

"Full of shit," we—me and fake-Alex—say at the same time.

Caden licks his lips, his eyes darting back and forth between us. Dammit.

"Can't you see?" the monster girl spews. "Anything I know, the chat-cornu knows it too. It takes stuff from my mind and uses it against us."

"Exactly!" I yell at Caden. "That's what it's doing right now. Wake up!"

I'm such a fool. The chat-cornu can read my mind. That's how he knew how to sit on the trail looking like Blue. How to act like Amka at the cabin. He even planted that vision in my mind of Amka hitchhiking here, using my own wishful thinking. Because, yeah. Some vile part of me yearned for her to come here even though I told her not to. Caden was right to worry I would ditch him for her again.

The monster with my face winks at me. Then, she moans and spits a bloody spray on the snow. "Come on, Caden. Let's get out of here."

Caden gives me the stink eye and starts his snowmobile. Why doesn't he just know I'm the real me? And more importantly, how the hell do I get out of this mess? I can't stand here all night having a fact-throwing contest with the chat-cornu.

"I'm tired of this shit." I kick snow at the snowmobile. "Fine. You *win*, you creepy bastard. You happy now?"

Caden pauses halfway through straddling his sled to cut me a conflicted glance, but fake-Alex pulls him down on the seat.

"Hurry up," she wails. "I'm hurting so bad."

I roll my eyes and stomp past them, giving the sled a wide berth. "I'm going home by myself on my magical damn snowshoes."

I hate leaving Caden behind, but I need to cross the threshold of the willows before the chat-cornu does and steals my identity for good. Maybe I could hide and yank it off the sled as they ride past? I've got no better idea at the moment.

The snowshoes cover a lot of ground as I stride downhill, so this plan might just work.

Caden's sled growls far behind. They're on the move. Within moments, the engine roars at my back. I turn my head to look, trip on the snowshoes, and sprawl on the ground. The sled's headlight blinds me. I'm toast. They're going to run right over me. I shield my head with my hands, for all the good that will do, and brace myself. The snowmobile stops an arm length away. Caden jumps down and kneels beside me. He doesn't have a passenger on the sled.

"Quick," he says, undoing the snowshoes' bindings and yanking them off my feet.

His presence is such a relief, even as pain floods back across my ribcage.

"How did you figure out I was me?" I ask.

A wicked grin appears on his lips. "You're the sorest loser I know. No one could fake that."

"Caden, come back!" The phony Alex comes running over the top of the hill, screaming like a banshee. "If you really loved me, you'd know I'm the real Alex."

"Huh," I tell Caden. "Ever heard me scream like that?"

"Not since that creepy Chatty welcomed us to kindergarten."

We both guffaw, but my laugh turns into a moan. Caden sobers up too.

Miss Phony charges down the hill, her fake pain seemingly forgotten, while mine is a fireworks factory in flames. The coyotes I heard earlier are getting closer, too. I know from experience that this is a bad sign.

"Time to leave." Caden lifts me by the armpits, hauls me onto the sled, and jumps on behind me. My hand finds the throttle and squeezes it all the way. Caden throws his arms around me to grab the handlebars, keeping me from sliding off the seat and helping me steer.

A blood-curdling screech drowns out the whine of the

engine. In the juddering side-view mirror, fake-Alex folds in on herself and shifts into a horrific horned lynx. A handful of coyotes—the underlings the chat-cornu sent to kill Blue—lope along, out to rip our throats.

Tree trunks rush by in the headlight's beam. A gale blasts my face and raises snowdrifts on our path, unnaturally fast. The sled launches off the drifts like a ship on rough seas, and we tilt dangerously on curves. Each jarring move is a wave of pain crashing down on me.

"Zwing! Where's Zwing?" I shout. If the chat-cornu and his murderous posse don't catch up, we might crash and break our necks before the chase is over. I try to release the throttle, but Caden holds my hand in place.

"It's fine," he shouts back. "I moved it to pass earlier."

While giant trees whoosh by like dark ghosts, I'm drowning in a pain-induced blur in which the coyotes' howls and the chat-cornu's screeches bang around in my skull like a bunch of knives in a snowblower.

Finally, the headlight sweeps the tangles of willows that mark the end of the trail—relief from an agony I'm hoping to survive. Caden nudges my hand off the throttle and takes full control as we hit the bottom of the ditch. We launch into the air then every bone in my body seemingly explodes as we crash-land onto the road. The sled tips to its flank. I hit the ground and slide to an abrupt stop against the snowbank on the far side.

"Alex?" Caden crawls over, hands hovering over my body, not daring to touch anything. "Alex. Speak to me."

"Ow," I reply. "This freaking hurts."

"Shit." He yanks his hat off and presses his forehead to mine. "I thought you were dead or something."

"We made it!" A ripping flood of joy births the most painful laugh that's ever passed my lips.

"Alex, I know you never listen to me, but this time please don't move," Caden says. "It might make your injuries much worse."

"Got it, Doctor," I croak. I don't want to move ever again. Maybe I've finally punctured that lung or even my heart. My mouth tastes like blood. "I think you should…go get help."

"I'm not leaving you alone." He fumbles inside his parka and pulls out his phone.

"No reception…here."

He still checks, waving the screen around.

"My house is unlocked. Go call your mom."

He puts his phone away in his pocket, then takes off his parka and covers me with it. "I'll be right back, okay?"

"Okay." I know he will.

He rights his sled, climbs on, and races away. After all the yelling, howling, and screeching, the stunning silence arrives too soon. The gale has died, and snowflakes prickle like needle tips as they fall on my face.

"I so wish you and I were still up at the cabin." Amka's disembodied voice wafts from the Devil's Tail. "Your kisses tasted so sweet."

Bitterness floods my throat. I kissed a monster. But it doesn't matter anymore. The curse is broken—I hope. I won't be fooled again, that's for sure.

A coyote yips, too close for comfort. A couple more

whine in answer. My body is on fire, but the tremor that climbs up my spine is pure ice. The chat-cornu can't step past the gateway of the willows, but the coyotes can come to finish me off. I don't think normal coyotes would do that. But if the chat-cornu is controlling them, then maybe they would? I can't see the line between reality and illusion anymore.

What's taking Caden so long?

A shadow creeps over the snowbank, pointy-eared but stockier than a coyote. Like a coydog.

"Blue?"

He whines, and the coyotes yip in response, sounding friendly rather than vicious. Could it be that they didn't kill him but instead protected him from the chat-cornu? Coyotes aren't the bad guys they're often made out to be. Shame on me for jumping to conclusions.

Blue approaches and sniffs me cautiously.

"Hey, you."

He grimaces, offering me that special wrinkled-nosed, toothy dog-grin he only ever showed Amka.

My eyes sting with tears. I never could stand a movie in which the dog dies in the end, not even *Cujo*. But I'm all for a story where the dog un-dies.

Blue sits a few steps away, facing the mountain. He's my guardian angel for now.

I slip in and out of consciousness while my other angels take forever to arrive. Blue slinks back to the forest when Caden rushes back on his sled.

"My mom will be right here." He covers me with a heavy throw he stole from the living room couch and puts his coat back on.

"G-goes r-really well with my new poncho," I joke through chattering teeth.

A moment later, Tina parks her car and runs out, fleece pyjama bottoms sticking out under her long winter coat.

"Search and Rescue is on the way, honey," she says, fussing with my blanket.

"My dad—"

"I'll call him as soon as we have you sorted out. Where are you hurt?"

"Um, everywhere?"

Tina checks my pulse with warm fingers, asks questions, and assesses me the best she can, but there isn't much she can do in the frigid dark. Her hand squeezes mine. She's as close to a mother as I ever had. I wish I could curl up in her arms, basking in her warmth like when she babysat me as a little girl.

The first responders arrive. I'm vaguely aware of answering more questions, of being strapped onto a stretcher, and being slid into the back of the rescue truck. Tina and Caden meet us back at the schoolyard, which doubles as a helipad.

"They're air-lifting you to Prince George," Tina says. "We'll see you at the hospital in a few hours."

"Caden?" I can't manage more than a whisper.

He leans close to me.

"Thanks for saving me," I say.

"Anytime. But you didn't do such a bad job yourself,

you daredevil." His strained smile is more soothing than whatever meds I've been given.

"Blue's alive. He's with the coyotes."

"I'll go look for him."

"No! Don't—"

"I won't go on the mountain, yeah, okay. I'll just set food out near the trail."

"Yes. Please."

Helicopter blades chop the air, first a distant hum, then loud enough to cut off our conversation. I'm loaded in like a piece of very fragile luggage and we take off. As the chopper soars into the night, I hover in a weird, weightless state. My body feels as insubstantial as a vague memory. My eyes are shut, but as if remnants of magic from the bewitched snowshoes still flow in my blood, I see—or sense—the Devil's Tail. A pack of coyotes haunts the slopes. Blue is with them. Higher up, the chat-cornu skulks around the Poltergeist Tree, not a beast of flesh and bone but a mere shadow.

I cast out for the real Amka. She's nowhere near Fort Cass, but wherever she is, I hope she's all right.

I hope I'll be all right too.

Chapter 25

I'm on my bed with the new phone Dad insisted I must have. My feet are warm inside my lucky purple-and-green socks, and the matching scarf is bunched up beside me like a giant caterpillar. When we're not in the same room, he messages me about every thirty seconds to make sure I'm being good and taking my meds. Serves me right, I guess.

In other news, Amka was never missing, or lost, or hitchhiking anywhere. Chloe, of all people, tracked her down for me after I barely escaped the Devil's Tail with my life—a reminder that our friendship was never officially over.

I've got Amka on the screen right now.

"You look like you've been to Hell and back," she says.

I smooth down my hair. "Five days on the hospital diet will do that to you."

Thank god I didn't puncture a lung, but I have three bruised ribs, a sprained wrist (the same I wrecked at the Lumber Games a century ago), and a collection of cuts and scrapes surrounded by bruises in all colours of the rainbow.

Laughing hurts. Breathing hurts. Hell, existing hurts, but I'm happy to be alive.

"Blue must have missed you," she says.

"Yeah, I think so."

He's curled up at the foot of the bed, having embraced the comfort of his life with me once again on the evening I came back from Prince George.

"You were brave to steal him back from the chat-cornu."

To most people, I sledded up the Devil's Tail to find Blue, was thrown off Zwing when the gear chain broke, and got lost in a freak windstorm. I told Amka the truth, except for the part where the chat-cornu impersonated her. I'd rather forget about it myself and treasure the real moments we shared instead.

"So…what have you been up to?" I ask. "You scared the heck out of me with your middle-of-the-night phone call and that Instagram post Chloe showed me."

"Do you think I was just another brown runaway girl?" Her half-smile says *what else is new?*

"Well, I…" It's more complicated than that, I want to say, but is it, really?

Though she doesn't owe me an explanation, I still wait, hoping for one. She doesn't give me any. I decide to be at peace with that.

The screen freezes and announces I have a slow internet connection. As if I didn't know that. I'd better hurry and honour my self-improvement list.

"Um, Amka…" I take a shallow breath because this is all I can manage. "I'm sorry I turned you down when you called for help. If anything had happened to you, it would have been my fault."

"I take responsibility for my own shit." She looks

straight into the camera, and it's as if her deep, dark eyes are touching my soul. "I really liked you, Alex, but I couldn't let myself like you too much, because, you know, I never meant to stay in Fort Cass."

This stings a little, but it's a sweet ache.

"It's all right. Your place is in Mississauga."

"Nope. I'm in Iqaluit with my grandpa. I'll go to school here after the Christmas break."

"Aren't you freezing your butt off over there?"

"Not in my grandma's seal parka."

"Cool." My own petroleum-derived winter outfit turned up in the dead willows across the ditch. If Caden hadn't recovered it, it might still be not-composting there a hundred years from now.

Amka tucks a strand of hair behind her ear. Her wrist is bare. Instead of her soul bracelet, a band of triangles, dots, and Ys is tattooed onto her skin.

Maybe what she was looking for all along wasn't some soulmate but a place where she belongs. I'm sure that wherever I go, Fort Cass will always be my place. I would have loved her to want to belong here with me, but not getting my way doesn't have to mean I've lost her.

A notification pings on my phone.

Mind if I come over? the message reads.

"I'll have to hang up," I say. "Someone's coming to see me."

Her eyes crinkle. "Tell *him* I say hi."

Look who's reading my mind now.

"Talk to you later, maybe?" she asks.

"Sure. That would be nice."

"Bye for now, then." She flashes a dimpled smile. "And stay safe from the chat-cornu."

"Yeah. I will. Bye." I hang up, and the weight of a mountain slides off my shoulders. The feeling turns to light-headedness as Caden's truck rumbles into my yard. I check myself on my phone camera. I do look like hell, but at least I'm in my moose-print pyjamas instead of some ragged old poncho.

We last saw each other the night I was admitted to the hospital, and I was so far gone all I remember is our agreement to keep the chat-cornu to ourselves. I hear the door bang closed and Dad's muffled voice through the floor. A moment later, there's a soft knock at the door.

"Come in."

Caden opens the door and smiles as soon as his gaze meets mine. "Hey, daredevil."

"Hey." Seeing him feels as good as catching the first glimpse of rain after weeks of sunshine.

He leans against the door jamb, arms crossed. "How're you feeling?"

"I'm a wreck. I hope I'll heal fast enough to beat you at the next Lumber Games."

"If you don't, they're looking for someone to wear the Chatty mascot suit."

"We should steal that creepy old thing and burn it." I pat the mattress beside me and carefully scoot over. "Are you coming in or what?"

He steps inside but hesitates near the bed. A half-moon bruise lingers on his cheekbone, the purplish hue a perfect complement to his green-gold eyes.

"Come on. You won't break me. I'm already broken."

He finally sits beside me, hands in his lap. I lean against him. The movement makes my ribs ache, but his closeness feels so good.

"I'm glad you came," I say. "Not just here now, but that night on the Devil's Tail, too."

"I'm glad you're alive." He slips his arm around my shoulders and lets it rest there lightly.

"And now, we all get to live happily ever after," I say.

He grabs my hand and rubs circles in my palm with his thumb. "Do we?"

By we, he means *us*.

His face is so close to mine. If I turned my head just a little, I could kiss him. It'd be soft, and sweet, and familiar. But for one thing, I can't twist my upper body without nearly fainting from the pain, and, for another, I very recently kissed someone I thought was Amka up in the mountain cabin.

Being fair to him is another item on my self-improvement list.

"I know I haven't been as good to you as I could have been," I say.

He looks at me, kind-eyed but not disagreeing. A charged silence stretches between us. I take a long, not-too-deep breath for courage. "I've been thinking that—maybe—we should step back and just be friends for a while."

He fidgets with a loose thread on the hem of his shirt as he takes in what I'm asking. "We're already friends," he says, his voice thick. "We've always been."

Tears of something like relief roll down my cheeks. I

wipe them with the balled-up scarf. "So…how far back are we rewinding?" I ask.

"How about…" He squints his eyes as if he's thinking hard. Then, the corner of his mouth lifts into a roguish smile. "That moment I beat you at the underhand chop?"

"Not fair! You already got the satisfaction of beating me once."

"Fine, then. How about that time I helped you start your sled after the games and you were pretending your wrist wasn't hurting like hell?"

"Another one of my shining moments. Someone should write a book about me." I try to laugh, but it hurts too much. I sniffle instead, the tears still threatening to spill.

Caden holds me a bit tighter, careful not to hurt me. He says, "Once we'd started your sled and stood in that exhaust cloud, you looked at me in such a way that I thought…"

"Yeah, I remember." I thought about kissing him. Maybe I should have, but I guess it's okay that I didn't. The next morning at school, we were as much to each other as we'd ever been. "That sounds good, Caden. Let's take it from there."

Maybe we're soulmates. Soulmates don't necessarily have to be lovers. Google says so—I looked it up on my shiny new phone. Even if we part ways for a while, we're bound to cross paths again and again. And whatever is meant to happen between us will happen when it happens.

"You know what?" he asks.

"What?"

He lifts my hand and examines the nasty friction burn

I got when I slid across the icy road. "You really are my favourite daredevil."

"And you'll always be my favourite paramedic."

Chapter 26

One afternoon a couple of weeks after the Christmas holidays, I'm with Melody and Dad in the living room, nursing a cup of hot chocolate and checking my new Instagram account. I've posted a picture of me wearing Karine's long-lost scarf. If she ever sees it, she'll understand I had a run-in with the chat-cornu and came out alive. I've been thinking about her a lot. When I'm ready, I'll try to find her and get in touch. The idea makes me nervous, but I have a feeling that it'll be sooner than later.

I pet Blue with the toe of my lucky sock. "Dad, did Karine ever tell you why she left—I mean, besides thinking the chat-cornu cursed me?"

He raises an eyebrow. He doesn't know I encountered her (sort of) on the Devil's Tail. Since he never believed in "all that chat-cornu crap," I've told him the same watered-down version I told almost everyone else.

Melody rises from the loveseat and ruffles her mahogany bob. "I'll go make myself a cup of tea."

"You can stay," I say.

She smiles kindly. "I'll be back in a minute."

"She left me a letter," Dad says as Melody walks out.

This adds up. In my vision inside the Poltergeist Tree,

I saw her write two letters, and only one of them was for me.

"Do you still have it?" I ask.

"Burned it. She said she was sorry for being an unworthy mother." He shakes his head, looking desolate. "Maybe I didn't know how to help her, but I sure hope I never made her feel that way. She was always so loving to you, even on her darkest days."

He sighs and stands. "She left a letter for you, too. I thought I'd give it to you when you turned eighteen, but I think you're grown enough to see it now."

He goes toward the basement door.

"Dad."

He stops, hand on the handle.

"I already found it." I wave my striped-socked foot. "Ran out of clean socks before the last Lumber Games, remember?"

"Oh."

"Worst hiding place ever! What were you thinking?" I smile to show I'm not angry at him, but he only says "oh" again.

"Basically, she said it wasn't my fault she left," I say. "I burned it."

He chuckles and comes to sit again. "Like father, like daughter, I guess."

My heart just about bursts. Maybe I look like my mother, but I love being like Dad.

"It's all good now," I reassure him. "Mostly."

I don't tell him the other details, but I still think about the chat-cornu a lot. I doubt the beast could trick me again, but it hasn't gone anywhere. It's probably still waiting for its ticket out of the Devil's Tail. Someday, someone else will go up there, and he will mine their muddled brain for vulnerabilities to use against them.

The window vibrates at the high-performance whine of a sled's engine.

"Caden's here. I gotta go."

"I should be going with you guys," Dad says.

"We'll be fine. See you in a bit."

"Be careful," he calls after me.

I smile at Melody on my way across the kitchen and pull on my winter clothes.

A few minutes later, Blue and I step outside. My ribs are still tender, but being able to take a deep breath of winter-cold air is wonderful.

Caden waits on his sled in front of the house, his face golden-tanned even though it's the middle of winter. Unlike me, he's still been able to enjoy the outdoors, while I've been almost too sore to get dressed.

"Hey," he says over the idling engine.

"Ready for our next wild adventure?"

The corners of his lips turn up. "If you're ready, I'm ready."

He stands to give me room to climb on behind him. We're off, going slow enough for Blue to keep up.

The summit of the Tail is veiled in clouds. We cross the ditch, and my stomach clenches as we pass through the willows. *Stay away from the Devil's Tail.* I see the words in my mind as Karine wrote them in her letter.

This is the last time I'm going up there, I promise…

Mom. I'm stronger now that I have allowed myself to grieve the loss of my mother. Me and Caden with Blue, in the daytime, we'll be fine.

The trail is gloomy, and the forest is still. I peer around us, wary of any trick the chat-cornu might try to pull. So far, he's a no-show.

There's Zwing, my untrustworthy sled, buried beneath a thick layer of snow. We park beside it and spend a while digging it out. That crackled, orange paint is a sweet sight. I've had plenty of idle time to shop for spare parts online. They're coming in the mail right now, and with some luck, I'll be able to ride a few times before winter's over.

Blue patrols the area, nose twitching and ears perked. He doesn't growl, so I think we're safe for now.

My single snowshoe still sits in the box, its twin buried somewhere on the mountain. The bewitched snowshoes are also nowhere to be found.

The spare canister of gas is still there, still full. I pull it out. "I've got an idea."

Caden sucks his teeth. "Tell me you're not thinking what I think you're thinking."

"Gabriel tethered the chat-cornu to the Poltergeist Tree. We're going to dispatch it for good."

"But what if—"

"We've got this, don't worry."

I climb back onto his sled and hug the canister to my chest, staring ahead. He shakes his head and gets on. We ride up into the mist. Four-legged shapes slink between trees. Blue yips and joins them. I resist the urge to call him back. I'm sure he'll return.

Escorted by our canine bodyguards, we follow the trail uneventfully until we reach the clearing around the cabin. The building's roof has caved in beneath the weight of the snow. In the next clearing, the Poltergeist Tree still towers.

I tap Caden's shoulder. "Let's stop here."

He kills the engine. We sit for a minute, watching the cloud of exhaust dissipate. Not a chickadee peep disturbs the silence.

"Can you wait for me here?" I ask. "I feel like I need to do this alone."

He clasps my wrist. "Be careful, okay? If anything happens, your dad will kill me."

"Yeah. I'll be careful."

Gas canister in hand, I plow into thigh-deep snow. I work up a sweat, but I barely feel the pull in my ribs as my breathing quickens. I stop near the tree's base. The hollow gapes before me. Inside are Gabriel's bones, the chat-cornu's pelt, and the bracelet Amka doesn't need anymore. I have no desire to see any of it. Axcalibur is still driven into the trunk, though, and I want it back. I yank it out in one solid pull, pleased to feel strong again—to finally be growing into my Awesome Alex persona.

I chip off some of the dry bark, then douse the pile with mixed gas. Holding my lighter at arm's length, I touch the flame to the woodchips. The fire whooshes to life, and I feel my eyelashes curl in the intense heat.

Caden waves me back to him. We stand at a safe distance, watching the flames crawl up the trunk. The shrivelled pelts in the boughs smoke and catch fire. Coyote howls close in on the clearing. Blue's voice is among them, not quite mastering the hunting song.

The chat-cornu, creepy as hell in its horned lynx form, bursts into the clearing.

I stumble backward, my heart pounding behind my bruised ribs. Then I notice he's not a beast of flesh and blood anymore. Just a silhouette, as insubstantial as a shred of northern lights in a snowy sky. I slip my arm around Caden. He squeezes my shoulder, and we take comfort in each other.

The coyotes retreat when they see Caden and me. Blue takes charge, ears pricked, head low, gaze intense. He might only be half-hunter, but he's also half-herder, quick and relentless. The chat-cornu dodges left and right but can't hold its ground. It blurs and nearly disappears when it moves too fast, like a candle flame in a gale.

"Come on, let's help." I stomp in the deep snow, swinging my axe. Caden grabs my free hand, and we block the beast's most likely escape route as Blue drives it ever closer to the tree.

In the hollow, the creamy pelt bursts into green-white flames. Yowling, the beast distorts as if trying to shapeshift. People's faces flicker over its own, and garbled words gush from its mouth—each cutting deeper than the last because they repeat in my voice the worst things I've said to the people I love the most. But I won't allow old hurts to fester anymore. I'll try harder and do better.

The best I can do right now is to finish what I started. I'd be strong enough to do it alone, but I feel even stronger with Caden and Blue at my side. We're holding the chat-cornu into a tight dog-and-humans half-circle. Melting snow sizzles on my mittens as flames shoot out of the hollow trunk. The beast, just a lynx with horns now, crouches and lifts a doleful gaze to mine.

For a flicker of time, I feel sorry for it. Maybe the people who made up the legend got it all wrong. Maybe pulling harmless pranks on people used to give it enough of a kick. Until Gabriel caught it in a snare and stole its skin. It doesn't excuse it taking my mother away from me, but we've all got to move on.

The chat-cornu is but a shadow now. The flames won't touch it, at least not in a physical sense, but they're getting way too hot and hungry for me. My skin feels like it's wanting to peel off my face.

Caden pulls me back a few steps, but I never break eye contact with the chat-cornu.

"You've done enough here." My voice trembles a little, and I'm not even embarrassed about it. What's happening here is totally wild. "It's time to go."

The chat-cornu gives me a cat wink, as if it agrees. Soon after, its disintegrating figure is sucked into the Poltergeist Tree like floating pollen dust into a whirlpool. The entire towering tree is engulfed. Bright green flames flesh it out like the branches of a majestic, living western hemlock. We retreat from the heat, Blue beating us to the edge of the clearing.

I drop to my knees and hug him tight. "You're such a good boy, Blue."

The three of us watch for a long time as the tree turns

into a blackening pillar licked by orange flames and grey-brown smoke.

"I think that's it for the chat-cornu," Caden says.

"I hope so." But what do I know? Maybe we annihilated it, or maybe we freed it. Maybe it'll go back across the ocean to haunt the land it came from. "Let's just get the hell out of here."

We're turning to leave when a thunderous roar shakes the ground and a spark-laden wind blows past us. The Poltergeist Tree has collapsed in a smoking jumble. I always knew it would fall someday, but I never thought I'd be the one to fell it.

We cruise down the mountain with Blue in the lead, stopping only long enough to hitch Zwing to Caden's sled with a tow rope. At the edge of the forest, the tangled willows are still dead and brittle, but a lone stem near the ditch displays tiny, white catkins. Last week's warm spell must have fooled it into awakening. Now that I'm willing to believe unbelievable things, I decide it's a good omen.

By the time we reach my front yard, the mist has cleared. We sit side by side on the porch, Blue lying down at our feet with a contented sigh.

The Devil's Tail turns to gold in the sunset—sharp as a fang, and as dangerous as any of its sisters. It can freeze you, bury you, or skid you off a cliff. There might still be ninety-nine ways to die up there, but I know in my bruised bones that the curse is gone.

You win some, you lose some, they say. Maybe so, but it's not that clear-cut. I'm learning that when the big prize slips away, what remains beneath the shards and dust is what I should hold dearest to my heart.

When all is said and done, I'm still just Alex. I don't know what the future holds, but whatever life throws my way, I'll grab the devil by the horns and give it my best shot.

The End

Acknowledgements

I'm privileged to live, work, and write on the land of the Lheidli T'enneh First Nation. As this land nurtures me on many levels, I'm hoping to treat it with equal kindness.

My writing journey began long before this story took shape in my mind. Many thanks to Ann MacIntyre, Norma Bakken, and Sophie Côté for your kind guidance and encouragement during my early attempts at writing novels.

Thank you to Ann Adams, Louise Ferrell, Catherine E. Clark, Paul Wedel, Richard P. Jacobs, Michelle Rogers, and Michael Helvaty for your precious feedback on the various drafts of *Devil by the Tail*. Mike, you appeared at the perfect moment, as if by magic, to help me see the story's unexplored potential. Thank you!

Elle Turpitt and Charlotte Sullivan-Swain, thank you for helping me refine the story's crucial opening pages. The same goes for you, Julie Blaho, and extra thanks for helping with the back cover blurb and, of course, your friendship.

I owe a great deal to my critique partners extraordinaire: Thea T. Kelley, Eric Diekhans, Emily Foster, and Robin Roberts. I don't know what I did to deserve you, but it must have been good because you're the absolute best! Your feedback, support, and friendship mean the world to me.

Special thanks to my sensitivity reader, Kaitlin Littlechild, for reviewing *Devil by the Tail* and addressing Indigenous sensitivity issues. Any blunders I've made on these pages are my own.

To my beta-readers Carolyn Kashner, Ryan Brandt, and Aysha Arias, thank you for sharing your thoughts on the final version of the manuscript.

I know I'm bound to forget someone. Thank you to everyone who helped me in one way or another on my writing path, especially the fantastic Scribophile writing community.

I appreciate the support from the whole team at Deep Hearts YA including John Robin, Craig Gibb, and Margaret Larson. Cali Kitsu, thank you for being so quick to answer my many questions and easing my publishing anxieties. Also, thank you, Craig and Cali, for creating the perfect book cover.

To my talented, inspiring daughters, Rafaële and Marie-Ève, thank you for bearing with me while I wandered around the woods of story-making and for calling me back to reality once in a while.

Mom and Dad, I wish you were here to celebrate this achievement of mine, but wherever you are, I know you're proud of me.

Finally, Normand, I can't imagine my life without you in it. Thank you for supporting all my dreams these past twenty-six years. I love you.

About the Author

Caroline Lavoie (she/her) is a French-Canadian writer who spends her days on the homestead, growing food and improbable tales from seed. Her short stories have been published in Cloud Lake Literary, Black Cat, and Haunted Words Press. Devil by the Tail is her debut novel. It was a finalist in CANSCAIP's 2022 Writing for Children Competition. Caroline lives in northern British Columbia on the land of the Lheidli T'enneh First Nation.

Website: carolinelavoieauthor.com

Also from Deep Hearts YA

Stone Feather Fang
A.G. Rodriguez

The gods—the cemi—have left the world of Ke', and their lush and verdant Andolin Islands are now inhabited by impious followers.

Teenage priestess Hildy Rios is tasked with saving her religion. In a special ritual called the Telling, she must somehow reawaken her people's love of the gods. Her effort is the last hope of her people: after this Telling, there will be no more chances, as the cemi will vanish into the past, their power forever lost to the world of Ke'.

The weight of her world on her shoulders, Hildy rewrites the Telling's story—and her own. She weaves a tale of her distant ancestor, a boy named Jenaro, blessed with the ability to see and speak to the cemi; a boy who, though long past, becomes as much a part of the present by way of the Telling's power.

For three days, Hildy brings to life the tale of Jenaro and his yearning for adventure, how he is haunted by the cemi of death, and who—like her—is fighting against the shackles of his family and society. For three days, Jenaro becomes real, and the power of the cemi to reach across time should be enough to convince Ke's people, but their impiety runs so deep…

Hildy and Jenaro. Two people joined by cursed blood, but separated by centuries of time. Only the cemi know how their tales will end.

Also from Deep Hearts YA

The Rest of Your Life Soundtrack
Benjamin Roesch

When teen musician Rainey Cobb gets noticed by a major record label, she's caught between her rock & roll dreams and her sick father's hope that she goes to college.

She finds a romantic diversion in Mia, a music-obsessed college dropout who makes the best mix tapes ever. But it's hard for Rainey to fully open her heart when she's not quite ready to show the rest of the world she's gay.

Signing a contract with the label should be a no-brainer. But they're also demanding that Rainey swap her Grunge-curious look for Gap-catalog styles and her edgy original songs for a more radio-friendly sound. They even offer to pay her dad's expensive cancer bills if she'll commit to their vision—but how much should a dream really cost?

Also from Deep Hearts YA

Cage of Nightingales
Elizabeth Hopkinson

In a highly structured eighteenth-century society, the city-state of Angelio is known for two things: its music and its guardian, the Archangel Michael.

At Angelio's music school—nicknamed the Cage of Nightingales—castrato singer Carlo is destined for fame at the opera…at the price of his freedom. Charity pupil Tammo hates the school and the restrictive future it offers, dreaming instead of escaping to live in the woods to charm birds with his flute.

When Tammo meets Carlo, their lives change forever. With the Archangel's help, they are granted the power to fulfil each other's deepest desires—but every gift demands a price.

As music opens doors to a glittering world beyond the Cage, the bond between them is tested by ambition, longing, and the fragile promises they have made. And their choices will shape not just their futures, but that of Celestina—a young aristocrat who will become entwined in their lives in ways neither of them can foresee.

Cage of Nightingales is a story of found family, and queer identity—featuring a tender portrayal of an asexual, nonbinary eunuch at its heart.